THE
DARKER
THE
SKIES

THE
DARKER
THE
SKIES

BRYAN PROSEK

CamCat
Books

CamCat Publishing, LLC
Brentwood, Tennessee 37027
camcatpublishing.com

Hardcover ISBN 9780744305548
Paperback ISBN 9780744305630
Large-Print Paperback ISBN 9780744305708
eBook ISBN 9780744305692
Audiobook ISBN 9780744305739

Library of Congress Control Number: 2022938377

Book and cover design by Maryann Appel

5   3   1   2   4

To all my readers, whose
support encourages me to continue writing.
Without you, I would be unable to share my stories.
I am continually humbled by your patronage.

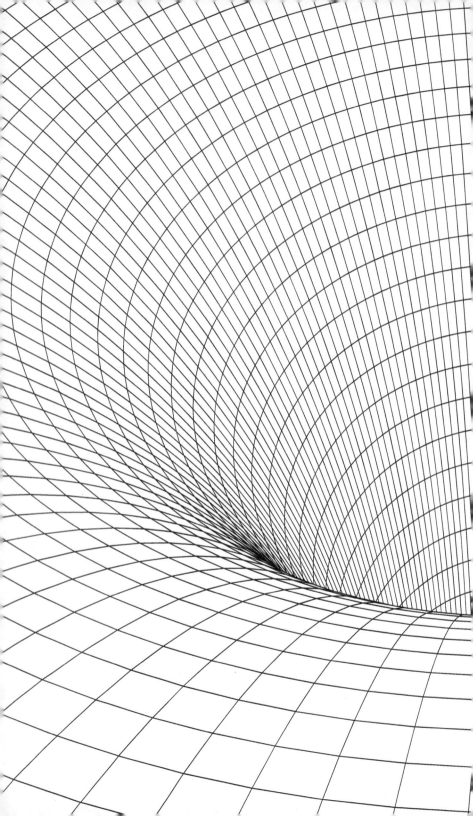

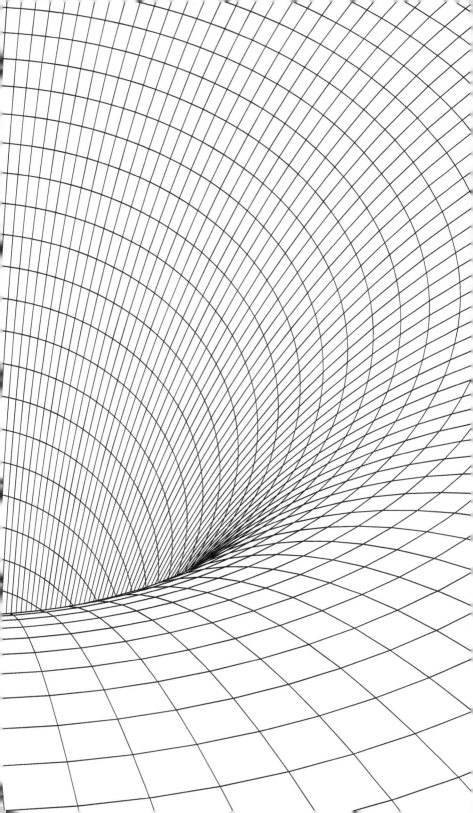

EARTH TIMES JOURNAL

March 14, 2187

This is Felipe Zapatero reporting on the discovery of a new planet in the Andromeda galaxy. As you know, the Andromeda galaxy, from which the Milky Way's planet Andromeda derives its name, is the closet galaxy to the Milky Way. In a statement released by the Presidential Mansion, scientists believe that the planet can sustain life. More importantly, because of the geological makeup of the planet, it is theorized that the planet could contain large quantities of hilaetite (pronounced hill-ay-ee-tight). Since it has been two years since the last discovery of a hilaetite crystal deposit in our galaxy, the need to find a new source of the crystal is becoming more important. Sources within the Legion say their hope is that the new quantum light fighter program will soon allow the Legion to develop the technology to reach the new planet that is being called Permidium.

PROLOGUE

Thirteen Years Prior to Romalor's Attack on Sector Four Headquarters

Alec Saunders flipped on the autopilot switch in the quantum light fighter and glanced at his copilot, Olga Vetrov. "This machine is smooth. I like it."

"Yes," Olga said. "EarthNX has outdone itself in designing this bad boy for the Legion. It's the first spacecraft to combine the fuel capacity and endurance of a military transport, the weapons array of the best tactical fighters, advanced shields, and quantum light drive."

Alec leaned back in his seat. "And the hope is that the program will eventually produce a ship that will reach Permidium."

"But until then, the edge of the Milky Way is as far as we're going," Olga said.

Alec stretched his arms. He wished they could go farther, but they were in the first manned vessel to go this far. With the planet Andromeda being the most remote planet in this region of the galaxy, nobody had had the desire to explore beyond it or had the ability to get there until now.

Olga continued. "The last unexplored region of the galaxy. We'll be famous, you know." She turned toward Alec. "Something you'll be able to tell that little boy of yours someday. It's Jacob, right?"

Alec smiled. "We all call him Jake."

Jake was Alec's pride and joy. Having lost his wife during childbirth, all he had was Jake. The memory of losing her was still painful. He didn't like to think about it. He looked straight ahead out the cockpit window. He loved how the stars seemed to zip by when traveling at quantum light speed. It helped take his mind off the struggles of raising a child as a single parent who was often absent. He felt more comfortable in space than anyplace else. He belonged there. He always thought he could live in space, just the stars and him.

Olga smiled. "I've seen pictures, He's a cute little guy. How old is he now?"

Alec had to bring his mind back to the present. "He'll be two in July. It wasn't easy leaving him for this mission."

That was the truth. His priorities changed when Jake came along. He realized that there was much more to life than being a Legion soldier and exploring space.

"I'm sure it wasn't," Olga agreed. "Who's keeping him?"

Alec checked their heading and adjusted the auto pilot setting. "My brother, Ben, and his wife, Jane."

The com buzzed.

Olga looked at the controls in front of her. "Sector Four headquarters is hailing us."

Alec leaned forward. "Put it on the screen."

Olga worked the controls, and the video screen in front of them activated. Alec could see a lady, whom he immediately recognized, seated at a table marked with the Legion seal. Behind her was a room full of Legion officers and privates sitting at various computers, some in groups and some alone. Still others were standing and talking or just observing. The camera was focused on the middle-aged, heavyset lady.

"Commander," Alec said, "is everything all right?"

"Yes, Captain," she replied. "I just wanted to check in with you one final time before we lose visual communication. How's the ride?"

Alec smiled. "Pretty sweet. I need to get one of these babies for myself." He patted the controls lightly.

The commander smiled. "You do that." She paused. "So, I take it you've had no troubles? Did everything go okay at Andromeda?"

Olga responded this time. "No issues with the flight or with the spacecraft, Commander. And refueling went smoothly at the planet. They seemed eager to help."

The commander leaned back in her seat. "Well, we did promise to share our intelligence with their government immediately, no matter what we find."

"I guess they have more at stake than any other planet since they're the closest to this region of space," Olga said.

Static lines cut across the video screen and the images jerked and distorted.

"I think we're starting to lose video, Commander," Alec said. "Switching to audio only." He worked the controls and the screen went dark.

Olga pressed the com. "Commander, we're now entering uncharted space. Not a star in sight. Turning on long-range scanners."

Alec looked out the window again. The complete darkness felt eerie. So different from the shooting stars that he'd seen not long ago.

Alec pressed the com. "We could lose audio at any moment. We'll be completely dark then. Headquarters won't be able to track us and we won't be able to relay any data."

"Understood," the commander replied, her voice breaking up. "That's what we expected."

Olga interrupted. "Captain Saunders, I'm picking up a reading on the long-range scanners."

"Can you tell what it is?" Alec replied. "A ship? Planet? Something else?"

"I can't tell for certain. It's too large to be any spacecraft we know, but not quite large enough to be a planet."

"Okay," Alec said. "Keep your eye on it."

The commander's voice crackled over the com. "Is the reading far enough away to be coming from the Andromeda galaxy? It could be Permidium. We've never scanned a planet at that distance. It could look deceptive on the scanner."

"Negative," Olga responded. "According to my readings, the object is still within our galaxy."

Alec worked the control panel. "Affirmative. I'm starting to pick up some faint sensor readings. It is definitely in our galaxy, and it's mobile, so it's not a planet."

He could feel the excitement start to build. His stomach started to churn. This was what he'd hoped for the moment he was selected for this mission.

This was what he had trained for. A new discovery.

The commander's crackling voice came over the com again. "I'm not picking up everything you're saying. You're breaking up. But it sounded like you said the object is mobile. In what direction is it heading?"

Alec looked at his sensors again, then at Olga as he pressed his com. "Straight at us, Commander."

Alec paused, looking at the instrument panel in front of him.

No response from the commander came, or none that was audible. "Let's try hailing it when we're in range."

"I've already started sending messages in case their scanners go farther than ours. No response yet."

"We're almost close enough for a visual," Alec said, turning to face forward. "Dropping out of quantum drive in three, two, one, now."

Olga immediately flipped the video switch. "Switching the view to exterior."

"Whatever it is, it's dropping out of light speed as well," Alec said, glancing at the video display.

A bright light filled the screen. Putting a hand over his eyes, Alec turned his head. Even with doing that, a splitting pain shot through his forehead. He separated two fingers to peek. Olga was in obvious pain as well, with her palms clasped to her forehead.

As Alec regained his composure, he lowered the display resolution to dull the light. They were close enough now to see the object more clearly. It was a massive spaceship. And the entire vessel emitted a clean, white light. It was like nothing he had ever seen.

The commander's voice was barely audible. "I repeat, do you copy me? I can still hear you, but you must not be receiving my transmissions." Alec couldn't make out what she said next but was able to discern one last sentence over the com static. "Headquarters will keep the coms open here to listen."

Olga worked the controls rapidly. "Still no response to our hail. What kind of spacecraft is it and where's it from?"

Alec didn't know the answer to either question. He checked the sensor readings again.

"That can't be," he said.

Olga turned quickly toward him. "Why? What can't be?"

"According to the sensor," Alec said, "ninety percent of the object consists of hilaetite."

"That's impossible!"

Alec frowned. "Impossible based on our technology. But apparently not based on theirs."

Suddenly, Alec heard a voice in a language he didn't understand. But the voice wasn't coming over the com. It was coming from space. From all around them. Amplified.

He peered at Olga. "Did you hear that?"

"Yes, but I couldn't understand it."

"Me neither. It must not be a language programmed into the translator chips."

Olga continued to work the audio com controls. "They aren't responding to any language we have in our program." She spoke faster now. Alec could hear the fear in her voice, just as he could feel the same fear himself. "I'm transmitting a message in every language in our database, letting them know that we mean no harm. But they won't respond!"

The voice came again. This time, even louder.

Alec monitored the sensors. His heart raced as he wiped a bead of sweat from his forehead. His voice was just short of a shout, even though Olga was seated next to him. "They're powering up weapons, whatever those weapons are. I'm raising shields."

This wasn't the excitement he was planning on. This was too much. If the ship contained that much hilaetite, he doubted their shields would do much good against the arsenal that it must possess.

Olga looked at Alec. "They must expect us to understand them, but since our responses are inaudible to them, they must think we're taking a defiant stance."

"So, let's not power up our weapons," Alec said.

"And I'm thinking we'd better get out of here."

"Agreed." Alec turned back toward his controls and powered up the subluminal engines. They began moving.

He heard the voice a third time. The decibel level was even higher. He winced and put his hands over his ears to stifle the sharp, piercing pain. But that did no good against the high pitch. He turned toward Olga, and she was doing the same.

Finally, the sound subsided, and Alec checked the sensors again. They showed the other ship's weapons at full power. As he reached for the quantum drive control, every system on the control panel went dark, then every other light in the quantum fighter blacked out. As Alec looked up at the viewing screen, a burst of bright light emanated from the spacecraft and shot straight at their fighter.

"Oh no," Alec said.

That light was the last thing he saw.

EARTH TIMES JOURNAL

July 12, 2209

This is Nigil Diggs and today is the one-year anniversary of the Battle of Craton, in which the Legion prevailed and halted Craton's attempt to use its new hilaetite-powered weapon against Earth. Over the past four days, we have talked about the heroes of the battle, but what about the villains? What ever became of them? Well, we all know that Romalor Leximer, the ruler of Craton, was killed in the battle at the hands of Jake Saunders. Edgardo Ramirez, president and CEO of EarthNX Corporation, was sentenced to life in prison. Marco Veneto, the president's chief Legion advisor, was also killed in the fight. Finally, there was Mr. Sloan. Nobody ever did figure out who he was, where he came from, the extent of his role in the plot, or where he went. The mysterious Mr. Sloan is still at large.

1

ANNIVERSARY DAY

Sloan stood straight and tall on the bridge of the lead pirate ship, his hands clasped behind his back, staring at the floor-to-ceiling viewing screen. In his suit and tie topped off by a black trench coat, he stood out from the crew of the ship. He was an imposing figure. That, along with his reputation, would put fear into the entire crew, as well as their captain. That put a grin on his face. He was confident that he was in control of not only this ship, but the fleet of spacecraft as well as the entire mission.

A small bluish dot was coming into view on the screen, growing larger as Sloan's ship approached. *This plan is a masterpiece,* Sloan thought. He had been putting the plan in place for almost a year, and on this day, Earth would finally belong to him.

An overweight, bald male sat in the captain's chair. Sloan continued to look at the screen as the man spoke in a scratchy voice. "We're approaching Earth, Mr. Sloan. Should I give the command to cloak, sir?"

That voice, so common in the captain's insectoid species, irritated Sloan. He also didn't like their yellow-pigmented skin. And what was the purpose of the black dots down each side of their face? Were insectoids born with those or did they put them there? At least there were a couple humans on the ship's crew, and even a Cratonite. That gave Sloan some confidence that things might get done correctly.

Given his distaste for the insectoid appearance, Sloan didn't turn around when he responded to the captain. "Cloak as you come out of light speed. Didn't you listen to the Permidiums who installed the device on your ships? You can't cloak at light speed. That will fragment the spacecraft." He turned to look at the captain. "But wait for my order to drop to subluminal."

Idiots, Sloan thought. *They are going to blow themselves up and kill me in the process before the battle even starts.* Maybe he should have led from one of the Permidium ships, where he would have been safer. No, he needed to be here with the pirate ships. The Permidiums knew how to fight as a unit. These pirate ships were from all over the galaxy. They only knew one-on-one dogfighting. That would come in handy later in the battle, but right now they needed to work as team, as one unit. They needed him.

Sloan turned back to the monstrous screen. He now could make out the familiar blue-surfaced ball painted with white brush strokes that distinguished Earth from every other planet in the galaxy. He wanted to reach out through the display and grab the ball in one hand and crush it. "Have you heard from the Permidium vessels? Are they in place?" He didn't address the captain by name or title. He didn't want to give him that respect.

"Yes, Mr. Sloan," the captain said. "All four Permidium vessels are in position, cloaked next to each of the four defense stations. Is there any way Earth can detect them?"

"Not with any technology in this galaxy." Sloan smiled again. *The Milky Way galaxy has never seen cloaking technology*, he thought. He recalled how he had persuaded the Permidiums to develop cloaking in the first place. With their planet located in the Andromeda galaxy, he knew the technology would never reach the galaxy he truly wanted to possess.

And the things the Permidiums could do with a spacecraft made 90 percent out of hilaetite. The destructive power of such a ship even impressed him, a little. The entire ship was a weapon. His only regret was that he didn't design the hilaetite ships first. But that really didn't matter; he had the Permidiums in the palm of his hand. A simple promise that he may or may not be able to keep was all it took. All other life forms were such fools and so easily manipulated.

This time Sloan turned and looked at the captain. "As planned, once the Permidium vessels take out the defense stations, half of your ships will hit Sector One headquarters and half will hit the headquarters of Sector Four. The other pirate squadron will take the headquarters in Sectors Two and Three." He stepped toward the captain. "Who is leading that squadron?"

The captain cleared his throat. "Abigor, sir. From Maul."

Sloan's eyes narrowed and his brow furrowed. "Maul? I've never heard of a planet Maul."

"Mr. Sloan," the captain said, "it's not really a planet. Maul is actually the remnants of a dead star near the edge of the galaxy. A harsh place to survive. I guess that's what made him a bloody scary pirate. He'll do anything to get what he wants."

Sloan stepped closer. "And you picked him to lead the squadron?"

The captain pushed back in his seat and turned his head slightly as if bracing for a slap or punch. "Well, sir, you see," the captain stammered, "he kind of picked himself. Nobody tells Abigor what to do."

Sloan stretched his neck, putting his head closer to the captain, and stared at him. "For your sake, you better hope he follows my orders."

Sloan turned again to face the display, shaking his head. He should have known the pirates couldn't follow a chain of command. He had thought that by putting the insectoid captain in command of them, he could rely on his orders being passed down through the ranks and obeyed. He didn't want to have to deal with the pirates at every level. Dealing with one was quite enough.

Sloan watched as the planet Earth slowly filled the viewing screen. "Have we reached the coordinates?"

"Your accuracy is amazing, sir," the captain replied. "We will in ten seconds, nine, eight—"

Sloan interrupted the countdown. "Prepare to drop out of light speed and cloak as you do."

"—three, two, one," the captain finished before turning his attention toward the helmsman. "Now!"

The helmsman kept his eyes on the controls. "Done, sir. We've successfully cloaked. Just outside the Sector One defense station."

"And the other ships?" Sloan asked the navigation officer.

"All in position and cloaked, sir," the navigation officer replied.

"Excellent," Sloan said with a smirk. It was finally time to put his plan into motion. He turned back toward the screen. "Split the display and patch us into the other three lead ships. I want to see what's going on at each Sector headquarters once we start."

<hr />

Private Samantha Simons sat alone at her post behind a slew of computers and video displays in the observation room in the Sector One central command building. Unlike most other privates who viewed watch duty almost like punishment, Sam stayed alert. She knew that the nine years of peace and quiet on Earth since Romalor had attacked Sector Four headquarters had made many in the Legion complacent. But not her. She took her job very seriously.

Sure, like everyone, she didn't fear a direct attack on the planet by pirates, even though Earth was technically at war with them. The pirates didn't possess the technology or means to carry out such an attack. But Sam had read all the reports from nine years ago, once the true reports were released. Nobody back then feared any sort of attack either.

So, she remained at the ready.

Sam took a sip of coffee, keeping her eyes fixed on the screens and monitors. A small blip on the radar monitor caught her eye. It was just outside the defense station. *I've never seen the radar do that before,* she thought. She quickly replayed the recording of the last minute of the radar and saw it again. Sam enlarged the video screen covering that area of space but saw nothing. She replayed that recording as well. Still nothing. She was probably just seeing things or wanting to see things. Maybe she took watch duty a little too seriously. No, she would follow procedure. She would inquire about any anomaly that she detected.

Sam pressed the com. "Sector One Defense, this is Sector One Central Command. Do you copy?"

A voice came over the com. "Go ahead, Central Command."

"Have you noticed any irregularities in space just outside the station?" Sam asked.

"Central Command, what kind of irregularities?"

Sam wasn't sure how to describe it. "Did anything show up on your radar monitor or viewing screen? I detected a blip on the radar a few minutes ago."

"A blip? I'm sorry, can you repeat?"

Now she started to feel embarrassed. Had her mind just created all of this out of boredom? Maybe she should just drop it. No, she had to follow through. That was protocol. "I thought I detected an object momentarily appear on my monitor, just outside your station. I'm sending you the coordinates now." She typed into the Legion mainframe the coordinates of the blip.

There was now a sharp tone in the voice coming over the com. "You thought you detected? Central Command, can you please clarify. Did you or did you not see something?"

Why won't they just answer? she thought. Sam tried to keep the irritation out of her voice. "That's what I'm trying to determine, Defense. Did you see anything on your screens? At the coordinates I just sent?"

After some silence, the answer came with nothing more. "Negative. Sector One Defense Station out."

Well, they aren't much help, Sam thought. She leaned back in her chair, her short legs allowing just the tips of her boots to touch the floor.

The next step in following the proper protocol when something was detected was to contact your superior. But maybe she saw nothing. Maybe she should just let it go. But did someone see something and let it go nine years ago? She pressed another com. "Captain, this is Private Simons in Central Command. I need to report a possible anomaly."

Sloan turned toward the captain. "Open a channel to the Permidium vessels."

The captain waved toward the insectoid communications officer, who then focused on Sloan.

"Done, sir."

Rather than walking to a com, Sloan spoke loudly, which wasn't hard for him. "The time has come. Soon Earth will be ours. You will have taken your first step in preventing this galaxy from taking over your planet." He paused for a moment. "And I will have the first planet in my new empire." This time he didn't smile. It was time for battle.

A computer-like, feminine voice came over the com. "This is the Conciliator of Permidium Vessel One, Mr. Sloan. We do not understand. We do not detect the transponder on this planet."

How irritating. Now he would have to persuade her to proceed. He could picture the conciliator on her bridge surrounded by her almost entirely female crew, their translucent bodies floating on the floor, all giving their input to the conciliator because that's what Permidiums did. What an inefficient way to rule. But they were intelligent. He had to give them that. He supposed that's what you get with a planet that's

90 percent female, lots of intelligence and lots of discussion. Unlike male rulers who tended to act on impulse before thinking or seeking advice, which made them much easier to manipulate. Had he come all this way for the Permidiums to back out now? He wouldn't let that happen. He would convince them to continue as planned.

"They likely have it shielded from detection," Sloan said, "or even hidden off the planet. Remember, the entire galaxy is in on this. Once we take Earth, we'll move on to the rest of the planets. Once the other planets see Earth's mighty defenses crumble, they will be lining up to beg us not to attack."

The com was silent for a moment. Sloan was irritated again by the delay, but not worried. If the Permidiums refused to attack, it would be an inconvenience and a delay in his plans, but it wouldn't stop him. He always had a backup plan.

The voice came over the com again. "Very well. Let us proceed."

Excellent, Sloan thought. He had to fight to hold back a grin. Even with their superweapons, the Permidiums were still under his influence and control. He wouldn't fail again. He looked at the viewing screen and spoke even louder so that his command could not be mistaken. "Proceed at once!"

Seconds later, brighter than anything he had ever seen, a blinding white light lit up the display. Sloan instinctively turned from the viewing screen, ducked his head, and closed his eyes. He slowly turned back toward the screen and blinked a few times. It took a couple seconds for his sight to return. Even then, the screen looked fuzzy until his eyes adjusted. He could see everyone else on the bridge trying to regain their composure as well. As his vision cleared, he saw nothing but space where one of Earth's four impenetrable defense stations had orbited just seconds earlier.

He had heard no explosion and there was no burning debris, not even a single piece of residue. Everything was gone: the station, the ship, and the Legion soldiers posted there. Sloan then recalled what the Permidiums had said about the use of their entire ship as a weapon.

It disintegrated whatever it hit. They had less potent hilaetite weapons on their vessels, but when they unleashed the full force of the spacecraft, nothing stood in the way.

The voice of her superior came over the com. "Go ahead, Simons. What do you have?"

Sam instantly forgot about the captain or why she had even contacted him. A bright light lit up the video screen monitoring the defense station and instantly the station's image and all readings disappeared from the monitor. She had to stretch to reach the reboot functions with her short arms. Why did she have to be so petite? She tried to reboot the video feed. Nothing. The cameras were working, but they just showed open space where the defense station should have been. The radar monitor showed nothing. All feeds from inside the defense station displayed static. Her heart raced. Sweat trickled down her cheek. Cool air chilled the back of her neck where her skin was left bare by her bobbed haircut. She leaned closer to the computers and monitors and rebooted all systems. Still nothing. No sign of the defense station.

Sam looked around the room and remembered she was alone. It was eerily quiet. She ran a hand through her strawberry-red hair, then pressed the com for the defense station. "Sector One Defense, this is Central Command. Do you read me?" She paused and waited. Silence. She pressed the com again. "Sector One Defense, are you there? Please respond." Again, nothing but silence.

Sam startled as her superior's voice came over the com. "Simons. What is it that you have to report?"

The viewing screen split into four sections. Sloan watched as hundreds of pirate ships poured into Earth's atmosphere near each of the four sector headquarters, with each group of pirate ships followed by a giant, bright white Permidium vessel. Not even a remnant of any of the Earth defense stations could be seen.

Sloan continued to watch the screen as he spoke to the captain. "Is the com still open?"

"Yes, sir," the captain replied. "I've left it open to all ships so you can direct the attack at all sectors."

Sloan didn't respond to the captain. Instead, he spoke loudly to his fleet. "Permidiums, remember, don't use excessive force unless I say so. I want as much of the planet intact as possible for my rule, and so we can find your transponder." He paused. "And stay within the sector headquarters in order to limit civilian casualties." He really didn't care how many humans they killed, but he wanted somewhat of a population as his subjects once the takeover was complete.

Sloan pointed to the screen showing Sector One. "Take out as many of those quantum fighters as you can before they get off the ground."

Legion soldiers raced from the buildings toward the hangars, while pirate gunships mowed them down with impressive accuracy. Sloan had to admit, these pirates sure could shoot. At the same time, torpedoes were launched from the gunships. Tails of fire trailed the air-to-surface projectiles heading straight toward the stationary fighters. With no pilots inside to raise shields, the fighters burst into balls of flames as the torpedoes took out two or three at a time. The unprepared Legion didn't stand a chance against his attack.

Sloan watched as one determined Legion soldier made it to his fighter and lifted off, only to be too slow to engage his shields. *An amateur*, Sloan thought. *Didn't the Legion train their men any better than that?* Oh well, the better for him. Sloan felt like he could hear the man's screams as he burned inside his crashing spacecraft. Sloan smiled. *The sound of victory*, he thought.

Still standing tall, facing the divided screen, Sloan scanned all four headquarters' grounds. "Over there." He pointed to several of the largest buildings on the Sector One screen. The buildings stood in a row near where all the light fighters had been positioned. "Send the coordinates of those buildings to our Permidium vessel. That's where their battleships will be housed. The battleship weapons will be no match for the Permidiums, but let's not let the Legion have even a glimmer of hope."

The feminine voice of the conciliator came over the com. "Would you like us to proceed against the marked targets with maximum force, sir?"

Sloan shook his head. Didn't anyone listen? "Yes, proceed, but not with maximum force. Just take out the buildings, not the entire planet!" *Idiots,* Sloan thought. No wonder the Permidiums hadn't expanded beyond their galaxy, even with all the hilaetite resources on their planet and the technology they possessed. They had absolutely no tactical sense.

No sooner had Sloan finished speaking when the Sector One viewing screen lit up as targeted buildings disintegrated in the same manner as the defense stations, leaving a barren crater in the earth.

Sloan's smile returned. "Now tell your other *conciliators*"—Sloan put emphasis on the foolish title—"to find and destroy the same buildings in each sector."

Sam regained her composure. "Sir, something's wrong at the defense station."

"What is it, Sam? I need . . ." The transmission of Sam's superior was cut short by an enormous explosion heard through the com. And then, static.

The explosion was followed by several more, which she heard without the com. Her building shook from the force.

Sam hit the red-alert alarm, which sounded on the inside and the outside of every building throughout the headquarters, although she doubted that it was necessary at this point. But sounding the alarm was protocol. With her superior incommunicado, Sam went up and down the chain of command trying to reach someone. Someone to tell her what to do. But nobody responded. The com wasn't just silent. It was dead. Nothing but static. She ran a diagnostic on the communication system, and everything came up clean on her end. It wasn't a problem with her com.

What was going on? Surely the pirates hadn't attacked Earth. They didn't have the resources. And how could they have gotten through the defense station? Whatever it was, it had to be a localized attack. Carried out by pirate sympathizers on Earth or pirates that had snuck in. But then why was the defense station not responding? And what had she seen on her monitor?

The beads of perspiration forming on her forehead were less apparent to her than the dampness growing in her armpits. She reached for the com again, trying to steady her shaking hand. For the first time in her life, she was truly scared. She was a Legion soldier, trained for this. She could not be nervous. She wasn't allowed to be afraid. But she was.

Sloan crossed his arms as he looked at all four split screens. The battle was going pretty much the same in all four sectors. If you could call it a battle. It looked more like a massacre, which was more to his liking.

As Sloan watched, he noticed the lead pirate ship in Sector Three, a sleek black-and-red fighter, veer out of formation and leave the rest of the group. *Where is he going?* Sloan thought.

The fighter was leaving Sector Three headquarters. That's exactly what Sloan had commanded not to do.

Sloan turned to face the captain and pointed toward the Sector Three screen. "Who is that!" he shouted. "And where does he think he's going? I warned you to control your people!"

The captain slouched in his chair. "That's Abigor, sir. I don't know where he's going or what he's doing." The captain started to tremble slightly. "I'm sorry, sir."

"Get him on the com," Sloan demanded.

The captain nodded toward the communications officer, who worked the com controls for a few minutes with no audible response.

Sloan's fingernails dug into the palms of his hands as he clinched his fists and looked at the communications officer. "Well? Anything?'

She leaned back in her chair and turned her face slightly as if preparing for Sloan to throw something at her. "No sir. No transmission whatsoever. He's ignoring my hail."

The tactical officer interrupted. "Sir, the screen. Abigor is attacking residential districts just outside Sector Three headquarters."

Sloan whipped around quickly to look at the screen, then turned toward the captain. "Send five ships to take him out. I don't mind taking out a few human civilians. In fact, it adds an exclamation point to our victory. But insubordination won't be tolerated." Sloan spoke more slowly. "This Abigor must be dealt with." Sloan paused and narrowed his eyes at the captain. "Or you will be. He's under your command."

The captain's voice was shaky. "Understood, sir."

Sloan liked the nervousness in the captain's response. He felt like he had gotten his message across.

Sloan turned around to look at the screen again as Abigor's fighter flew in the direction of Sector One, out of range of the video, followed by five pirate fighters.

Sam pressed the com, knowing that this call was the final step in the predesigned Legion procedure for an attack on a sector headquarters. She prayed that there would be a response on the other end.

"Dark Forty, this is Central Command. Do you copy?"

Sam held her breath as the com was silent.

"Come on," she whispered to herself. "Come on. Please answer." The silence felt like minutes, but she knew it was only seconds.

"I copy, Central Command. This is Dark Forty. What's going on up there?"

"Thank you," Sam whispered again. Then she spoke into the com. "I don't know, sir. We're under attack. I can't reach anyone, including the defense station or the commander or any other Superior Guards." She didn't know what else to tell him. She had never come close to being in this type of situation before. She hoped he would know what to do next.

"Copy that, Central Command," was the response. "I'll let the Captain know. It sounds like it's his decision to launch or not."

As Sam started to press the com again, her head suddenly filled with pressure, feeling like it was about to explode. In the same split second, a deafening groundburst pierced her ears as she flew off her chair. Her body and face smacked into the near wall as the opposite wall opened up, debris and flames flying everywhere. Her face went numb and her ears were filled with a loud ringing. The point of impact must have been just outside the wall. A couple feet to the right, and Central Command would have been eliminated, along with her.

Sloan smiled as he watched the battle. His pirate ships along with the four Permidium vessels had things well in hand. Soon, victory over Earth would be his.

The captain interrupted Sloan's thoughts. "Mr. Sloan, the ground appears to be opening up in that deserted area over there." He pointed to the bottom of the screen showing Sector One. "It's happening in all four sectors."

Sloan's smile turned upside down as he clinched his hands into fists. "No, that can't be," he said to nobody in particular. He watched as a whole division of quantum fighters flew out of the opening in the desert ground. He turned and glared at the captain. "Why didn't I know they had underground hangars?"

The captain squirmed in his seat. "Sir, our scouts never picked them up. The hangars must be new, and the Legion kept it discreet."

Sloan stepped toward the captain with his fists still clinched.

"But sir," the captain said, "there's no way we could have known."

Sloan stopped short of the captain. "With a little intelligence you could have." He turned back toward the screen and spoke softly to himself. "No use having a battle of wits with an unarmed person."

A year's worth of planning. Planting scout spies around each Legion headquarters, and scouting Earth, all to be wasted because the pirates couldn't do their job. He could have attacked with just the Permidium vessels a long time ago if he wanted to wipe out the entire headquarters. He should let the quantum fighters take out the pirates before having the Permidiums intervene, but he still needed the pirates. And then there's the renegade pirate, Abigor, killing civilians. Civilians that would become his subjects. *Insubordinate idiot*, Sloan thought.

Sloan spoke louder now, still facing the screen. "Get me the Permidium conciliators on the com. Now I'll have to use more force." He paused. "And along with that, it'll take out more infrastructure." He turned back toward the captain and glared again. "And the cost to rebuild is coming out of the pirates' compensation."

Sam's hearing started to return as she lay on the concrete floor of what was left of the Sector One Central Command building. Her head ached and the side of her face stung. She touched her cheek and winced at the pain, then she looked at her blood-soaked fingers. Her face must be cut pretty badly, but she didn't have time to deal with it now. She put one hand on a toppled desk, and pulling herself up, she grabbed her ribs with her other as a sharp pain shot through her side.

After righting herself, she staggered toward the open wall, using piles of broken computer equipment and wrecked furniture for support as she moved. From her vantage point, with the debris in front of her, all she could see was the smoke-filled sky through the opening. Just as she started to climb over the debris, bright flashes lit up the sky, with more explosions to follow. She turned her head and closed her eyes as the blinding light penetrated the thick smoke. The vibrations from the explosions shook the piles of debris.

Sam was slowly losing her balance. She fell backward and reached for a metal rod sticking out of a pile, but her hand caught only air. The back of her head smacked the concrete floor, and pain penetrated her skull like a knife. She lay there, at first stunned. Then her vision turned fuzzy and dim. She wanted to let go, leave the pain, leave the fear. But no, she had to fight. She had to remain conscious. If she passed out, she was likely finished.

Who was around to help her?

She needed to give her brain something to do. She focused on the situation. She had never seen a weapon put out light like that. Who was attacking Earth?

Her head throbbed as she pulled herself up once more and started to climb, this time making it over the debris pile. She stepped through what was left of the central command building's east wall and coughed with every breath as her lungs tried to force out the inhale of smoke; residual smoke from weapons fire and from burning buildings and spacecraft, mostly Legion. The sight was like something out of an old doomsday movie. Fire and burning debris as far as she could see. Not a building standing. And not a single person walking. The sky was filled with spacecraft. All types. But not a Legion fighter was in sight. They had to be pirates. But how?

Standing out from all the other vessels was one giant ship, glowing bright white.

Sam's attention was pulled back to the ground when cries for help reverberated from the toppled buildings. No doubt, Legion soldiers being buried alive. Her heart sank. She lost all sense of time. All fear and anger dissipated, leaving her with a nothingness, an emptiness.

Who did this? She thought. *Did the entire planet look like this?*

She stood there as tears rolled down her cheeks.

Sloan surveyed the viewing screen. All sector headquarters were clear. Not a moving Legion soldier, aircraft, or spacecraft in sight. The Permidiums had quickly dispatched the new Legion fighters. They were efficient killing machines, Sloan had to admit.

"All pirate ships, fall back," Sloan commanded. "Send in the transports with the ground troops. Secure all four headquarters." He paused for effect. "I want no Legion soldier left alive." He paused again. "All four Permidium ships are with me. We have one final target."

This would be the exclamation point on his attack. This would show not only Earth but also the entire galaxy that he was unbeatable. This would put fear in the hearts of every species on every planet.

Sloan smiled to himself. "Discontinue the split screen. I want a full view of what's in front of us."

The four Permidium vessels came into view on the screen as they fell in line with his pirate ship. The sky was free of any Legion fighters. They all must have been sent to defend the four headquarters. That worked out as planned. The ground was quiet as well. He expected that too. Everyone would be deep underground by now, where they thought they would be safe. He smiled. They thought wrong.

Sloan looked at the captain. "Is the com still open to the Permidium vessels?"

"Yes sir," the captain said, with more confidence now that the battle was in hand.

Sloan spoke loudly. "All four vessels are to focus the hilaetite weapons at maximum strength on the coordinates that I gave you."

One of the conciliators spoke in response. "But sir, that will blast a hole miles deep. How does that achieve our objective? I believe we are in a position to demand the planet's surrender. They no longer have a fighting force."

Sloan clinched his fist, the anger swelling inside him. Did he have to go through this again? He spoke through clinched teeth. "Did I not tell you that we must permanently cripple this planet if you want the other planets to fall in line? Have I not gotten us this far? Just do what I say and you will get the transponder."

Again, silence. Sloan shook his head. They were discussing it, getting everyone's input. How much more frustration could he take? He just needed to keep his eyes on the final prize. He waited.

The com crackled. "Very well, Mr. Sloan. We will proceed."

At last, Earth would be his. Sloan smiled and turned toward the captain. "Zoom in on the coordinates that I gave to the Permidiums. The focal point is in the center of this sector. Right there." Sloan pointed to a spot on the display.

The captain looked up at the screen. "Mr. Sloan, that's the Presidential Mansion."

Sloan's smile widened. "I know."

EARTH TIMES JOURNAL

July 8, 2209

This is Nigil Diggs, and just four days from today will be the one-year anniversary of the Battle of Craton. Many of you can still recall exactly what you were doing when you learned about this epic battle that took place at the Planet Craton. After learning what was at stake in the battle, we all were in shock and disbelief at how close our own planet Earth and everyone on it came to total annihilation that day. Except for those in the government and Legion that were involved in the events leading up to the battle, nobody knew what was going on. If not for Legion Privates Jacob Saunders and Cal Danielson, as well as Vernition Ambassador Diane Danielson, Earth would be no more.

2

***

J ake Saunders leaned back in his swivel chair on the observation
deck. He loved the view from the glass bubble: stars and space in
every direction, except for the planet Vernius directly in front of him.

"Have you been reading the *Earth Times Journal* lately?" Cal Danielson said. "They're all over the Battle of Craton anniversary. They're
calling it Anniversary Day. It's crazy. We're still heroes you know."

"Nope, never read it," Jake said.

"Are you going back to Earth for the anniversary?" Cal asked.
"They're planning a parade in every sector. I'm going the day of,
assuming Diane and I get everything set for the Imperial Majesty's
birthday celebration. I was voluntold by Diane that I had to help her
prepare."

"Another nope. Hadn't planned on it. I'm happy just hanging out
on Vernius."

"Unless Diane goes," Cal said with a smile.

Jake was overcome with a feeling of warmth. Cal was right.

"Tell me again why I asked to be transferred to the Vernius out-post," Cal said. "Oh, right, so *you* could be close to my sister."

Jake leaned back farther, interlocking his fingers behind his head. "That's why *I* volunteered. I don't know why *you* did."

Jake thought back to a year ago, when he'd first heard that Diane had been appointed the Vernition ambassador, potentially a lifetime position. He was certain he would never see her again. He remembered how his heart ached. He had never even told her how he felt about her. How things had changed in a year.

Cal worked the controls on the instrument panel in front of Jake and him. "I guess somebody had to keep an eye on Diane and you." He turned toward Jake. "Frank warned us that this would be a bor-ing job, but man, that's an understatement. Generally, decorated war heroes that can pick their next assignment choose high-ranking public jobs, especially when they've been promoted from private to captain. They don't pick manning a two-person outpost outside the most docile planet in the galaxy. Earth is currently leading a galactic war against the pirates, and Vernius is Earth's closest ally. Even with all of that, there isn't a single threat against Vernius, a planet with zero defenses of its own. Come on, you would think there would be some excitement here."

Jake spun his chair toward Cal, still leaning back and resting his head in his hands. "That's because Vernius has nothing anybody wants. They have lots of technology, but the pirates wouldn't know how to use it even if they stole it." He laughed. "Besides, we get to hang out in this observation room most of the time or take a nap or grab something to eat on the lower level. Then fly down to the planet when our shift is over. What a life!"

Cal refocused his attention on the instrument panel, frowning, and picked up his portable transponder. He started working his thumbs on the controls, effortlessly.

"Are you still playing that combat game?" Jake asked.

Cal stared at the transponder intently, his thumbs moving franti-cally. "It's called *Intergalactic Combat*," he said.

"Never mind," Jake said, "you just answered my question." He paused. "And see, you get to play all your little computer games with this assignment. What are you complaining about?"

Jake continued when Cal didn't respond. "Isn't that the black market game that uses real military technology and codes from various planets? You've had that thing at least a year."

"Ah crap, lost again," Cal said, tossing the transponder on the small shelf to his left. "Yep, that's the game. And if it wasn't for this game, we would have never cracked Craton's code and shut down their weapon. This game saved Earth!" Cal sat up straight. "The manufacturer just uploaded new technology to all active devices. I haven't beaten it since they did that." He paused. "And for the record, it's never been proven that the maker gained access to the technology through the black market."

"Still, it's probably illegal to even own the game?" Jake said, shaking his head.

The com buzzed before Cal could respond. Cal quickly pressed the com button and Diane appeared on the viewing screen.

Jake immediately sat up in his chair. Her dark brown eyes still mesmerized him. She was absolutely the most beautiful person he had ever seen, and the love of his life. Even after a year, his heart raced every time he saw her. He could see that she was at some type of conference or meeting. People were mingling in the background with tables set up for what looked like a formal presentation.

"What's up?" Jake asked. Then Jake remembered his plan. He couldn't act excited to see her. He slouched back in his seat.

Diane smiled. "Oh, nothing. Just checking in on you two hardworking Legion soldiers. I have a few minutes to kill before the Imperial Majesty gives her speech on the effects of the pirate war on the economy of the planet. Anything exciting going on up there?"

Jake tilted his head toward Cal. "Cal lost at his video game again."

"At least I'm not napping," Cal said, looking directly at Jake.

Diane sighed. "Will you boys ever grow up?"

One of the Vernitions came up to Diane and whispered in her ear. She turned for a moment and then looked into the video again. "Hey, I have to run. Are we still on for tonight, Jake?"

Jake leaned farther back and looked up. "Oh, yeah, I forgot. At the V-Bistro? Is that right? What was the time?"

Diane furrowed her brow. "Um, yes, the V-Bistro. You picked the place and the time. You said nineteen hundred so you would have plenty of time for your relief team to get settled in and for you to make it back down to the planet. You forgot already?"

"Sorry, it's not that big of a deal, is it?" It was a huge deal. All he thought about all day every day was seeing Diane in the evening. But his plan was to throw her completely off so that she would be shocked when he finally proposed to her.

"Okay," Diane said very slowly. "Whatever." She paused. "I might be running a little late with everything going on here."

Perfect, Jake thought. Diane was never late for anything with him. So, his plan was working. Now he had to act like he didn't care if she was late.

Jake spoke without looking into the video com. "No worries. I don't mind. I'll be ready whenever you are."

Diane hesitated and a Vernition placed his hand on her shoulder. "I have to go."

The screen went dark.

Cal spun his chair toward Jake. "Are you going to ask her tonight? Your hard-to-get, I-don't-care-anymore game has gone on too long."

Jake pulled a large diamond ring out of his pocket. He loved how one tradition had not changed through all the years. Diamond engagement rings. "No, not tonight."

"Dude!" Cal said. "What are you waiting for? That wasn't the sweetest good-bye she just gave you. I think you might be going a little too far with this plan of yours. And it was a pretty stupid plan in the first place, if you ask me."

"Has she said anything to you about it?"

Cal shook his head. "No, no. We don't talk about you and her. But I can read between the lines. You need to stop dragging this out."

"I just want it to be the perfect time and surprise her when she least expects it," Jake said.

"So, when is the perfect time?"

"Anniversary Day," Jake replied.

Cal scrunched his eyebrows. "Anniversary Day? Whose anniversary?"

"You know, in four days," Jake said, leaning toward Cal.

Cal sat up straight. "You want to propose to Diane on the anniversary of the Battle of Craton?" Cal shook his head and rolled his eyes. "How romantic."

Jake leaned back and spun his chair. "That's also the anniversary of the first time we said *I love you* to each other."

Cal nodded very slowly. "Oh, right, while standing next to Romalor's dead body. Still not romantic. But you get an A for effort, my friend."

"But that's not all," Jake said as he leaned forward. "I booked a weeklong luxury space cruise, stopping at the four planets ranked by the *Earth Times Journal* as the best couples' vacation destinations in the galaxy. And I had your dad ask Diane if she could take the week off to help him with some things at his new house in the Sector One countryside." Jake picked up his data pod, poked the screen, and handed it to Cal. "I have the tickets right here. I'm just waiting for the confirmation from the company."

Cal took the data pod. "I thought you never read the *Earth Times Journal*." He looked down at the data pod screen. "Again, an A for effort, but another mistake. These tickets are for Jake and Debbie. Who's Debbie?"

Jake grabbed the data pod out of Cal's hand and looked at it. "Crap, you're right. My travel agent must have messed that up." Jake leaned back again. "I'll get it fixed before we go. The point is, I have it all planned out."

Cal shook his head. "I still think you're playing with fire with this whole act."

The com buzzed again. Cal pressed the button, and Frank Cantor appeared on the screen.

Jake sat up quickly. "Frank! To what do we owe the pleasure? Long time no see."

Jake gave up a long time ago on addressing Commander Cantor properly. He never knew his father, losing him in a quantum light fighter explosion when he was not quite two. Then, at fourteen, he watched his uncle Ben, who had raised him, die at the hands of Romalor. Even though Frank was still their commander through Sector Four, after that, Frank had become his father figure. Without him, Jake had no idea how he would have survived after Ben's death.

Frank removed the unlit cigar from his mouth. "Are you cowboys still taking the easy route, hanging out in the saloon above Vernius? You're missing all the Wild West action out here."

Frank used every television analogy from the old American westerns that he could. Jake grew up watching rerun after rerun of almost every western movie and television series ever made. He had to admit, he enjoyed them too. John Wayne was Frank's favorite actor from the day, and so he became Jake's favorite too.

Jake smiled. "You know it, boss. We're enjoying the good life. When you're a war hero, you can get these cushy assignments."

Cal jumped into the conversation, smiling as well. "Besides, somebody has to look after Vernius."

Frank shook his head, removing his Stetson. "If anyone deserves a cushy assignment, it's you two, after all the outlaws you've had to gun down."

Jake leaned toward the com. "What about you, Frank? Commander of an entire Legion headquarters, turning down President Buchanan's offer to be his chief Legion advisor, and you're out there fighting in the middle of the pirate war. Shouldn't you be the one taking it easy?"

"You know me, boys. I'm not going down sitting behind a desk. I'm going out guns a-blazing. Even the Duke filmed his final movie while he was dying of cancer."

This time it was Jake who shook his head.

"You're one of a kind, Frank." He paused. "Where are you, anyway?"

Frank leaned back. "On some deserted rock that used to be a planet. Now, it's half gone from erosion or asteroids or something. It's pretty barren. Anyway, we think it's close to the pirate stronghold, so we set up shop here."

Cal swiveled his chair back and forth while he talked.

"Yeah, you're the top commander in this pirate fight, I hear. Eight of the sixteen Legion divisions are off Earth and in the arena under your command. That's pretty impressive."

Frank gave a sheepish grin. "I don't know how impressive it is. With all this firepower, we still can't seem to get the upper hand on these pirates. They're getting help from somewhere. We just can't figure out where. They're too organized to be running this campaign on their own." Frank shifted in his seat. "You know pirates. A small faction may work together, but they're always in it for themselves and too selfish to combine forces. And that brings me to the reason for contacting you cowboys."

Jake straightened his back. "Fire away."

Frank leaned forward, put his cigar in his mouth for a few more chews, then placed it in an empty ashtray on a portable metal desk. "I hoped you two might be able to help me track down a lead on where most of these pirates are holed up. We figure if we can locate their headquarters, we can find out who's helping them. If we can cut off the head of the rattler, that should kill the snake."

Cal leaned forward.

"Great idea. It has to be nearly impossible, fighting these random pirate ships when they're using guerrilla warfare tactics. They just hit the transports or military escorts and run."

"Exactly," Frank replied. "It's just like fighting a group of bandits that you can't see. They strike and then head back into the hills. If we can take out whoever is organizing them, they should fall apart."

"Without the Legion having to find and destroy every single pirate ship," Cal added.

Jake looked at Cal. Cal always impressed him. Not only was he a technology whiz, but he was always the strategist too. Jake was the shoot first, ask questions later person. Cal was the thoughtful one. Jake appreciated that. Cal had saved him on more than one occasion by making him stop and think before pulling out his sepder and firing.

"Bingo," Frank said.

Jake's eyes lit up. "So where are we off to? What do you need us to go check out?"

Jake had enjoyed the easy life this past year. And that's the way he acted around Cal and Diane. He had enough of fighting after the Battle of Craton and killing Romalor. Or at least he thought he did. Truth be told, he was growing bored. He wanted to spend the rest of his life with Diane. He wanted to settle down and raise a family. He wanted that more than anything in the universe and he wouldn't do anything to jeopardize that dream.

He'd lost eight years of his life thinking about nothing except revenge against Romalor and he'd almost lost Diane in the process of seeking that revenge. He wouldn't make that mistake again. But deep down inside, he was much more like Frank than he cared to admit. He was a fighter. He needed action to keep him going. After a year sitting around at this outpost, he felt his blood flowing faster just thinking about going on an assignment.

Frank raised a hand, palm toward the screen. "Slow down there, horsey. I didn't say anything about going anywhere. I just need you to look into some intel."

Jake sank back in his seat. His excitement was gone. It was good to feel his blood pumping again, even if it was just for a moment. But this was probably for the better anyway. He had a date with Diane that night and would be proposing to her in just a few days. That was his life now. That was what he truly wanted.

"What intel?" Cal asked.

Frank cleared his throat. "We intercepted a transmission from one of the pirate spacecraft. We have been trying to intercept any communication we can among them but have not had any luck until now. They seem to run silent. We came across this transmission more by accident." He paused and shifted in his seat. "The problem is that it's coded."

Cal interrupted. "But we have programs that can break pretty much any code in the galaxy, especially since everyone in the galaxy has a translator chip implanted in their ear. That gets decoding over the first hurdle. Every language in the galaxy has been recorded at some point. Doesn't the Legion have access to that data?"

"Yes," Frank said. "In fact, it was the Legion who made most of the recordings. Our surveillance technology is second in the galaxy to only Vernius." He paused. "But that's just it. None of our programs can decipher it. They've either found an extremely advanced code for an existing language, which I doubt, or they're using a language not in our database. And I can't see how that could be. But either way, this code is far more advanced than any pirate capability."

Now it was Cal's face that lit up. Cal loved challenges like this. As much as Jake missed the heat of a battle, he could tell that Cal missed technological challenges even more.

Cal stood up, still looking into the viewing screen. "You got it, Frank. Send over the communication and I'm on it!"

Jake cleared his throat rather loudly, looking at Cal.

Cal looked at Jake and then back at the screen. "I mean *we're* on it."

Jake smiled. "I'm just joking, pal. We all know that this is all yours."

"I'll have the information sent to the Imperial Majesty's main-frame," Frank said. "She's already said that you can work in their tech center. They have equipment that puts the Legion's technology to shame. Let me know if you can figure it out." Frank stood up, put his hat back on, and picked up his cigar. "I gotta ride on out of here. It was good to see you cowboys again. And be careful out there."

EARTH TIMES JOURNAL

July 9, 2209

This is Nigil Diggs. We'll be celebrating the one-year anniversary of the Battle of Craton in three days. Today I want to talk about an unsung hero of the battle. He is the mysterious elderly blind man on the planet Craton who led Jake, Cal, and Diane to Romalor's superweapon in the first place. The man gets only a brief mention by Jake Saunders in the reports that were made public. Nobody knows who the man is or how he had obtained his information. And while I am sure the Legion hasn't been roaming Craton looking for him, he hasn't been seen again. Earth owes a big thank-you to this man, whoever he is.

3

THREE DAYS EARLIER

Ezekiel paused as he stepped out of the passenger hold of the transport ship. He scratched his scraggly gray beard and ran a hand through his matching hair. He then tilted his head back, looked up, and opened his eyes. He saw nothing but darkness. But he could feel the warmth of the two suns on the dark skin of his arms, his neck, and his face, and most comforting, on his eyes. Slowly, his vision started to return. The first sight was blurred tree leaves. They faded in and out as his eyes tried to focus. He allowed the rays of the suns to penetrate deep into his retinas. He blinked several times and with each blink the leaves became sharper. He continued to stand beside the spacecraft, looking upward, until the yellow sky and lavender leaves came clearly into focus. What a beautiful sight it was. It had been so long since he had been home. And so long since he could see. A bright orange-and-red pokemo bird darted across his line of sight. *Beautiful,* he thought. His vision was perfect. In all his travels, he had found no place like the planet Lotox. How he wished he could stay here. Not only did he miss the yellow sky, the lavender grass and trees, the peace and quiet of few vehicles and cities, and the sweet smell that always lingered in the air, but it was also the only place that his damaged eyes would allow him the pleasure of sight.

His reflective moment was broken by an old crackling voice. "Ezekiel, how was your trip?"

Ezekiel lowered his head to make eye contact with the man and smiled. "Purss, my friend, the trip was uneventful. It's so good to see you."

Purss opened his arms and embraced Ezekiel. Ezekiel noticed Purss's bright white robe next to the drab appearance of the same garment that he wore. But then again, he hadn't actually been able to see his clothing since the last time he was on Lotox.

Purss pulled back. "We have much to discuss. Much to catch up on. But that must wait. The Chamber is already assembled. We've been waiting for you. I'll have your things sent to your home. Come, let's walk to the palace."

Ezekiel knew the matter was urgent, but he had hoped he could go to his house for a bit before addressing the Chamber. But the decision wasn't his to make. He had to comply with the Chamber's wishes.

Ezekiel walked in stride with Purss, his hands folded in front of him. The uneven stone street underneath his sandals made walking difficult, but even that felt comforting. It felt like home. He had no idea of the number of miles he clocked walking these streets for the three hundred twenty-four years of his life, but he would love to never have to leave this place again. He took in the small stone structures that lined the road and side alleys and the people mingling about. No vehicles in sight. Only people.

Purss looked straight ahead as he talked. "I trust that your sight has returned as usual?"

"Yes, indeed," Ezekiel replied. "It is as clear as ever. How I missed the colors."

Purss smiled agreeingly. "Even if you could see outside Lotox, I don't think there's any place quite as beautiful."

"Agreed," Ezekiel said. "In my travels, I have learned that the vegetation on most planets is green. How odd."

Ezekiel noticed that the building at the next intersection looked different. He thought for a moment, trying to remember. "What happened to the café that was on the corner?"

Purss responded as they continued to walk. "You have been gone for a while. The café closed nearly fifteen years ago. The young folk like their meals a little faster."

Ezekiel raised an eyebrow as he surveyed the crowd, noticing many people dressed in clothing from other planets rather than the traditional white robes of Lotox. "And I see they like a different wardrobe as well."

"Yes, my friend," Purss said, clasping his hands together in front of him. "The times are changing. And it's becoming more difficult to maintain the ancestral code. The younger generations want to explore. They're leaving the planet more often." He paused. "But we have good people. There have been no other incidents."

Ezekiel lowered his head as they continued to walk. "But this one incident is bad enough to last a lifetime."

"Yes, it is. Bad enough to last many lifetimes."

Ezekiel remembered the route to the palace perfectly. But even if he didn't, he could look up from anywhere in the city and see its smooth coral rock towers reaching high above the smaller stone structures. As they reached the center of the city, they turned right. Ezekiel paused to take in the view. He always loved the sight as he made that final turn. How the narrow streets suddenly opened up into the expansive courtyard leading up to the palace steps. The fountains still danced with sparkling white water. People mingled. A group of children were playing catch. Other children were playing in one of the fountains. The suns' rays reflected off the colorful courtyard stones.

The palace and its courtyard were the pride of the city. Actually, as Ezekiel thought about it, since this was the capital city, they were the pride of the planet. He could recall all the city gatherings in the courtyard. The festive weddings where bright, vibrant-colored clothing was worn. A wedding was one of the rare occasions for which he could don his purple robe. A live band would play while guests danced. He could almost smell the sweet aromas of the cakes and pastries that covered the tables lining the edges of the courtyard. To cap off the wedding day celebration, fireworks would light up the night sky. But he remembered the difficult gatherings as well. There were the protests, which were few and far between, but never involved any violence. There was never any violence on Lotox. Well, except for the incident.

Ezekiel's thoughts were again broken by Purss's voice. "Shall we continue? They're waiting."

He and Purss remained silent as they crossed the courtyard. Ezekiel squinted as the light from the two suns reflected off the massive white marble doors of the palace. Before climbing the steps to the portico, he paused to take in the citrus berry grove to the left of the palace. The red blossoms set against the lavender leaves of the trees made one of the most picturesque sites in the galaxy, and probably beyond. The red flowers would soon turn into the sweetest berries that a palate could taste, but until then, people enjoyed the cinnamon spice fragrance they produced.

Ezekiel and Purss stepped through the entrance into the foyer. Their footsteps on the black and white marble floor echoed against the thirty-foot arched ceiling. Ezekiel would like to have strolled through the palace to see if anything had changed since his last time there, but he knew the Chamber was waiting in the meeting hall immediately to their left. He would have to sightsee later.

Upon entering the meeting hall, Purss sat at the seat just inside the door at the end of a large cavernwood table. Ezekiel made his way past Purss and the ten other Chamber members, all sitting quietly, and took his normal seat at the other end.

Ezekiel again noticed the contrast of his dingy robe, now stained almost brown, to everyone else's.

He liked the formality of Chamber gatherings. No time wasted with greetings even though he hadn't seen the Chamber for years. The members simply acknowledged his presence with a nod, which he returned.

Purss spoke to the group. "Thank you all for gathering so quickly at the news of Ezekiel's return."

The other ten Chamber members simply made eye contact with Purss.

Martock, a bald, heavyset man, looked at Ezekiel and then turned back toward Purss. "Of course, Chancellor. Ezekiel's duties are of the utmost importance not only to Lotox, but also to our Black Eye galaxy, and the entire universe."

"Yes, very true, Martock," Purss replied.

Esau, a frail, elderly man, lifted his head the best he could and peered at Ezekiel. He spoke slowly in a small voice. "Tell us, Ezekiel, what has Mr. Sloan . . . I understand that's the name he goes by now. What has Mr. Sloan been up to?"

Ezekiel leaned forward. "Yes, Esau, Diabolus has been going by the name Sloan outside our galaxy. As for what he has been up to, well, a lot has changed since my last report. Allow me to update the Chamber."

Purss urged Ezekiel on. "Please proceed."

Ezekiel rested his forearms on the table. "As I indicated in my last report, I tracked Diabolus through several galaxies. He appeared to be scouting them out, talking mostly to the not-so-reputable beings in those galaxies, and plotting. But he never took any hostile action." Ezekiel adjusted his position in his chair. The high-backed granite seats in the meeting hall were never very comfortable. "However, that changed when he entered the Milky Way galaxy. He plotted with two of their strongest planets, pitting them against each other. I believe he was attempting to gain control of the military of one or both planets."

Martock interrupted. "To what end? Did he succeed?"

Ezekiel raised a finger. "From what I gather, he is trying to take over the entire galaxy. But no, he did not succeed." He paused. "This time."

"Did you have to interfere?" Purss asked.

"Very minimally," Ezekiel said. "I made contact with only one person: a human named Jake Saunders. I pointed him in the right direction to assist him in thwarting Diabolus's plan. But I am certain that he suspects nothing."

Esau slowly raised his head again, which was obviously difficult with his extreme hunchback. "You said *this time* and *is trying*. Is he not finished?"

"Unfortunately, I think his plan is far from over," Ezekiel said. "I have observed him with the Permidiums."

Martock interrupted again. "Permidium? In the Andromeda galaxy? The hilaetite planet?"

"Yes," Ezekiel said. "The very one. I fear he may be forming an alliance with them, possibly even tricking them into attacking the Milky Way galaxy. It seems the planet Earth is his main target. It's a very formidable planet in the galaxy and holds a lot of resources."

Cleoptara sighed. "We cannot allow him to rule a galaxy. He won't stop there. He'll want to control more and more planets, more and more galaxies. And once he's conquered all he can, or all he wants, what's to stop him from making Lotox his next conquest? Or worse, destroying us?"

Ezekiel always admired Cleoptara. Only one hundred fifty-two years old—middle-aged for Lotox—she was the youngest member, and one of five women on the Chamber. Despite her young age and youthful appearance, she possessed as much or more wisdom than her senior colleagues.

Martock leaned forward and addressed Cleoptara. "Our ancestral code forbids us to interfere with the happenings outside Lotox. You know that."

Cleoptara's dark brown eyes squinted at Martock. "But we've already interfered. Diabolus is one of us. We need to do everything in our power to prevent any further interference by him. Our intellect, strength, and resourcefulness are far superior to any other species. And Diabolus has proven to possess more of each of these qualities than any of us."

Esau raised a quivering hand. "I agree with Martock. We cannot interfere. We can only observe. That's what we commissioned Ezekiel to do. And he has already crossed the line with this Mr. Saunders.

The members started talking at the same time, some siding with Martock and Esau and some siding with Cleoptara. Ezekiel had trouble making out who was on which side. He couldn't remember when the Chamber was so split on a matter.

Purss picked up the gavel in front of him and slammed it on the table. Ezekiel flinched at the echo in the large room from the hollowness of cavernwood. The room fell silent.

Purss spoke in a loud, firm voice. "Ezekiel, what is your position?"

Ezekiel remained silent. He wanted to pause and reflect in the quietness. He turned to the window behind him overlooking the bustling courtyard.

Ezekiel let his mind wander back to the day that the courtyard wasn't so full of people and festivities.

Ezekiel was the last to leave the palace that evening after the special Chamber meeting that decided the fate of Diabolus. Diabolus was the first and only Lotox citizen to rebel against the ancestral ways and code. Diabolus thought that Lotox should use its superior power and intellect to overtake other planets, even other galaxies, for Lotox's gain. So, when the Chamber refused, he decided to take matters into his own hands. But rather than starting a rebellion against the Chamber, Diabolus decided to simply achieve that gain for himself. After all, he possessed more of every Lotox trait than anyone before him and to date, after him. Every trait except foresight. The monopoly on that attribute belonged to Ezekiel.

Purss's voice brought Ezekiel's mind back to the present. "Ezekiel, are you all right?"

Ezekiel slowly turned back toward the table. "You asked for my position on the matter. The ancestral code does forbid interference with the lives of other species, but it does not forbid interaction. We may visit other planets, other galaxies, as we do. We are just not allowed to use our power to alter their ways, whether for the better or for the worse. But Cleoptara is correct. Diabolus has already done that." Ezekiel paused and looked around the table at each face.

He had the attention of every Chamber member. And his foresight told him that they would ultimately agree with whatever action he suggested.

That was his gift. Diabolus had extraordinary strength to go along with the rest of his Lotox attributes, but Ezekiel had foresight. He knew things. Not like those who claimed to read people's minds or claimed that they could predict the future. Those people were just guessing or using tricks. Ezekiel just knew. He didn't know how, just that certain things simply came to him.

"The ancestral code is also flexible. It contemplates the changing times. And times are changing, as is evidenced by our younger generations wanting to get away and explore the opportunities in this vast universe. Therefore, the Chamber must change in its interpretation of the code." He paused and scooted closer to the table. "There will likely be more interference incidents as more of our people leave Lotox. So, the Chamber must change and adapt, or be left behind. Our younger generations will ignore the ancestral code altogether if we do not allow it to evolve with our people."

Purss rested his elbows on the table. "So, are you suggesting that we do whatever is necessary to stop Diabolus?"

Ezekiel frowned. "No, not whatever is necessary. We should still intervene to the least extent possible in the affairs of other planets, but our primary objective should be to prevent Diabolus from any further interference."

Esau interrupted. "But the Chamber commissioned you to only observe Diabolus to determine what his intentions might be. With your keen foresight, you were the perfect person for that. If we are now going to try to oppose Diabolus, we will need someone much stronger, or an army. Lotox isn't equipped for that. We have no crime here, no violence. We have nobody trained in such matters."

Esau was correct. That was the problem they had when Diabolus escaped from the planet in the first place. They had few weapons and no means to contain him. Lotox used its intelligence and technological advancement only to develop what was necessary, like its FTL drive propelling its spaceships three times faster than any other known vessel, its perfect crops and domestic animals for food, and its perfectly balanced society with a one hundred percent employment rate, a maximum of forty hours a work week, and no individual poorer or richer than another.

The only weapon it had ever developed was the departiculator, a device that emitted an invisible and undetectable energy wave that extinguished its unfortunate victim. Located at the security facility out in the countryside, it could target any vessel or object coming within firing range of Lotox.

But it wasn't portable, so it could not be used against Diabolus. Its sole purpose was to protect Lotox from an invasion. A purpose that it had served very well.

Ezekiel looked at Purss. "Is it ready?"

All eyes again turned toward Ezekiel.

Martock wiped a bead of sweat from his brow. "Is what ready?"

Purss spoke before Ezekiel could say anything more. "It is. It hasn't yet been tested, but we have no reason to believe that it won't work. The technology is sound."

Ezekiel had just descended the palace steps when he saw several guards escorting Diabolus out of a side door of the palace. Only two of the guards were armed with small plasma guns. After all, there was never a need for weapons on Lotox, and the departiculator took care of any enemy that approached. Diabolus's wrists were bound in shellmetal cord, one of the strongest materials known. But his hands were bound in front of him, not behind him. Looking back, it was another mistake chalked up to inexperience. Ezekiel didn't know where they were taking Diabolus since they had no jails or prisons on Lotox. By the time Ezekiel reached the courtyard, Diabolus had made his escape before his eyes. It only took a matter of seconds. Why hadn't he foreseen it? In one swift move, Diabolus reached his bound hands up and over the head of the guard walking directly in front of him, throttling the man's throat as he turned to face the two guards with weapons. Diabolus was so fast that he positioned his captive between himself and the guards by the time they fired. Both plasma bursts hit the guard, shielding Diabolus from the beams. Diabolus pushed the then deceased guard into the others, grabbed the plasma guns, and snapped the barrels off. He severed the shellmetal cord like a piece of string and made quick work of the remaining unarmed guards with his bare hands. His strength was impressive.

Ezekiel snapped back to the present, realizing that everyone was waiting for him to speak. "Will it work as was planned? As you know, no other known sedatives work on Lotox people."

"It will," Purss said. "Our best scientists have developed the serum. But the main active ingredient comes from the root of the angel flock plant, which you know only grows on Lotox and is rare. So, we could find enough to make only two doses. One dose should knock out Diabolus long enough to transport him back here. The neck is the ideal target. That should put him out in seconds. In the head could kill him, as it works on the brain. Any other part of the body will work, but the scientists couldn't say how long it will take to kick in. And remember, it is lethal to any other species in any amount."

"And the holding cell?" Ezekiel asked.

"It's complete as well," Purss replied. "Underneath the security facility. It's deep enough that there's no escape."

Ezekiel didn't want to resort to such means, but what choice did they have?

The rest of the Chamber murmured restlessly to one another while Purss and Ezekiel talked.

Martock finally spoke up. "Why hasn't the rest of the Chamber been made aware of these plans?" He glared at Purss and Ezekiel. "When did you two start to plan this?"

Purss responded. "The minute we sent Ezekiel on his mission to observe Diabolus." He paused. "And we kept it between us to protect the rest of you, the Chamber, and the ancestral code. If word of this serum got out before we had developed it and the people of Lotox protested"—Purss paused and looked around the table—"the rest of you would have deniability and only Ezekiel and I would be to blame."

Cleoptara finished Purss's thought. "And the Chamber would remain intact."

"And the code," Ezekiel added.

"Why tell us now?" Martock asked.

"We are telling you now," Ezekiel said, "because now that we have the serum in hand, the need for the Chamber's knowledge and support of the mission outweighs the risk of a protest."

"Well, I still don't like it," Esau rasped sternly. "Such measures are strictly forbidden by the code."

"Like it or not," Ezekiel replied, "It's our only option at this point if we are going to stop Diabolus. We know what his plans are, and I don't think there is any other planet with the knowledge or means to stop him."

The murmurs started up again as everyone stated his or her objection or support, and the noise grew louder and louder until Purss slammed the gavel on the table again. The room immediately fell silent.

Ezekiel stood up. "My position on this matter is that I must give Diabolus a final warning to stop what he's doing and return to Lotox.

And if he refuses, then my mission changes from observing Diabolus to injecting him with the serum and returning him to Lotox."

"Why are we sending only one person for this task?" Cleoptara asked. "Wouldn't two or three or even an army have a better chance of getting close enough to inject Diabolus? And what if something happens to Ezekiel?"

Ezekiel started to respond but was stopped by Purss's raised hand. He sat back down.

"Because with each person we include," Purss said, "the risk of interference with a society and discovery of our plan by Diabolus increases exponentially. We need to be discreet about this and catch Diabolus by surprise. To our knowledge, he has no idea that we've been following him."

The heads around the table nodded in agreement—all except Esau and Martock.

"Good," Purss said as he looked around the table. "Let's have an official vote on the matter. The motion before us is for Ezekiel to follow, confront, and, if necessary, inject Diabolus with the serum and bring him back to Lotox. Esau, you may begin."

Esau reached out and picked up a black marble and a white marble from a saucer on the table in front of him. Very slowly, he got up and wobbled his way to a long, narrow table along the wall. On the table sat two containers that had been used for votes for as long as Ezekiel could remember: a blue-and-red-swirled vase with a small opening at the top for marbles and an identically shaped gray vase. White marbles signified yes votes and black marbles, no.

Each member, having been given two marbles, would vote on the measure using the first vase and discard the other marble in the second one. With all the technology and intellectual ability that Lotox possessed, it could easily surpass any planet in the universe by constructing giant cities, communications systems, transportation, anything. Yet, their cities contained small stone buildings and uneven streets; most people walked or rode imported horses or native woolly musks because the Chamber limited fuel to that necessary for vehicles, air-craft, and spacecraft; and they voted using marbles. He laughed to himself, but he liked it that way.

Shielding his marbles from everyone's view with his hand, Esau dropped one in each container. One by one, the other Chamber members followed suit, until everyone had voted. Ezekiel watched as Purss then picked up the blue-and-red vase and emptied the contents in a large saucer on the table for everyone to see. All white marbles except for two.

Purss spoke first. "The motion passes."

Ezekiel and Diabolus were the only people who remained standing. As their eyes met, Diabolus lowered his head and glared as he started toward Ezekiel. Ezekiel still remembered every word of their short conversation.

"Diabolus, you don't know what you're doing. Stand down. The Chamber is only trying to help you."

"I don't think so," Diabolus replied as he continued toward Ezekiel. "The Chamber wants me to disappear. All I want is for this planet to use its scientific know-how for itself for a change. We have the strength and intellect to expand our control throughout the galaxy. But the Chamber is too cowardly to do so."

Ezekiel recalled his response. "But that is not our way. Our way is peaceful. Lotox has no desire to conquer a galaxy. It's enough that we are safe and left alone on our planet."

Diabolus smirked. "Then I'll go find my own galaxy to rule."

"You're strong, but not that strong, Diabolus. You can't do that alone. We won't let you."

Chills still went up Ezekiel's spine as he recalled seeing Diabolus's smile grow wider and more cynical as they stood face-to-face. "You won't let me? You can't stop me. And trust me, I won't have to do it alone."

Ezekiel again didn't know why he had no foresight into Diabolus's plans. "What are you talking about?"

Diabolus's smirk disappeared. "See, old man, not even you can predict what I'm going to do. But I still don't think I'll take any chances. I don't need you getting in my way."

Before Ezekiel could move, Diabolus had grabbed him by the throat and waist and heaved him over his head. Ezekiel lost his ability to breathe and was overcome with fear as Diabolus tossed him like a rag doll. He put his hand to his throat, the pain from Diabolus's grip lingering.

The last thing he remembered of the encounter was seeing the corner of the fountain quickly approaching his face before he was thrown headfirst into the stone base.

When he came to, he knew he was in a surgeon's office, fear overwhelming him again as he slowly opened his eyes. He saw nothing but darkness. The surgeon was able to partially repair the damage to his eyes but told him that it would always take the light of the two suns of Lotox to stimulate his retinas enough for his vision to return.

***

Martock was glaring directly at Ezekiel. "Looks like you got your wish. Now you can go after Diabolus and get your revenge on him for taking away your sight. That's what you really want, isn't it?"

Ezekiel stood and looked directly at Martock. "Make no mistake. This is not my wish and I have no desire for revenge. Trying to take down Sloan is the last thing I want to do."

EARTH TIMES JOURNAL

July 10, 2209

This is Nigil Diggs, and we are two days from the one-year anniversary of the Battle of Craton. Today I want to highlight the behind-the-scenes hero of the battle, Frank Cantor. Frank was the gunslinging, Stetson-wearing cowboy commander of Sector Four. If not for his last-minute message delivered to President Buchanan, the command to attack Craton would have never been given to the Legion, and Romalor's weapon would have been activated directly at its target, Earth.

4

TWO DAYS EARLIER

Frank exited the transport onto the surface of the planet Aquarii. His boot crunched the fine gravel that was once part of the barren rock that made up most of the planet's surface. He could see nothing but jagged black stone outcroppings and cliffs in every direction except one. Straight ahead, down in the valley, he could barely make out part of a large body of water and small green forest along part of the shore. The rock cliffs blocked his view of the rest of the water.

A petite woman with dark skin dressed in her Legion uniform, holding her sepder, stood next to Frank. "Commander, all of the troops have disembarked. We have about a quarter of the division here."

As Frank surveyed the landscape, he spoke through clenched teeth, which were holding his unlit cigar. "Private"—he glanced at her name tag—"Jackson, this place looks like the ugly in *The Good, the Bad and the Ugly*."

Jackson tilted her head and furrowed her brow. "What's that, sir?"

Frank frowned. "Never mind. Tell the stagecoaches to mosey back up to the shooters, where they'll be safe until we're ready to call in the cavalry."

Jackson raised an eyebrow. "Sir?"

A thin, freckled man whom Frank knew, Private Hanks, stepped forward. "Commander, she's new to your command."

Frank raised his chin in acknowledgment.

Hanks responded to Jackson. "Tell the transport ship to leave the planet and wait just outside the atmosphere with the quantum light fighters until the commander gives the evacuation order."

Frank looked straight ahead into the valley and took the cigar from his mouth. "That's what I just said."

Jackson scowled at Hanks and then looked at Frank. "Yes, sir."

Frank wondered if they were right or if they could be walking into some sort of trap. Lately, the Legion had been tracking pirate space-craft returning to Aquarii after attacks on transport caravans. But it seemed too easy. After all that time, why was the Legion now seeing so many ships returning to one place? Pirates liked to scatter after an attack. Could the Legion have found a pirate stronghold? Possibly the nerve center of the pirates and their allies? Or could it be a setup? He wished he could wait for Cal to decode the intercepted message, but he needed to move now, while the clue was fresh. And there was no guarantee that Cal would be able to decode it anyway. He would just have to be cautious.

A woman approached Frank. He recognized her as a Superior Guard from Sector One, Ava Cruz.

"Commander," Ava said, "the unit is assembled and ready to move out on your command."

Frank bit on his cigar again and stared at the forest in the valley. "So, Captain, the only readings of life on this planet come from that forest?" He motioned with his head.

Ava looked down at the forest and then back at Frank. "Yes, sir. In fact, that forest is the only sign of vegetation, let alone other life, and it isn't a very large forest. The rest of this place is rock. Odd for a planet with an atmosphere similar to Earth's."

Frank rubbed his chin. "That's what I thought." He turned toward Ava, removed his cigar, and used it to point to the far end of the valley. "You take half the unit, circle around to that end of the valley, and enter the forest from there. I'll take the other half and drop down there by the water and follow it to the trees on that end. Stay in communication. The outlaws have to be holed up in that thicket somewhere."

Ava stood erect. "Yes, sir."

"And Captain," Frank said. "Stay alert. This could be a trap."

Abigor put his palms on the table and leaned in to read the map more closely, his long blond hair falling around his face. "With all the technology around, is a paper map all that we pirates can afford?" He looked up at an older human female of Asian descent standing across the table from him. "You do know that by definition, pirates *take* things? We could *take* a more technologically advanced map than this piece of paper."

The woman spoke through gritted teeth. "Paper is safer. The Legion is intercepting every communication these days."

Abigor straightened his muscular, six-foot three-inch frame and used his hand to brush the hair back from his red eyes. His head almost touched the log roof in the dimly lit one-room cabin, the only building he had seen on his first visit to Aquarii. "Then tell me again, Ning, why should I join this war? I have no dog in this fight."

Ning turned her attention to the other person in the room, a Cratonite pirate standing at the end of the table. "Dolf, please explain to Abigor what we are trying to do in this war."

Dolf, who was short for a Cratonite, straightened up and puffed out his large chest with its third pectoral muscle. He spoke in a gravelly voice. "We are doing what pirates do: steal for profit and kill when somebody gets in our way."

"It's more than that. Much more," Ning interrupted, leaning her short, plump body against the table. "All you Cratonites are alike, only thinking about currency and killing. Do you think all these pirates from throughout the galaxy have united for something as simple and shortsighted as that?"

Dolf snarled and stepped back from the table.

Ning turned to Abigor. "We are fighting this war for something far greater. In the end, it will be the pirates who control the galaxy. Every planet will bow to our demands. We will no longer be looked down on or have to hide. We will be respected." She leaned closer. "We will be feared."

Abigor slapped the table and laughed. "Who fed you that line? Pirates are too shortsighted and too selfish. We'll never unite long enough to achieve dominance of the galaxy. And even if we did, how would we rule? Everyone would be in it for himself." He paused. "Excuse me. And herself."

Abigor knew exactly how pirates thought and what they desired. After all, he was one, although he thought of himself as a little above the others. He was a pirate out of necessity, not choice, having been abandoned as a teen on a barren rock that wasn't even a planet and forced to steal and scavenge to survive.

Kill or be killed. And he worked alone, not with a crew like other pirates.

He narrowed his eyes at Ning. "So, I ask you again: If I am going to join this fight of yours, what's in it for me, and who is organizing it? I know that no pirate has the ability to pull all of this together." He gestured at the map. No single pirate had the skill, leverage, or strength to persuade or coerce all the pirates to join forces. And there was no way that pirates would form any type of committee to democratically make decisions.

Ning squinted at him and remained silent.

Abigor knew she was holding back information. He wouldn't back down. He stepped toward the door. "Fine. If you won't tell me, then I'm gone. I don't need you or your band of renegades. Do I need to remind you that *you* asked me to this meeting, not the other way around?"

Ning held out a hand. "Okay, fair enough. I'll tell you what I know."

"You really don't know who you're following, do you?" Abigor said over his shoulder, smirking. "And they say that you're the sagacious one."

Ning stepped forward in what he perceived as an attempt to regain control of the conversation. "He goes by Mr. Sloan. He's not from around here. But he is very persuasive."

Abigor stepped back toward the table. "Persuasive? What did he promise you? The galaxy?" He smirked again.

Dolf responded before Ning could. "As a matter of fact, yes. That's what Ning told you earlier. He has an ally from another galaxy. With the full force of the pirates and his ally, we can defeat every planet."

Abigor looked at Dolf. "And then this Sloan and his ally just walk away, leaving the pirates in charge of the galaxy. He gets nothing out of it."

Dolf glanced at Ning and then back at Abigor. "Well . . ." He rubbed his forehead. "We . . ." He paused. "We didn't talk about that."

"And you didn't think that was important?"

"No," Ning said sternly. "The important thing is that we unite as a force. And Sloan was able to get us to do that."

Abigor eyed Dolf and then Ning. "Who's we? Do the two of you represent all the pirate factions?"

Ning shook her head. "No, Sloan was able to pull all the factions together. Almost every pirate commanding a spaceship agreed. Those who haven't joined yet are the ones we couldn't find to meet with Sloan." She looked at Dolf and back at Abigor. "Dolf and I were charged with finding you and bringing you on board." She paused. "So there. Now you know everything that Dolf and I know."

Abigor wasn't sure what to think and how much of this to believe. He didn't feel that one person could unite all the pirates. And how could he have an ally powerful enough to take over the entire galaxy? But he was intrigued. What did he have to lose if he joined the fight? If they won, then he would share in the spoils. And if they lost, he would be no worse off than he was now. A lone wolf looking for his next meal.

Abigor ran his hand through his hair. "Okay, I'll join your cause or whatever you're calling it, but on two conditions." He paused.

"I'm listening," Ning said.

"I work alone. Nobody is on my ship and I don't set foot on any other ship."

"I don't see that as a problem," Ning replied. "What's your second condition?"

Abigor placed two fists, knuckles down, on the table. "I take orders from nobody. Not even your Mr. Sloan. So, I command any group or squadron that I'm a part of." He was certain that Ning didn't have the authority from Sloan, whoever he was, or the other pirates to grant the second condition. But he knew she would agree to the condition in order to claim to the others that she had accomplished her task, and she would pass along the message. He would deal with the topic when it came up later.

Ning took a deep breath. "Fine, I will inform Mr. Sloan."

That wasn't a yes, but that was as much as Abigor expected.

Frank started down the rock cliff as the last bit of daylight faded. He, along with Privates Jackson and Hanks, were in the lead. They didn't need climbing gear, but steep, rocky terrain forced them to descend on all fours in spots. It was treacherous, even with the bright white light of Frank's night vision goggles. It sure beat the eerie green glow of the older version, though.

Hanks whispered, "You know, most commanders don't take *leading their troops* so literally. They usually bring up the rear, where it's safer."

"Well." Jackson's foot slipped on a rock as she started to speak. Frank reached down toward her and she quickly grasped his hand and regained her balance. Jackson continued. "As I started to say, most *commanders* don't even go into battle."

Frank replied quietly while he bit on a fresh cigar and continued to walk or crawl. "These are different times. The West has never been wilder. Besides, I would much rather ride the lead horse so I can spot the bandits and take the first shot than ride in the wagon at the back."

"I think I'm learning your language, sir," Jackson said with a soft chuckle.

Frank never thought much about the way he talked. He knew he used old west analogies, but they had become second nature to him. He didn't think of it as another language. It was natural.

Frank placed a hand on a boulder to balance himself as he crouched down. The fallen boulders were the Legion's last foxhole until they could reach the trees about two hundred yards away. They had made it down the cliff without incident. Frank removed his night vision goggles. *Good*, he thought. *Pitch black.* They would need the cover of darkness if they were to make it along the beach to the forest. He was glad they had donned the dark uniforms. He dabbed his forehead with his sleeve to remove the sweat, careful not to remove his face paint. The air was thick and close, with no breeze whatsoever, which was surprising with such a large body of water in front of them.

He regarded Jackson. "You wait here as everyone passes. Direct them to spread out along the trees once they clear the shoreline. It should be about two hundred yards toward the far end of the lake. You bring up the rear. Once you hit the trees, buzz me once on the com. That'll be my smoke signal to move forward."

Jackson gave a quick nod. "Understood sir."

Frank paused. He almost expected an ambush at any moment. Every sense was on high alert. He hunched over as he moved forward, leading the team from the rocks, along the shoreline, and into the trees, his sepder, in gun mode, at the ready. It was quiet as he crept into the forest, his night vision goggles lighting the way. Not a single leaf moved in the stale air.

His shirt stuck to his back. It was even more humid in the woods. Frank pulled his collar up to dissuade the large mosquito-like insects that seemed to go for the neck. He stepped gingerly to avoid cracking a stick or rustling the leaves.

Frank stopped and motioned for everyone to spread out, right and left. He wanted to cover as much ground as possible in a solid front line. If the pirates were on this planet, they would be in here. At least that's what the readings showed. Cruz and her team would be coming from the opposite direction. The valley was narrow and the forest not that large. Whatever number of pirates were here, the Legion would find them. The question being, what was the number?

Frank whispered into his com. "Captain, we're in the trees."

Ava responded, also in a whisper. "Roger, sir. We just entered as well. All's quiet."

"Copy that. Keep me informed," Frank replied. Something had to give soon. There wasn't that much ground between Cruz and him.

Frank looked up at the thick canopy as he continued to slowly move forward. The Legion intel was accurate. Quantum fighters would be useless down here.

When he turned his gaze forward again, he thought he noticed a light. He slipped off his goggles and sure enough, a dim light shone through the trees in the distance.

Cruz came over the com. "I see a light. Dim, but it's a light. Straight ahead."

Frank replied. "I see it too. Stay spread out but move toward it. We'll do the same."

Frank signaled with his hands to continue forward. Hanks, who was closest to Frank, passed the signal along.

Frank was proud of how stealthily the Legion was moving. Even so, his shoulder muscles tightened as he moved from tree to tree toward the light.

Frank tensed at the sound of leaves rustling overhead. In one quick, smooth motion he looked up and raised his sepder, aiming it to fire. He let out a sigh when he saw a canalopy, this planet's version of a parakeet.

Frank and his team were about thirty yards from the light source when his com buzzed. It was Ava. "Commander, we're here. The light is coming from a small cabin. Looks like one room. No movement inside. I'm moving in for a closer look."

"Copy," Frank said, "but stay alert. It could be an ambush."

Frank was growing less concerned about this being a trap, as they hadn't seen a thing, and pirates didn't have the discipline to stay quiet and hidden that long. The more plausible explanation was that there hadn't been very many pirates on the planet, and those who had been there were now long gone.

Frank had started to move forward when he was blinded by a flash of light—made even brighter through his night vision goggles—which was followed by a deafening explosion. The concussion knocked him over, his sepder dropping into the forest underbrush. He lay there for a moment, his head throbbing, unable to see, trying to regain his bearings. *What just happened?* he thought.

His sight was the first sense to return. He flung off his goggles. The forest burned in front of him where the flash of light had illuminated his surroundings just moments earlier. He felt around for his sepder, found it; then, pulling it under him, he put his weight on the firearm and used it as a crutch to help him stand. He leaned against a tree to steady himself. His hearing slowly returned. Shouts came from all directions, then plasma guns and sepders shot from where the fire burned. The Legion soldiers to his right and left were slowly getting up as well, while those in the rear were rushing forward to meet the front line and take defensive positions. *They're well trained,* Frank thought.

"Commander, are you okay?" someone shouted.

Frank didn't know where the voice came from, but he wiped the dirt from his forehead with the back of his hand and said, "Yeah, I think I'm still in one piece."

Hanks moved toward Frank. "Sir, what happened?"

Frank didn't respond. Instead, he pressed his com. "Cruz, is your team still standing? What's going on over there?"

Silence.

Frank tried again. "Captain, do you read me?"

Silence again before the com crackled, and then a male voice spoke. "Commander, is that you? We've been hit hard and are under heavy fire."

Frank could barely hear over the blasts of the plasma guns coming through the com.

The voice continued. "Captain Cruz is dead. So is over half our team. The cabin was set to detonate. And we have pirates coming down on us from the trees. They're everywhere."

There was no time to mourn Cruz or her team members because seconds after the voice finished, war cries came from the trees overhead, followed by flashes from plasma guns and the frightening sound of plasma bursts raining down around him.

Before Frank could move or say a word, a hole burned through Private Hanks's chest. At the same time, a sharp pain shot through the back of Frank's head. He grew dizzy. He attempted to steady himself with his sepder but to no avail. After a few wobbly steps, he toppled over. He heard shouts from the Legion and sepders returning fire. The pirates had outsmarted him. They had been disciplined. They lured him right into their trap. Then they waited for his back line to move forward before dropping from the trees. *How did they learn such tactics?* That was Frank's last thought as he watched the butt of a plasma gun coming toward his face. Then everything went dark.

EARTH TIMES JOURNAL

July 11, 2209

This is Nigil Diggs, and tomorrow is the big day, the one-year anniver-sary of the Battle of Craton. We have talked about the heroes of the battle, and tomorrow there will be parties and celebrations all around the planet to honor those heroes. Tomorrow will be my final report on the events of that fateful day a year ago and those involved in the conflict. Tomorrow, I will feature the villains who came so close to destroying the planet Earth. I hope you have enjoyed my special feature on this epic battle.

5

ONE DAY EARLIER

Jake punched the light fighter into quantum drive. It felt good to be flying again, flying into space. He had forgotten how much he missed it.

"Keep an eye on the sensors for pirates," Cal said. "We can handle a couple in this beast." He patted the control panel, "But we don't want to encounter a fleet."

"Already have one eye on it," Jake replied. He turned toward Cal. "Okay, we have some time before we reach the coordinates. Now, can you tell me what you found that we had to leave so quickly? And shouldn't we be contacting Frank?"

"Okay, yes, let me explain." He paused. "I couldn't crack the code used in the communication that Frank sent using any methodology or formula in the Legion's or Vernius's database. So, I developed a program that would search both databases for any possible language outside our galaxy that was input into Legion's or Vernius's tech system. The Legion picks up signals from time to time that we don't know from whom or from where they came. Vernius probably does the same. When we do, we input them as possible foreign languages. I also put together a secondary program that would then run any hit and determine if it's a possible match for the code in the communication." Cal turned back to the control panel and changed their course slightly.

Jake checked the sensor readings. All clear. "And you found . . ."

"I recognized one of the hits that my program spat out. I knew I had seen it before and then, bingo! I remembered. That hilaetite ship we encountered last year chasing Veneto. If you recall, they spoke in English, but the words came from space, from outside our spacecraft, not through our com."

"I remember like it was yesterday," Jake said.

Cal scooted to the edge of his seat. "Right, and the reason our and Vernius's existing programs didn't pick it up was because it wasn't translated using our translator chips. The hilaetite ship somehow broadcast what we heard in English."

Jake raised an eyebrow. "This is all pretty ingenious, but what does it have to do with deciphering the code Frank sent you or why we're in such a rush?"

Cal held up a hand. "Patience. I'm getting there. Our programs still couldn't use that information to crack the code. There was a missing link. That is, a missing link until I recalled that I had my portable transponder with us when we met the hilaetite ship, with Intergalactic Combat opened up from Diane and I using it to crack Craton's system. And the transponder picked up the actual language coming from the hilaetite ship before they translated it into English. I altered one of Vernius's decryption programs using the readings from the transponder, and it worked." Cal clinched his fist. "The altered program deciphered the message."

Jake could feel himself losing focus. Cal was brilliant at figuring out things like this, but too brilliant to explain it quickly and succinctly. "Great job, buddy, but again, what did the transmission say, and why haven't we contacted Frank?"

"Okay, okay," Cal said excitedly. "I still couldn't translate it word for word, but it was a message from a hilaetite spaceship like we saw, since the output signature is exactly the same as the one my transponder picked up a year ago. It was a broadcast message to the pirates, coordinating them to a rendezvous point for the initiation of an attack. That's why we're in such a rush. I don't know how much time we have. I figured we could hit the trail, as Frank would say, and I could fill you in along the way."

Jake felt his heart quicken.

He didn't want anyone to be the target of a skirmish and he certainly didn't want any casualties, but the talk of a fight, the possibility of seeing combat action again, got his blood flowing. He straightened in his seat. "An attack on whom? Where?"

Cal shook his head. "The transmission didn't say, but it gave the coordinates for the rendezvous." He paused. "The planet Titan."

Jake's excitement for battle immediately turned to a feeling of dread. There was nothing good on Titan. "The pirate planet? I guess we should have guessed."

"Yep, that's the one," Cal said. "And that's where we're heading. Maybe we can pick up another transmission or find out something that will give us a clue as to what or who is being attacked and when. It should be easy to find the rendezvous point since there's only one city on the entire planet."

Jake interrupted. "Yeah, Tortuga. And what a pleasant place I hear it is. Filthy and full of drunken pirates."

"Exactly," Cal said. "Tortuga was the Legion's first thought as the pirates' headquarters, but they quickly dismissed it. The only pirates on the planet were too drunk to be planning any war. At least the pirates were smart enough to figure that would be the first place the Legion would search for their headquarters."

Jake checked the instrument readings. "Yeah, and that's why they probably picked it for this get-together, figuring the Legion has written off Titan. But what about Frank? Weren't we supposed to report our findings to him? The Legion should be checking this out. Not that I'm complaining."

"Yes, we were supposed to," Cal said, "but I can't locate him. I got in touch with a couple of his officers. They said he was leading an away mission last night and they hadn't heard from him. They didn't know anything about this transmission and said the Legion was spread too thin right now to help. So here we are."

Jake again started to feel the excitement swell inside him. The dread of Tortuga was overcome by the chance to take some action, to do something useful. But he also had become much wiser than he was just a year ago. He knew the importance of a team and the risk of going into a fight alone. "So, we're on our own? Does anyone even know where we're going?"

"Yes and yes," Cal replied. "We are out here alone, so we need to be careful. This needs to be a surveillance mission, not one of your lone-wolf attacks. Okay?"

Jake had already made that determination. "You got it, buddy. My lone-wolf days are over. But who knows we're out here?"

"Diane cleared the mission through the Imperial Majesty. Her security detail, which is the closest thing Vernius has to a military, knows we're heading to these coordinates. So, we're flying under Vernius's flag, not the Legion's."

Jake chuckled. "A lot of good that'll do us if we run into trouble. The combat experience of the Imperial Majesty's security is halting a protest or two."

Cal shrugged. "Well, it's better than nothing."

It was easy to find a remote place to land on Titan. Jake set the fighter down in a clearing well outside Tortuga. He had never been to Titan before and immediately noticed the lush trees, green spaces, and hills. The foliage reminded him of Earth.

Cal reached behind his seat and pulled out a bundle of clothes. He tossed a ragged shirt and cloak to Jake and kept an old shirt, cloak, and pair of pants for himself. "Put these on. It'll help us fit in. As soon as I figured out where the coordinates would take us, Diane grabbed these for us." Cal looked at the instrument panel and then pointed to Jake's right. "Tortuga should be that way, through those trees."

As they made their way through a thick pine forest, Jake breathed deeply, taking in the fresh air and pine scent. He turned toward Cal. "What are we looking for, exactly?"

Cal chuckled. "Good question. Two possibilities. I brought the portable scanner in case there's another encrypted transmission. It'll pick it up and we can decipher it."

"I'm guessing they aren't going to chance another broadcast message since they've already set the rendezvous point."

"Agreed," Cal said. "That leads me to the second possibility. We need to look for pirates who look out of place in Tortuga."

Jake laughed. "You mean sober?"

"Yeah, that's a good sign," Cal said. "We should find groups of more serious pirates. I'm assuming they'll be gathering to somehow receive and relay instructions."

Jake climbed over a fallen tree. "And an even better sign would be if one or two people from the hilaetite ship were to come down to give instructions. We don't know what they look like, but I'm sure they would stand out."

"Right," Cal said as he climbed over the same tree. "Once we find a target, we can play the part of pirates looking for the meeting."

A twig suddenly snapped. Jake stopped and looked behind them. Were they being followed? Everything was quiet. He slowly turned, looking in every direction, as well as up into the treetops. Nothing. But he had an odd feeling, like he was being watched.

"What's wrong?" Cal asked.

Jake was quiet for a little longer, listening. He shook his head. "Nothing. I thought I heard something, but it was probably just some critter."

"But there's no wildlife on Titan."

Jake processed that fact but didn't respond. That did explain why it was so quiet in the woods. Not even a bird chirping.

"Let's keep moving," Jake said. "And you better keep that scanner hidden when we get to Tortuga." Jake jerked his head toward the device in Cal's hands.

"Don't worry. I have that covered." Cal pulled a faded leather pouch from his shoulder and dropped the scanner inside. Then he pulled his cloak back, revealing his sepder attached to his waist. "And we need to keep these hidden too. Pirates don't have sepders."

Jake shrugged his shoulders. "Unless they steal one."

As the pine grove turned into a thicker hardwood forest, Jake could faintly hear indiscernible noises in the distance ahead of them. "We must be getting close."

Another stick broke behind them just as leaves rustled to their left.

Jake looked at Cal. "Did you hear that?"

"Hear what?" Cal replied.

"You said there are no animals here?"

"Right," Cal said, "no animals, no native species, nobody except the pirates that hang out in Tortuga."

There was someone out there following them, watching them. Jake could feel it. He could hear it. At least two people, maybe more. He turned around and yelled, "You can come out now. What do you want?"

Cal's eyes widened. "Who are you talking to?"

Four pirates stepped out from behind trees, two human and two with blue skin. Unmistakably from Neptune. They all looked serious and very sober.

A heavyset bearded human said, "You two need to leave in that quantum fighter you came in. You aren't welcome here."

Jake whispered to Cal, "I guess playing the part of a pirate isn't going to work with these guys."

"Yeah," Cal said, "and I doubt they would believe us if we told them that we stole the fighter."

Jake raised his voice. "We have business here. We aren't leaving. You can either help us or get out of our way."

The four pirates moved closer. The same pirate spoke. Jake took him to be the leader of the group.

"If you do not leave now, then you will remain here permanently, to rot, you Legion pigs. We will kill you just like the hundreds of others of your kind that we've killed in this war."

Three of the pirates drew sabers, and one drew a long knife.

At first Jake tried to figure out how to subdue them without killing them. They could have simply been Tortuga pirates looking for some rough fun, so he couldn't kill them, but yet he couldn't let them go to warn others who Cal and he really were. But that all went out the window. They were part of a pirate war. By their own admission, they'd killed Legion soldiers. Jake could feel his senses heighten. His muscles tensed in excitement and then relaxed as his training took over. He drew his sepder.

Cal drew his as well and said softly to Jake, "No shooting. We're too close to Tortuga to make that kind of noise."

Jake threw Cal an affirming glance and flipped his sepder into sword mode. He wasn't angry. He had finally learned in his battle against Romalor to control his anger. He was focused. He was a Legion soldier. He hadn't fought in a real fight for almost a year, but he'd never stopped training. Even on Vernius, he'd trained. He saw only the four men around him. He heard only their movement. He felt the hilt of his sepder in his hands. He breathed slowly, lowering his pulse. Every sense in his body was now heightened, ready to fight. He'd missed this feeling.

Jake wanted to draw three of the pirates toward him, leaving only one for Cal. He knew he had better odds against three than Cal did against two. He moved toward the three pirates on the left. Cal went for the one on the right.

The leader simpered through his thick beard and said, "You're making a big mistake. But it's *your* life."

As Jake closed in, the pirates spread out from one another.

Good, Jake thought. The farther apart they were, the easier it would be to fight them one at a time.

The lead pirate raised his saber, ran toward Jake, and swung. Jake blocked and countered with a series of sepder strikes—high then low, high then low, to the right, left, right, left.

All blocked.

Jake sensed one of the pirates approaching from behind. He turned quickly—with his sepder raised to block, which he did perfectly—with an immediate counterstrike, slicing across the blue skin of the pirate's bare chest. Dark green blood oozed from the wound.

The third pirate was on him now, and the lead pirate was still on his back side. He immediately turned, swinging his sepder in the process. He connected with the unsuspecting third pirate, slicing his outstretched hand clutching a knife, leaving his hand dangling from a small strip of flesh as the knife fell to the ground.

Jake felt a sharp sting in his bicep as the lead pirate connected with a saber strike. Blood trickled through his sliced shirt sleeve. Luckily, it was his left arm. He could wield his sepder in either hand, but he was stronger with his right. The wound hurt, but he had felt much worse. He blocked out the pain, and without missing a beat, he turned and delivered a quick counterstrike, connecting with the pirate's forearm just below the hilt of his saber, striking bone. The pirate grimaced and swiftly flipped his saber to his other hand, blocking Jake's second strike.

Nice move, Jake thought.

Jake blocked two counter swings from the lead pirate, then immediately turned to face another onslaught from the blue-skinned pirate, whose chest still seeped blood. Jake alternated blocks between the two pirates as he backed up. He didn't like the position he was in, on the defensive. But one pirate was hurt badly, and the other was using his weak arm. Both injuries forced them to swing high. He had to take advantage of that.

He heard someone approaching from behind. It had to be the pirate who wielded a knife. He would have to get close in order to strike Jake.

Jake waited and listened as he continued to block the other two pirates' swings. He now knew both attackers' weaknesses. He would exploit each one in turn. He heard the final step of the third pirate, sensing him at his back. Jake dropped to one knee, ducking the high saber swings. As he dropped, he pivoted, bringing his sepder down, and then, thrusting it upward, he drove it deep into the pirate's chest before he could bring his knife forward.

Jake continued in the same motion, pulling out his sepder. As he spun, he rose toward the chest of the blue-skinned pirate, head butting him in his open wound. The pirate fell backward as Jake thrust his sepder into his neck with his right hand and grabbed the falling pirate's saber with his left, careful to avoid the blade, which was pointed toward him. Jake thrust the saber underhand and backward into the oncoming lead pirate's stomach. He turned to see the lead pirate clutching the embedded saber with both hands, his eyes wide and blood trickling from the corner of his mouth. Jake just stood there and watched the pirate stumble backward, then fall.

Everything was quiet. Jake turned around quickly and saw Cal approaching. The other blue-skinned pirate lay motionless on the ground beyond.

"You okay?" Jake asked.

"Yeah, thanks," Cal said. "But that arm of yours doesn't look so good."

Jake glanced at his arm. "I'll live. It gives me a more authentic pirate look."

Jake and Cal continued toward Tortuga uninterrupted. The shouts and music grew louder the closer they got. Jake could smell the stench coming from the city, a mixture of alcohol, sweat, and vomit. Titan's sun was setting as they reached the outskirts of the municipality. The dimly lit narrow brick streets and buildings reminded him of pictures he had seen of London, England, in the early 1900s. Most of the buildings were dark. He couldn't tell what they were used for. Maybe small businesses or houses. Or more likely they were abandoned. But on every street there was at least one well-lit building filled with music and shouts and screams, and, most likely, plenty of alcohol. Jake added the smell of rotten food to the list of unpleasant aromas wafting through the air.

The two men paused when they neared the center of the city.

"How are we supposed to find pirates that look like they're actually here for the rendezvous?" Jake said. "All of these pubs look and sound the same."

Cal smiled. "Looks like we have some bar hopping to do. We're going to have to check them all out until we find something."

Jake shook his head and muttered, "Oh joy."

After about the fifth pub, Jake concluded that they all looked and smelled exactly the same, from the drunk pirates stumbling around, to the cards and dice gambling, to the scantily dressed women. He couldn't decide if they more resembled an English pub, as he first thought, or an old western saloon from Frank's John Wayne movies. The only difference was the selection of music and the variety of instruments, although the songs rose to the same decibel level in each establishment.

By the time they hit the eleventh pub, which was on the far side of Tortuga, the night was well past the halfway point, but the pirates were still going strong. Jake sensed something different in this pub. The music was softer, and there was less shouting. Most of the occupants were sober pirates quietly gambling.

People barely raised their heads when Jake and Cal walked in. They made their way to the large bar, found two empty stools, and ordered what they learned from their experience at the previous pubs was the only nonalcoholic drink on the planet, aura ale. Jake took a sip of the spicy beverage and set his mug down on the rugged wood bar. He wasn't sure what type of wood it was. Probably pine, since pine trees seemed to be so abundant on Titan.

The bartender placed his large, overweight frame in front of Jake and Cal as they sat there silently. "You two seem like you're looking for someone."

Jake and Cal looked at each other. Jake perked up. Maybe this was the break they had been looking for.

Cal replied, "Or something. Can you help?"

The bartender wiped his sweaty brow with the rag he was using to dry mugs. "Do you have something to tell me?"

He had to be asking for a password or phrase. Jake looked at Cal, wondering if he had any ideas.

Cal didn't miss a beat. He replied again, speaking softly, "Look, we've traveled from the other side of the galaxy. We barely picked up the transmission of the rendezvous and coordinates. We couldn't make out anything more. We really want to take part in the attack and take out those Legion pigs. Can you just tell us where the meeting is? We'll even slaughter a few pigs just for you."

Jake watched the bartender for a reaction. Wow, Cal laid that on pretty heavy.

The bartender froze for a moment, eyed them, and then gestured toward a dark corner to the left of the bar, where Jake could make out wooden stairs. "Left at the top. First door on your right."

Jake shot him a final glance, and the bartender moved on.

Jake leaned toward Cal. "I think we might have found what we've been looking for. Let's go."

Cal stood up. "Yeah, fortunately . . . or unfortunately."

As they started up the steps, a gravelly voice came from the darkness on the other side of the stairs. "You two looking for something?"

Jake peered around the stairs. He could make out a lone table in the corner with an old, dark-skinned man sitting at it. The man stared into his mug. Jake could barely make out the gentleman's face in the darkness through his shaggy gray beard and long hair, but he looked familiar.

"You head on up," Jake said to Cal. "I just have a feeling I need to talk to this guy." He pointed toward the old man.

Jake approached the man and sat down cautiously in the chair opposite him as Cal proceeded up the stairs.

"Have we talked before?" Jake asked.

"Maybe."

Jake knew the guy from somewhere. It was right on the tip of his tongue.

"Why did you ask if we are looking for something?" Jake asked. "What makes you ask that? Do you know something I don't?"

The old gentleman, motionless, continued to stare at his hands cupping his mug. "So many questions, yet so few answers. Be careful what you seek, for you may not like what you find."

Jake could feel the agitation building inside. He didn't have time for this. And it seemed to be getting hotter in the pub. His shirt stuck to his back when he leaned forward.

"Look, if you have something to say, say it. Otherwise, I need to go upstairs with my friend."

Just as the last word left Jake's mouth, it hit him. Craton City. This was the old man in the pub in Craton City who had helped him find Romalor's weapon. How could that be? He didn't know how, but it was the same person. He knew without a doubt. Maybe this guy really could help Cal and him. But he remembered that he always talked in riddles, never giving a straight answer.

The gentleman raised his head and looked at Jake with glassy eyes. "Are you prepared for what you might find upstairs? Once you start down that path, you will not be able to return."

Jake remembered that the man was blind.

"What do you know about what's going on upstairs?" Jake asked. "That's the pirates' rendezvous to discuss what and when they are going to attack, isn't it?"

"If it is, what can you do about it? Can you alone stop it? You're just one person fighting an unknown enemy, alone."

Jake shook his head. "I can try. There's still plenty of Legion soldiers out there. I just need to gather them. And the enemy is known. They're a bunch of unorganized pirates and a hilaetite ship from somewhere."

The old man lowered his head toward his drink wrapped in his hands. "This goes deeper than you know. It goes back to an old enemy of yours and your father's."

Jake couldn't believe what the guy had just said. *An enemy of his father's?* His father was a typical Legion soldier, killed in a quantum light fighter accident in deep space. What did that have to do with anything going on now?

"What do you mean by an enemy of my father's?" Jake demanded.

The old man shook his head slowly. "That does not matter now. What does matter is what you do next. A lot of lives may depend on your decision."

Jake raised his voice. "Tell me what's going on. Where's the attack? You're the one that started talking to me. Do you have any useful information?" Once again, his pulse quickened. He heard the agitation in his own voice.

"You must figure it out on your own. I cannot choose for you. I can only warn you. The galaxy needs you, Jake Saunders. But if you choose to help the galaxy, you may lose the one closest to you."

How does he know my name? Jake thought. *Did I tell him on Craton?*

"I'm a Legion soldier. Of course, I'm going to help my comrades, and the galaxy, if I can," Jake said.

"Very well, then. I leave you with two pieces of advice." The gentleman paused, then appeared to look up at Jake. "Don't be afraid to accept the aid of one you believe to be your foe. And when the time comes, you alone cannot defeat the one behind all of this."

Jake shook his head. "What foe? I cannot defeat who alone? Why do you speak in riddles?"

The old man took a sip, then sat quietly, his face once again tilted toward the mug.

A crash from upstairs startled Jake. In one smooth motion, Jake jumped from his seat, kicking the chair aside and pulling his sepder from underneath his cloak. Seconds later, Cal burst into the balcony hallway, his sepder drawn.

Cal shouted, "Let's get out of here!"

Jake glanced at the table in the dark corner. The old man was gone.

A hoard of pirates raced after Cal, wielding various styles of swords, knives, and battered guns.

Cal leaped over the balcony railing as one of the pirates fired his plasma gun. The first burst sailed just over Cal's head. The second burned a chunk out of the railing. Cal landed feetfirst on the bar below and rolled onto his side and off the bar, again landing feetfirst on the floor.

Impressive move, Jake thought.

Everyone on the pub floor cleared to the sides or dove under tables, knocking over chairs and spilling drinks in the process.

Jake met up with Cal and raced for the door. He swung the door open and then froze, Cal bumping into him. Four pirates, all from different planets and dressed in matching military-style uniforms—much better than any of the pirates they had seen on Titan so far—blocked the doorway. Each one had a newer-looking plasma rifle aimed at Jake and Cal.

Jake and Cal went back-to-back, their sepders drawn. Jake slowly swiveled his head back and forth between the military pirates blocking the door and the pirates in the pub behind them. There was nowhere to run. They were completely closed in and extremely outnumbered. And based on what had just transpired, the pirates didn't want to simply capture them. They were out for blood. If the pirates started shooting, they would hit each other in the crossfire. But if he and Cal fired first, he figured the pirates would throw caution to the wind, not caring if they took out one another.

Their best option was to try to fight their way out the door using their sepders as swords.

"Any ideas?" Jake said to Cal.

"Nope," Cal said. "How about you?"

"Just one," Jake said as he lunged for the pirates in the doorway.

The four pirates jumped to the side. A tall man in a black trench coat and black boonie hat pulled low over his face took a quick step forward and grabbed Jake's outstretched arm by the wrist. Jake's forward momentum stopped immediately. He had never seen anyone move so quickly.

He tried to yank his arm free, but he couldn't budge it. He threw all of his weight backward, but the man still held firm, seemingly without any effort. Pain shot up Jake's arm from his wrist as the man squeezed hard. The pain in his wrist and arm grew until he could no longer feel his hand. His fingers opened and his sepder dropped to the ground.

Cal turned and drew his sepder back to strike the man but froze when two of the pirates stepped forward and stuck their plasma rifles in Cal's face.

Jake used the man's leverage to raise himself up in a jump and drop-kicked the man in the chest. A sharp pain pierced Jake's knee as his leg snapped back toward him and he fell to the ground.

The man placed his boot on Jake's chest. The pressure was immense. It felt like his lungs were collapsing. Jake couldn't breathe. He gasped for air but none came. He grabbed the man's leg, but it was like trying to move a tree trunk.

His opponent spoke slowly. "Are you finished?"

With guns pointed at Cal's head and this person's unmovable foot on his chest, Jake had only two options: give up or never breathe again.

Jake grimaced and spoke the best he could. "Yes."

"Good," the man said, "we have some things to discuss."

Both anger and fear coursed through Jake's veins as he recognized the man. *Sloan.*

———————

Jake sat on a makeshift concrete bench in a cold, damp cell. Water trickled down the three walls carved into a rock hillside and puddled on the stone floor. Cal leaned against the iron bars that made the fourth wall. With the dim lightbulb at the steel entry door, Jake could see at least three other cells in the block, each one occupied by drunken pirates.

Jake rubbed his nose. The place smelled of mold and urine. "What happened in the room in the pub?" he asked.

Cal straightened up. "They found out who we were. I think they found the pirates in the woods, and then our quantum fighter." He paused. "Everything was going fine. I fit in perfectly. Then one of the pirates got a com call. I don't know what he was told, but he pulled out his sword and looked directly at me. I tried to play dumb, but he didn't buy it. The others followed suit, so I pulled out my sepder and, well, you saw the rest."

Jake already assumed that's about how it went down. They should have been more careful.

"We have to get out of here," said Cal. "Before the com call, I found out about the attack. They're attacking Earth tomorrow! We have to warn the Legion."

Jake jumped up, his heart racing. Earth was the last place he thought they would attack. "Earth? Are you sure?"

"Positive," Cal said.

"But how?" Jake asked. "How can a bunch of pirates get through Earth's defense shield?"

Cal started to pace as he talked. "That's not all. The Permidiums are with them."

"Permidiums? Permidium is in the Andromeda galaxy," Jake interrupted.

"Correct. That's where the hilaetite ship we saw was from. When Earth first discovered Permidium, we knew hilaetite was a plentiful resource on the planet, but *plentiful* is an understatement. Apparently, the entire planet is practically made of hilaetite. I never put two and two together until now, that the hilaetite ship was Permidium. And we saw what such a ship is capable of. Our defense shield may be no match for them."

Jake shook his head. He couldn't believe what he was hearing. "And now I guess we know the connection between the pirates and Permidium."

"Yep," Cal said, "our old friend, Mr. Sloan."

"Or better said, our old enemy." Jake paused. "The old man was right."

"What was that?" Cal asked. "You said something about that old man. Did you find out anything from him?"

Jake thought for a moment. He thought about telling Cal about his conversation with the man, but there really wasn't anything helpful for the current situation. "No, not really."

Cal continued talking, "And with Sloan leading this . . . well, we know what he can do. He helped Romalor get through our defense shield, so I'm sure he can figure out a way to get through it again."

"But what would Permidium want with our galaxy? Why are they involved?"

"That was my exact question," Cal said. "It has something to do with my transponder. Apparently, Sloan has convinced the Permidiums that I recorded some highly confidential data of theirs when we were chasing Veneto and ran into the hilaetite ship a year ago. I have no idea what that would be or if it's even true. All I remember is that I had the Intergalactic Combat game open." Cal stopped by the cell's bars and grabbed one. "Sloan told them that the transponder is on Earth."

"So that's how Sloan's getting the Permidiums to help with the attack. So they can recover the transponder. But where is the transponder?"

Cal lowered his head. "In our quantum light fighter."

Jake pierced his lips. "Which Sloan and the pirates now have."

Cal spoke solemnly. "I'm afraid so."

Jake grabbed an iron bar in each hand and squeezed. "Sloan won't give it to the Permidiums, though. That's his carrot to keep them fighting for him. We have to get out of here."

But Jake knew that escape was hopeless at the moment. They were stuck in a solid rock cell.

6

ANNIVERSARY DAY

President Jack Buchanan sat behind his desk in the West Room of the Presidential Mansion looking at an all-too-familiar sight: his advisors seated around him ready to discuss another crisis. These were the most powerful and influential people on Earth, almost all of whom had been with him his entire term in office.

Now in his tenth and final year in office, he wanted to go out on a positive note, not on the losing end of an attempt to resolve another challenge to Earth's survival. He had gathered his advisors once more to make a final decision on the options they had discussed yesterday. He hoped that after a night's sleep everyone would be able to think more clearly and give his or her succinct opinion.

But if the rest of the team was like him, then they didn't sleep much last night.

Armin Dietrich, sitting to Jack's right, broke the silence. "Mr. President, everyone is here except Ms. Brown." As his chief of staff, Armin could pretty much run one of Jack's meetings without him. Jack liked that, but he couldn't give Armin that much control. Because of

Armin's disposition, people wouldn't give him the same deference they would give Jack.

Jack looked at Armin. "Have you heard from her?"

If it were anyone else, Jack wouldn't worry, but Aretha Brown was the perfect senate leader. She had never been late for a single meeting with him. But maybe she was just stuck somewhere in the Anniversary Day festivities. All of the sectors had celebration plans for today.

Aretha kicked the door of her hover car, then limped away from it shaking her foot, trying to get rid of the pain. *That was stupid,* she thought. But what luck that her car would break down in the middle of nowhere in the Presidential Sector. Now she was sure to be late for the President's meeting. And she was never late for anything.

Her earlier meeting at Sector One headquarters had run over, way over. She left in such a rush that she had forgotten her portable com. *Another stupid move,* she thought. Could her day get any worse? She climbed back inside her car and tried the car's com again. No luck: it was as dead as the rest of the car. She climbed out and surveyed the landscape. No other cars or aircraft in sight and nothing but dry desert in every direction. Fortunately, she always carried plenty of water in the trunk when making long road trips. She would just have to sit tight and wait for someone to pass by and, hopefully, stop. Surely a passerby would recognize her. After all, she was the leader of Earth's senate.

Clarisse Chirac stood up and walked toward a table in a corner set with hot tea and coffee. "Mr. President, I'm sure Aretha has a good reason to be late. You know her. She's never late for anything." She poured a cup of coffee. "Anybody else want a cup? We could be in for a long day."

Jack felt bad for even involving Clarisse in the meeting. The pirate war, as it had come to be known, had little if anything to do with her, as the chief civilian advisor. But he valued her opinion so highly that he wanted to hear what she had to say. "You may be right, Clarisse. This might be a long one."

Jack turned to a short, thin man seated directly opposite him. "Min-jun, while we wait for Aretha, why don't you update us on the status of the Legion, where they are posted. That will be directly relevant to the decisions we'll be making today."

Min-jun Park was a solid chief Legion advisor and very trustworthy. Jack needed that, after Marco Veneto and the events of a year ago. The whole planet needed that. He still would like to have seen Frank Cantor accept the position, but he wasn't surprised in the least when Frank turned it down.

Frank wasn't the type who could sit behind a desk all day. Even as a sector commander, he still led away missions. That was very risky for the Legion, but Jack allowed it because, well . . . because Frank was Frank.

Min-jun sat up and straightened his tie. He spoke in a heavy accent from his home region, the former South Korea. "Yes, sir. Right now, half of the Legion forces are off the planet involved one way or another in the war. The Alpha and Charlie divisions from each sector are out, leaving the four Beta and four Delta divisions on the planet. The Delta divisions are made up of mostly young privates and cadets, so that doesn't leave much here besides our defense stations."

Jack frowned. "That's the same as the last report. Have any locations changed?" He generally liked the formality of Min-jun, always thorough and starting from the top, but today he wanted to get directly to anything new.

Min-jun looked down at his data pod, then back at Jack. "Well, sir, all four Alpha divisions are now under the command of Commander Cantor in Orion's Belt. We've narrowed down the location of the pirates' nerve center and believe that it is located in one of the star systems there. Most likely in the Mintaka system. If we can neutralize their command center, we could very well end this conflict."

Jack raised an eyebrow. "At least we've narrowed down the location since the last report."

Armin interrupted: "But keep in mind sir, it's only a calculated assumption that the command center is in Orion's Belt, and even more of an assumption that it is located in the Mintaka system."

Jack looked from one advisor to the other, waiting for Min-jun to say something. He didn't. Min-jun was much more reserved than Marco ever was. Marco would have jumped all over Armin for stepping into his territory and following up on his report. Jack did like not having to deal with that conflict anymore.

Still looking at Min-jun, Jack continued. "And the Charlie divisions?"

Min-jun cleared his throat. "The four Charlie divisions are spread throughout the galaxy under the commands of the division's superior guards. They're trying to ward off any pirate attacks and protect cargo transports going from planet to planet."

Clarisse sat down with her coffee. "What are the other planets doing about the pirate attacks? Isn't this a joint planetary effort?"

Armin spoke before Jack had a chance to. "It's supposed to be, but we clearly have the strongest military in the galaxy right now and are supplying the bulk of the forces. Vernius and us are getting hit the hardest. And you know Vernius has no military. The two of us have lost more transports than the rest of the galaxy combined. Craton is still recovering from the events of a year ago. And everyone else seems to be using most of their military to protect their home turf from pirates."

"So, we're the only planet out there protecting transports and looking for the pirates' command center?" Clarisse asked.

"That's about it in a nutshell," Jack said. "And the reason we are all here today. And as far as we know, the pirates have organized and are doing this on their own, is that right? No other planet is backing the pirates?"

"That is correct, sir," Min-jun replied. "We have found no evidence of any other involvement, although Commander Cantor recently found a lead that may point to possible involvement by a third party. He's looking into it."

Aretha leaned against her car and took a sip from her bottled water. The sun was starting to burn her skin. It felt much warmer than when she'd first stopped. She adjusted her sunglasses and shook her head at her stupidity and bad luck.

A bright light out of the corner of her eye caught her attention. It looked as if the sun was reflecting a glare off of glass or something shiny. But the light was moving. It was at an extremely high elevation, moving in a downward direction. She had nothing better to do so she retrieved her subspace imagery scanner from the trunk. It could be set to any location within the hemisphere and an image would be reflected off subspace drones positioned just outside the atmosphere and pictured on the scanner. Of course, the charge on the scanner was almost dead, and she couldn't recharge it with her hover car, given its condition. Oh well: she would use what power it had left to check out the light. She set the scanner to the light's approximate location. As the light got closer to the ground, she saw that it was over Sector One headquarters. The longer she studied the light, the more it looked like it was being emitted from an object, not a reflection from the sun. She didn't know of any Legion aircraft or spacecraft that gave off that type of light, but then again, she had never observed Legion ships from this vantage point.

As she zoomed in, she could make out hundreds and hundreds of small dots moving all around the light. Suddenly the light magnified in a flash a thousand times brighter than it had been. A second later, even from that distance, she heard what sounded like an explosion and felt the ground tremble. *What on Earth is going on?*

"This is a good segue into our meeting," Jack said. "We might as well get started. We can fill Aretha in when she arrives."

Jack scooted his chair forward and leaned his forearms on the edge of the desk, his data pod in front of him. He continued, "The first couple items on my agenda are old business that we can knock off quickly."

Jack wanted to get to the heart of the meeting. He needed to make some decisions and he wanted input from his staff. He really wished Aretha was here. He glanced at his data pod. "First, have we confirmed that the recent EarthNX upgrades to the defense shield are functioning properly? The last thing we want is a pirate invasion of Earth."

Armin spoke up. "I'll take this one. Yes, sir. I confirmed it with the new EarthNX president and CEO. By the way, they finally filled that position left open by Edgardo Ramirez. Anyway, Earth is safer than ever."

Jack looked at Min-jun. He wanted to hear it from his chief Legion advisor. "Min-jun?"

"Agreed, sir."

"Good," Jack said. He shifted in his seat. "Second, any change in what we think is the reason for the pirate attacks?"

Armin and Min-jun exchanged glances. "I don't think so, sir," Armin said hesitantly.

Before Jack could say anything further, Clarisse spoke up. "I guess I might be of some use. Aretha and I just discussed this." She straightened in her chair. "There isn't anything new, but we have received further confirmation. It's pretty clear that the pirates are after hilaetite. Since the processed hilaetite stores on Pergan are running low and since there are no more crystals out there, the value of hilaetite on the black market has exceeded the value of any product in the history of the galaxy. And prior to the passage of Treaty five two seven four, hilaetite was used in various products, like our sepders, making those products high-value targets."

Jack interrupted her. "So, the pirates are after any goods that contain hilaetite."

"Exactly," Clarisse said.

Jack noticed one of his bodyguards by the door putting his finger to his earpiece attentively, then speaking into his com. The guard's forehead wrinkled and his eyes shifted rapidly.

"Okay, on to new business," Jack said to the room, but stopped short when the bodyguard whispered something to another, who in turn came toward Jack.

The guard spoke softly, although Jack was pretty sure everyone could hear. "Sir, we need to get everyone to the underground combat room immediately."

Jack stood. "What's going on?"

The bodyguard replied, "We just received word from Sector One and Sector Four headquarters that both are under attack. Sectors Two and Three headquarters are off-line, sir, and can't be reached."

"What? Attacked by whom?"

Two other bodyguards closed in around Jack while one still standing by the door responded to Jack's question. "They don't know, sir. Best guess is pirates, but that hasn't been confirmed."

Armin rushed toward the door. "We really should be going, Mr. President. The combat room is the safest place for me. I mean for us. I mean for you, sir."

Jack didn't respond. He didn't like doing anything out of fear, but protocol during any type of attack or even a threat of an attack was for the President and his staff to retreat to the combat room underneath the Presidential Mansion.

It was the safest, most secure, and most technologically advanced venue on the planet. In the combat room, the president had better access to the planet's computer systems and weapons than anyplace else on Earth.

Everyone gathered their things, including their data pods and other computer devices.

Armin paced at the door with his hands in his pockets, speaking to anyone who would listen, or more likely trying to convince himself. "We'll be fine in the combat room, it's almost two miles below the surface. There isn't any weapon that can penetrate that far."

———

Aretha watched the reflected imagery on the scanner in horror. Flashes of fire lit up the ground where Sector One headquarters would be. She realized Earth was under attack and there wasn't a thing she could do about it. The bright light and dots were enemy spacecraft. They continued to maneuver over Sector One. She could now see streams of smoke billowing from the ground underneath the spacecraft. She couldn't tell if any of the dots were quantum light fighters or other Legion ships, but she assumed the Legion was fighting back.

It probably wasn't all that long, but it seemed like hours before the enemy spacecraft started to dissipate. That is, all of them except the bright light. That one was heading in her direction as her scanner went dark.

Aretha tossed the dead scanner in the hover car and tried the com again, even though she knew it wouldn't work, and it didn't. Completely dead. Her planet was being attacked and all she could do was watch. She could now see the "bright light" spacecraft clearly with her naked eye as it approached and passed over her position, but she still couldn't make out anything. It was at too high an altitude. But it was enormous. Larger than any mechanical object she had ever seen. The light it emitted was pure white, also brighter than any light she had seen. It was like trying to look at the sun. She couldn't stare directly at it.

Her hands started to shake, and her throat went dry and tight when she realized it was on course for the Presidential Mansion. She followed it by sight as it passed in front of the sun, its light still discernable.

She held out hope that it would pass over the Presidential Sector, but that hope dissipated when she saw three other identical lights converging on the location of the Mansion.

"Heaven help us," Aretha said out loud as the four ships came to a stop. She couldn't see for sure from that distance, but she was certain that the ships had halted above the Presidential Mansion. A few minutes later, all four ships lit up with the magnified light. Aretha instinctively covered her eyes. Even from that distance and wearing sunglasses, the brightness painfully blinded her to the point of tears. A second later she heard the explosion, much louder than the one she heard coming from Sector One headquarters. Aretha fought to maintain her balance against the tremoring earth. With her eyes covered and her legs wobbling, she tried to step forward and grab her hover car, but the earth finally won, and she fell face first into the sand.

7

THE OCCUPATION

B ernie walked outside to investigate the faint sound of explosions. He could see specks in the sky off in the distance above Sector One headquarters. Every now and then a distinct white light flashed from a much larger object.

As the specks maneuvered around one another, some dropped from the sky into the smoke now cascading up from the ground. Sector One was under attack. No doubt.

Even though Bernie was retired, his Legion training kicked in. He quickly and calmly moved back inside, not panicking. He sat at the desk in his den and flipped on his com to see if there were any reports from the Legion. Nothing. Still calm, he clicked through the channels. Every channel was either silent or had nothing but static.

Bernie ran his fingers through his thinning hair. What should he do? He had an aircraft equipped with some smaller plasma guns, but no missiles or anything large. Could he help? No, he didn't even know what was happening. Flying into headquarters' airspace without any intel in an ill-equipped aircraft would be suicide.

He would wait and see if the fight came to him.

Bernie turned toward the window. The streets of the country subdivision were becoming populated with residents leaving their white domed houses to peer in the direction of the Legion headquarters. People needed to get off the streets. If the attackers moved into the country, the residents would be picked off like ducks on a pond.

The sound of small plasma blasts sent Bernie diving to the floor. The blasts peppered the streets. He had seen plenty of combat and death throughout his Legion career, but the sound of civilian shouts and screams from the street made the hair on the back of his neck stand up. The sounds of running feet were mixed with cries for help and moans of those already beyond assistance.

Who would do this to civilians? Bernie thought. It had to be the pirates.

As quickly as the plasma blasts started, they stopped. He heard just one ship pass over. By the roar of its engines, he figured it was a spacecraft, not aircraft, so the attack must have come from off planet.

Just as he got to his feet, he heard the spacecraft returning for another pass. He dove again. Pain shot through his right knee as it caught the desk when he hit the floor. He put both hands over the back of his head, waiting for the plasma blasts. He tried to control his breathing as he was taught. But it was harder at his age. Sweat dripped from his face. He didn't want to admit it, but he was scared.

Bernie continued to wait for the second barrage of plasma fire, but it never came. Instead, he heard the spacecraft landing in the middle of the street. He slowly pulled himself up, using his desk as leverage. Limping to the window, he pressed the auto-window console long enough to close the metal blind halfway. With one hand rubbing his aching knee, he hunched over to look out, staying clear of a direct line of sight through the window.

The street was empty but for the several corpses who moments ago were his neighbors. Two people were crawling toward their houses: Leonardo, an older gentleman who lived two houses down and across the street, and Anna, a young widow who lived next door with her two little boys.

A tall, solidly built man stepped out of the black-and-red ship, his long blond hair blowing in the wind. His red eyes seemed to pierce through anything he looked at. As his feet hit the pavement, he pulled a plasma handgun from the inside pocket of his tan duster and shot Leonardo, burning a deep hole in his back.

Bernie closed his eyes for a moment. What ruthless, senseless killing.

The man quickly walked toward Anna, aimed his gun, and shouted, "I am Abigor. You people get out here right now with your valuables. Don't hold back. I'll know."

The smell of burning flesh permeated through Bernie's window screen as he watched two men from down the street, each brandishing a plasma rifle, take up defensive positions behind parked hover cars about seventy-five yards from Abigor. Bernie couldn't figure out why the pirate was acting alone, though. They always worked in groups, or pairs at a minimum.

Bernie breathed slowly again, his fear turning to hope as he developed a plan. He went to his safe for his firearm. With the two men at one end of the street, maybe Bernie could flank the pirate. He would have to go out his back door because the pirate was in the street just outside Bernie's house.

Bernie placed his palm against the safe lock, but he didn't hear the familiar click. He rubbed his sweaty palm on his pants and tried again. Nothing. He blew on his palm to dry it. No good. He felt his heart race. Why couldn't he control his breathing, like he used to do in the Legion? He hated getting old. He rushed to his desk and fumbled through a drawer. Where was the backup combination? He had never used it.

Bernie startled at the sound of plasma rifles firing. *I'm too late for my plan*, he thought. If only he could have coordinated with the two men.

The street was quiet for a moment. Maybe the men were successful. Bernie cautiously made his way back to the half-open window, not knowing if Abigor was still alive and where he might be. Crouching by the window, he wiped sweat from his forehead. A barrage of handgun fire opened up down the street. Abigor was standing behind a tree and one of the men was lying next to the car, his face charred. The other was slumped over the vehicle. Bernie couldn't see where he had been hit.

Abigor slowly walked back toward Anna, who still lay in the same spot, his gun in the air, shouting. "If I don't see fifty people in the street with valuables in ten seconds, this young lady gets her face burned off." He pointed his plasma gun at Anna.

None of the people were likely to leave the relative safety of their houses after what they had just witnessed, let alone fifty. Bernie's safe was unbreakable and he had no time to search for the combination, so he had no weapon. But he had to do something, even if it meant that this was the end for him. Maybe he could buy some time for Anna and draw the pirate's attention so someone else could attempt a shot at him.

He watched his shaking hand press the interior door keypad. His nervousness frustrated him even more than his rapid breathing. He used to be so calm under pressure.

Abigor stepped closer to Anna. "Time's up."

Anna shielded her face. "Please don't. I beg you. I have two little boys."

Abigor's face remained stone cold as Bernie stepped through his door. Not a single person had come out of their house.

"Leave her alone," Bernie demanded.

Abigor slowly raised his head and eyed Bernie with a smirk. "Or what?"

That was as far as Bernie had gotten with his alternate plan. He had drawn the pirate's attention, but now what could he do? He had to talk. Try to get the pirate into a conversation.

"What do you want with our valuables?" Bernie asked. "We're just a bunch of poor folks living in the country. You picked the wrong place to loot."

"Oh, don't you worry. I'll loot all the other places on this pathetic planet." Abigor looked around and shouted, "You're all a bunch of cowards." Then he turned back toward Bernie. "You're the only one who came out, but you didn't even bring anything to save the girl." He raised his gun, aiming it at Bernie. "I guess I'll take you next."

Doors started to open all up and down the street with people stepping out. Nobody carried anything.

A woman down the street shouted, "You'll have to murder us all then."

Abigor, keeping his gun trained on Bernie, slowly rotated his gaze with wide eyes and raised eyebrows.

Abigor quickly regained his composure and turned his attention back to Bernie. "I will do just that, starting with you." He stared at Bernie.

The sound of ships flying very low distracted everyone, including Abigor, and they all looked up. One spacecraft broke off even lower than the others. Bernie couldn't tell what planet it was from, but it had the markings of a pirate ship.

Abigor's stare stayed with the spacecraft as it buzzed past. His eyes darted back and forth between Bernie, Anna, the others, and the group of ships, which appeared to be circling back.

Abigor lowered his weapon, quickly ran to his own ship, climbed in, and departed moments before the group of ships returned.

Bernie's gaze followed them as Abigor quickly outpaced the others. Maybe that explains why he was alone. Could he have been a renegade pirate?

Bernie and the others turned their attention to Anna and checked for survivors among the casualties.

8

VERNIUS

Diane made her way down the lavishly decorated hallway in the Imperial Majesty's palace. Her footsteps were silent on the plush red carpet. She still couldn't believe the news that Earth was invaded yesterday. And according to the account she heard, the invasion was a success. That meant that Earth was now under someone else's control. *How was that even possible?* she thought. *The Legion defeated? Was it the pirates?* She had heard from Jake and Cal that only about half the Legion remained on Earth. The rest were dealing with the pirates in space. And what about Jake and Cal? Where were they? Were they okay? She hadn't heard from them since they left to check out the coordinates. The more she thought about it, the more her anxiety increased. A bead of sweat trickled down her back.

She had to speak with the Imperial Majesty. Diane hadn't had a chance to talk to her since the news of the attack reached Vernius. Things were chaotic, to say the least. With its closest ally and its only line of defense, Earth, now in the hands of an enemy, Vernius could easily be the next target. Without any means of defense and no military, Vernius needed to come up with a plan, and quickly. As Earth's ambassador, she would be the primary person the Imperial Majesty would look to in order to develop that plan. But did she know what to do? Was she trained and prepared for this? She wasn't sure. Her hands started to shake. She stopped in an otherwise unoccupied stretch of hallway. She took a deep breath, and then another. She thought about Jake and Cal and what they must be going through right now. She was glad they weren't on Earth. She wasn't certain about the current state of her and Jake's relationship, but she was certain that she still loved him. Right now, though, she needed to focus on the task at hand. She asked herself again, Was she trained and prepared for this? This time the answer was yes, of course she was. First and foremost, she was Legion.

Diane entered the outer office, which housed the Imperial Majesty's assistant. It was decorated with the best desk and furniture in the galaxy. Red carpeting adorned this room as well. Currently, the outer office was empty, but Diane could hear voices coming through the closed door that led to the much larger main office. Two different voices. She recognized the Imperial Majesty's voice, but who was the other person?

"Are you threatening me?" the Imperial Majesty's tone was more commanding than Diane had ever really heard. "How did you get in here anyway?" She paused. "And where are my guards?"

"I go wherever I want to go," the other person said, deep and calm.

Chills ran down Diane's spin. It was a man, and she had heard that voice before, but where?

The other voice continued. "Your pathetic excuse for guards are useless against me. And yes, I am threatening you. If I can take down Earth with its glorious defense shield and Legion, how much easier do you think it will be for me to take over Vernius?"

The Imperial Majesty interrupted. "YOU invaded Earth? Why would I believe that? The word I received was that it was a bunch of pirates along with a couple unknown ships. Who are you, a pirate?"

Diane could almost hear a smile in the other voice. "It was four ships, and they aren't unknown. They are Permidium, armed with enough hilaetite to destroy your planet at my command. And one of their ships is sitting just outside your atmosphere as we speak. I'm sure your scanners picked it up before I got here. How do you think we penetrated Earth's shield? Do you really think pirates could have pulled that off alone?"

Diane knew that voice. Who was it? *Think, Diane, think.* She wondered whether she should continue to eavesdrop. Maybe she should just knock and interrupt or leave and come back. No, she couldn't leave. This was urgent. She had to talk to the Imperial Majesty, but she needed to hear what this man had to say, and he might stop talking if she disrupted them. She looked over her shoulder to make sure the assistant wasn't returning, then she stepped closer to the door.

"Permidium?" the Imperial Majesty said. "Why would the Permidiums come to the Milky Way galaxy?"

"Exactly," came the other voice. "Why would they come here? Well, I'll tell you why. Because of this."

He must have shown something to the Imperial Majesty, who replied, still very confidently, "A transponder? You're still not convincing me that you caused the attack."

"Not just any transponder," the man said. "This transponder was taken from one of the Earth's Legion. It contains intel, recorded a year ago, on how one might destroy the Permidium ships. As long as I hold this device, the Permidiums will do anything I say."

That had to be Cal's portable transponder. And if this man had it, he probably had Cal and Jake too. *Oh no,* Diane thought. She wanted to burst in and find out where Jake and Cal were. But she couldn't. She had to listen and try to learn as much information as she could. Then she could use that to help find Jake and Cal.

The Imperial Majesty must have been starting to believe him, because her tone softened. "Who are you, anyway, if you aren't a pirate and you aren't Permidium? And what do you want?"

The man's voice stayed eerily calm and steady. "What I want and what I WILL get is this galaxy." He paused. "Who am I? You wouldn't understand if I told you. But you can call me Sloan. Mr. Sloan."

Diane gasped, then caught herself and froze so as to not make another noise. She suddenly felt very warm. *Sloan? Not again,* she thought. She, like many others, had hoped he had disappeared for good.

The Imperial Majesty seemingly recognized the name as well. Her tone went from soft to conciliatory. "Mr. Sloan, why didn't you say so earlier?"

"So, we can do it the easy way or the hard way," Sloan said in his deep, dark voice. "I would hate to destroy this magnificent structure we are in and all the other buildings and technology on this planet. I could use it in my new empire. I could even see Vernius as my home base."

Clearly, he was playing on the Imperial Majesty's pride.

Sloan's voice grew even darker. "But make no mistake, if I have to destroy your entire planet, I will do so. I can always rebuild it."

"I understand, Mr. Sloan. I can give you my word that you will receive no resistance from Vernius. In return, can I ask that you leave my people alone and let them go about their business as usual?"

Diane shook her head. Sloan scared her as well, and she'd heard what he'd done to Earth, but the Imperial Majesty was completely spineless. Vernius needed to take a stand. After all, it was the most technologically advanced planet in the galaxy. Surely, they could come up with something. Instead, she was disgusted. Disgusted with the Imperial Majesty giving up so easily. Disgusted with herself for aligning with the Imperial Majesty. And most of all, disgusted with Sloan. She could still see him on the video in Romalor's command center as clearly as if it was yesterday, ordering the deaths of Jake, Cal, and her.

But maybe she was wrong about the Imperial Majesty. Maybe her cooperation was just a ploy to buy more time.

Diane heard Sloan coming closer to the door as he spoke. "Your Majesty, as long as you and your people cooperate with me, you have my word that your people will be left alone." He paused. "And who knows? I might even make you my number two. Now I must be going. I have a meeting with some new prisoners tomorrow."

Yeah, right, Diane thought. She could trust Sloan about as far as she could throw him.

Sloan started to move again. He was now right by the door. Diane bolted out of the outer office and into the hallway. She still needed to talk to the Imperial Majesty, alone. And she had to find Jake and Cal to help them and tell them what she'd learned. They had to be alive. They just had to. But most of all, she had to find a way to get the transponder from Sloan. If the hilaetite ship that she, Jake, and Cal saw a year ago was a Permidium ship, then the Permidiums were as powerful as Sloan said. If the transponder was what was controlling them, then she had to get it out of Sloan's hands.

Diane made certain that Sloan had left the palace before she made her way back to the Imperial Majesty's office. She sat on one of the two sofas in the middle of the room, waiting patiently for the Imperial Majesty to finish whatever she was doing on her computer at her desk, or with as much patience as she could muster up. Diane knew better than to interrupt, but she also knew that time was an issue. Her hands anxiously rubbed the blue suede couch seat back and forth, first against the grain which darkened the spot, then with the grain, smoothing the suede back to its light blue color. Diane had to find out if the Imperial Majesty had a plan, but she couldn't let on that she had overheard her conversation with Sloan. And Diane had to find out if the Imperial Majesty knew where Sloan was keeping the transponder.

The Imperial Majesty rose and strolled slowly toward the sitting area, her long red-and-white frock trailing, her hands clasped in front of her. Her pale skin and petite frame made her arms look like sticks protruding from the large open sleeves of her garment. Diane stood as was proper to show respect. The Imperial Majesty sat on the couch opposite Diane. She looked like a tiny human who never saw the sun, but that was the typical build of Vernitions, both male and female. Diane wiped her palms on her pants as she sat down again.

"Diane, what can I do for you?" the Imperial Majesty asked, her face expressionless as usual.

Diane wished she could have seen the expression on her face when she was angry with Sloan.

"Your Majesty," Diane said, "we need a plan to defend Vernius now that Earth has been captured. We don't have much time. Vernius could be the next target. I have a couple ideas I would like to run past you."

Diane didn't have any ideas, but she figured this was the quickest way to see the Imperial Majesty's hand. Knowing how the conversation ended with Sloan, the Imperial Majesty would either tell her about Sloan and her plan or she would try to cut her out of the loop. Diane was the only one who would challenge any directive of the Imperial Majesty. That was part of her job. So, if the Imperial Majesty wanted the people to not oppose Sloan, she would either need to get Diane on her side or remove her from the equation by keeping her in the dark.

Diane's heart sank as she listened to the Imperial Majesty's response.

"No," the Imperial Majesty said in her soft voice, "it's too dangerous to oppose whoever attacked Earth. If Earth couldn't defend itself, it would be mass suicide for us to try to do so."

Diane leaned forward. "But I thought we could rally the remaining planets and mount a joint defense, and . . ."

The Imperial Majesty raised a hand to stop Diane. "Diane, I know for a fact that the rest of the galaxy is already planning on falling in line. They don't want to experience the fate of Earth. All but Craton, that is."

Diane must have missed that part of the conversation with Sloan. What a brilliant plan of Sloan's. Take out the alpha planet first, and the rest of the galaxy is his, without raising another finger.

"But, with all due respect, Your Majesty—"

Diane was halted again by the small yet powerful hand. "This isn't a democracy, like your Earth. I've made up my mind. And I've already started diplomatic negotiations to position Vernius as a key strategic player in the new galaxy order."

Diane felt the heat rise in her body. She thought of Jake and Cal in a prison somewhere, being beaten, or worse. She clenched her fists, trying to keep her emotions in check. "Your Majesty, you can't do that. You can't give in so easily."

Unfazed by the anger in Diane's voice, the Imperial Majesty continued to sit calmly on the couch. "I can and I will. I have to think about the safety of the Vernition people first and foremost."

Diane couldn't take it any longer. She jumped to her feet, arms straightened at her sides, fists still clenched. "The safety of the people? You're feeding them to the wolves." Diane's anger burned. She could feel her face turning red with heat. She pointed at the Imperial Majesty. "You have no idea who you're dealing with. You've made a pact with Satan himself. You can't trust Sloan!"

For the first time, the Imperial Majesty displayed emotion. Her eyes widened in surprise, then narrowed in anger. "How did you know I was talking with Mr. Sloan? You've been eavesdropping! I think we're done here." She rose, turned her back on Diane, and quickly returned to her desk.

9

FRANK

Frank slowly regained consciousness only to feel a steady pain in his forehead. He thought his head might explode from the pressure. He opened his eyes only to see blurry surroundings. He could feel dried blood on his face. He tried to move his hand to rub his eyes and aching head, but it wouldn't budge. He tried again and realized his hands were bound behind his back. What had happened, and where was he? That's right, he and his team had been looking for the pirates' stronghold on Aquarii. The Legion was ambushed. He had been outsmarted, and he remembered the butt of a gun targeting his face. That must be why his head was throbbing. No, that wasn't all. He had been in a cage on Aquarii, in and out of consciousness, but for how long? He recalled eating and drinking some, but that was all he could remember. And where was he now?

He raised his head as his vision started to clear. He was in some sort of dimly lit interrogation room with only a few chairs and a filing cabinet. A lingering smell of sweat permeated the musty room. He was seated in a chair, his legs also bound together. He tried to swallow but his throat was parched, his lips dry. He could have used a drink of water right now, but he doubted he would get any. Pirates weren't known to be merciful. He assumed that's who had him. What about the rest of his team? Were they okay?

What a fool he had been to lead them into a trap. A trap that he even suspected. He let his head drop as he closed his eyes to try to ease the pain stabbing his temple.

He startled and raised his head when the door burst open. Two pirates in military-looking uniforms entered and stepped to either side of the door. They were followed by a tall man in a black trench coat who had to duck as he passed through the doorway.

One of the pirates closed the door as the trench-coat man turned a chair backward, placed it in front of Frank, and sat down, leaning his elbows on the back of it. "Commander Cantor? I believe that is correct? May we have a little discussion?"

Frank's mind spun and his head continued to throb. Who was this guy? How did the guy know his name?

"How about a swig from a canteen first, hombre?"

The guy wrinkled his forehead and sat silent for a moment. "The name is Sloan. You can call me Mr. Sloan."

Frank's senses heightened and he stiffened his neck at the sound of that name. It couldn't be Sloan. He knew a lot about Sloan from Jake, Cal, Diane, and from the events of a year ago, but at the same time, he and everyone else on Earth knew so little about him. Sloan was back? Why was he involved in the pirate war? But if Sloan was behind this, that did explain the discipline of the pirates on Aquarii and their organized attacks.

Frank cleared his throat. "What gang of bandits do you ride with? And what cow town are we in?" he said, looking Sloan up and down. "You don't look like you've been on a horse during this shootout."

Sloan raised an eyebrow. "I beg your pardon. Just what language do you speak, Mr. Cantor? And I'll be the one asking the questions in this conversation."

Frank gave a halfhearted chuckle. "Ask away, pilgrim. But I can't promise you any answers."

"Hombre, pilgrim—such colorful names," Sloan replied. "And I have ways to make you answer." He paused. "Mr. Cantor, we are on Titan, in Tortuga. There, I gave you something. Now why don't you give me something in return?"

Frank half grunted and half laughed. "And just what might that be?"

Sloan leaned forward. "Hasn't there been enough bloodshed in this war? Let's end this conflict before any more lives are lost. I know a good portion of your Legion is still out there. Call them in and we can discuss a mutually beneficial arrangement that lets you and what's left of your Legion live."

Frank blinked and shook his head to stay focused. The pain still pressed against his skull. "And why would I do that? You may be in command of the pirates and won the little skirmish on Aquarii, but this isn't the Alamo. We aren't bottled up and surrounded." He paused and leaned forward. "Now, where is the rest of my division?"

Sloan straightened his back. "Mr. Cantor, it seems you've been out of it for a while. I do believe your leverage has disappeared and you don't even know it."

Frank tried to think what Sloan could be talking about. How long had he been out? It couldn't have been long enough for anything drastic to have happened. Sloan was bluffing. *That's what he does*, Frank thought. *He feeds off of fear.*

Sloan held out a hand to one of the guards, who gave Sloan a large data pod pulled from his jacket. He touched the screen a few times, then raised his eyebrows. "Ah, yes, here it is." He turned the pod around and held it up to Frank. "This was recorded two days ago."

Frank dropped his head in an attempt to seem disinterested, but he was in truth very curious about Sloan's "loss of leverage" comment. He had to watch. He looked up without raising his head. It was a recording of a spacecraft's viewing screen, a very large screen.

It was a view of one of Earth's defense stations. Sloan wouldn't be showing him that if there wasn't more to it. Frank's muscles tensed. He tried to remain nonchalant, but he had a bad feeling about what Sloan might have done. He continued to watch as the screen lit up bright white. Bright enough through the data pod to make him flinch. When the light dissipated, he breathed a sigh of relief. He expected to see a devastated defense station, but instead, the view simply panned out to space. He could see nothing but the stars.

Frank raised his head. "So, what was that all about? Trying to scare me with a light?" He paused. "Now, what have you done with my people? Even pirates must have some sort of ethical code for captives, especially those who've surrendered."

He really didn't believe there was anything ethical about pirates, and from what he knew about Sloan, he didn't believe Sloan had an ethical bone in his body, but he had to ask the question again. His team had to be held somewhere. As outnumbered and as surprised as they were, he was certain they would have surrendered, especially once he went down. He just wanted some assurance that they were being treated properly.

Sloan said nothing. That made Frank uneasy again. Instead, Sloan pulled the pod back, tapped the screen a few times, and then presented it to Frank once more.

This time Frank paid attention, keeping his head up. If he played along with Sloan, maybe Sloan would provide him with some information about his team.

There was no grin on Sloan's face as he spoke this time. Rather, he gave Frank a "game over" look. "That was a view of space where your defense station once was. All your defense stations shared the same fate."

The words didn't register at first. If anything, Frank figured it was another bluff. After all, a person could do anything with digital feeds. But Frank's world collapsed as he watched the screen now. It showed a barrage of pirate ships, all sorts of makes and classes, invading Earth.

He recognized the Legion headquarters, or what was left of it. The Legion was being obliterated. There were very few quantum fighters getting off the ground, and those that did were immediately shattered. Ground forces were being taken out just as quickly and easily. How was this possible? How did they destroy the defense stations? Was the Legion asleep in the saddle? Was he that gullible? After all, he was one of the highest-ranking Legion officers. The Legion should have been better prepared. *He* should have been better prepared.

Frank couldn't say anything. He just let his head drop again and closed his eyes. All those Legion deaths were on him. He didn't think things could get any worse, until Sloan continued.

"And you are correct, Mr. Cantor. Your team did surrender like cowards. But you'll have to go back to Aquarii to find them. Pirates don't take captives."

At that, Frank's heart raced. His self-pity turned to anger. They had slaughtered his entire team. He raised his head, his eyes wide, and mustered every bit of strength left in him as he lurched forward in rage. "Sloan!"

But the binding on his hands and feet held and he toppled over, his already damaged face planting into the concrete floor. Pain shot through his skull from forehead to crown. All he could do was lie on the cold surface with the metallic taste of his own blood filling his palate.

Sloan stood and shook his head. "This man is broken. He will give us nothing. But he will be quite useful for getting information out of Danielson and Saunders. Bring him."

At those words, Frank's heart broke. Sloan had Jake and Cal too. And all because he had brought them into this. His eyes filled with tears, and through all the pain, he felt a drop gently roll down his cheek before it fell a short distance to the floor, mixing with a splatter of blood.

10

THE ESCAPE

It was hard to keep track of time in the cell without any sense of day and night, and without a timepiece, but Jake calculated that they had been locked up for about three days. He and Cal had no contact with anyone except a couple pirates locked up in the other cells who clearly weren't part of the war, and the guard who brought them stale bread, water, and occasionally some sort of meat. What was the state of Earth? Did it get attacked? It was eating him up not knowing.

Jake sat on the edge of one of the two cots that were brought into the dank cell. He was starting to grow used to the damp, moldy smell permeating the cavern.

The steel door to the cell block scrapped against the rock floor as it began to open. It was too early for a meal. Probably bringing in a prisoner. That would be good. Maybe he and Cal could get some news from somebody new from the outside. Two guards stepped through the door followed by a tall figure in a black overcoat. Sloan.

Stopping outside their cell, Sloan looked down at his shoes. The water trickling down the cell walls was puddling outside the barred door. Sloan's wingtips were a couple inches deep in it. His large, imposing figure loomed just outside the cell door as he stared in the way that only Sloan could.

"Are you two tired of this place yet?" Sloan asked as his gaze went from the cell ceiling to the floor, and then took in each of the walls. "I figured I would give you some time to get used to your new home before I came to you with my proposition."

Cal started to say something. But Jake stood, stepped in front of him, and spoke first. "Oh, I don't know. It's kind of growing on me." Jake looked around. "You know. The natural look."

"Then maybe I should leave you both here to rot," Sloan said as he started to turn away.

"No, wait!" Cal said moving forward quickly. "What's your proposal? Your attack on Earth failed and you need us to do something so you can save face, right?"

Sloan smirked. "Quite the opposite. You're looking at the new unofficially elected president of Earth United. I believe that's the title you use." He chuckled. "Such colorful names."

Cal grabbed the cell bars. "You're lying. There's no way you could get past the defense shield."

Sloan raised an eyebrow. "Oh, I can and I did. I believe you've seen firsthand what the Permidiums are capable of."

Jake was still astonished at what Sloan was able to find out. Sloan had to know of Cal's, Diane's, and his encounter with the Permidium ship a year ago.

How else could he know about the transponder?

Cal hung his head and stepped back.

Sloan continued. "That's a good segue into my proposition. Why don't you two join me? You seem to have a knack for getting in my way. You would be an excellent addition to my team. What else do you have? Earth is mine, and the rest of the galaxy is now falling in line. You have no place left to go even if you did get out of this drunken pirate prison and off this disgusting planet."

"No way, Sloan," Jake said. "Not on your life. I would much rather rot in here with these pirates"—he waved his hand toward the other cells—"than do anything with you. Each one of these pirates is ten times the person you are." Jake turned and walked to the back of the cell and stopped, facing the back wall. He watched Cal and Sloan out of the corner of his eye.

Sloan turned his attention to Cal.

"Same goes for me," Cal said. "You can go back to wherever it is you came from."

Cal must have struck a nerve unintentionally. Sloan's eyes narrowed.

Cal raised an eyebrow. "Where did you come from? You probably weren't wanted, even there."

With the speed and agility of a large cat striking its prey, Sloan reached through the cell bars, caught Cal by the throat, and pulled him against them. Cal's face was jammed between two bars. He gasped for breath.

Jake raced toward Cal and tried to pull him free. He grabbed Sloan's hand to pry it from Cal's throat, but he felt Sloan squeeze harder. Sloan was too strong. Jake used both hands and threw his body weight into the effort. But like a crocodile jaw clamping down on its prey, it was impossible to force open. In the midst of the commotion, a tinge of fear ran down Jake's spine. Never had he felt such strength in anyone, and especially in a single hand.

Rage showed in Sloan's eyes. "Don't you ever speak of my home again. I will return there someday and they will bow to me. I will show them." He thrust his face nose to nose with Cal. "Right after I take over your entire pathetic galaxy, you worthless excuses for life forms."

Sloan released his grip on Cal. He fell to the ground grasping his throat with both hands, choking and coughing.

Sloan stepped back and turned toward one of the guards. "Bring me the other prisoner."

The guard left through the steel entry door.

Jake helped Cal to his feet. "You okay?"

Cal nodded, still holding his throat.

"Another prisoner?" Jake whispered.

The steel door swung open again, and the guard returned with a prisoner who was hunched over, bloodied, dragging one of his feet, and had his hands tied behind his back. His Legion uniform was dirty and torn.

Sloan grabbed the man by the hair and pulled his head up.

Jake's eyes popped open wide. He barely recognized the face with the swollen black eye and cheek cracked open. "Frank!"

"Good to see you cowboys," Frank said in a slurred voice, one side of his jaw barely moving.

Jake and Cal moved to the cell door.

Jake grabbed the bars. "Are you okay, Frank? What have they done to you?"

Jake knew what they had done. They had beaten him to near death. But the question just came out.

"I'm fine," Frank slurred again. He spit blood. "It takes more than this bunch of bandits to keep someone like the Duke down."

"More colorful words," Sloan said. "I thought you all knew each other. What a lovely reunion." He stepped toward the cell. "I know the strongest part of your Legion was off planet when we attacked Earth. And now I need to know where they are located. And since you two won't join me, and your friend here"—he tipped his head toward Frank while still addressing Jake and Cal—"won't give up the information, then you two will tell me what I want to know, or I finish off"—he paused, then continued—"the *Duke*, right here in front of you. Is that clear?"

Sloan made a fist, pulled it back, and again with the speed and strength of a cat, sent it flying into Frank's jaw. The sound that came from Frank made Jake quiver. At the same time Jake heard coins bounce on the rock floor several times until they stopped in the pool of water just outside the cell.

But they weren't coins at all. They were teeth. Three of them.

Frank dropped to his knees and struggled to speak. What came out was even more slurred than before. "Don't tell him a thing. That's an order."

Jake's heart was breaking. At the same time, he could feel the anger swelling up inside him. He had to control his anger as he had learned to do. And he had to keep his emotions out of it. He was a Legion soldier above all else. He could not give the rest of the Legion away, even if he and Cal knew where they were, which they didn't.

All hope wasn't gone after all. From what Sloan said, there were plenty of Legion troops who survived or escaped the attack. And if Sloan wanted their location so badly, there must be enough of them to have him worried.

Sloan made a fist and cocked his arm again, aimed at Frank's face.

Jake wanted to tell Sloan something to make him stop, even if it was a lie. He wanted to help Frank, but he couldn't. He had to remain quiet. But how much longer could he stand there and watch Frank be beaten? And how much more could Frank take?

Sloan eyed Jake, turned up the corner of his mouth, and let his fist fly. It looked like a rocket, connecting with Frank's forehead. The sound of knuckles hitting flesh with such force was sickening. The skin on Frank's forehead opened up, splattering crimson red over Sloan's hand and coat sleeve. Frank, still on his knees, fell foreword, his head bouncing as his face hit the wet stone floor. He lay motionless.

Sloan pulled a hand towel from inside his coat and wiped off his knuckles, which looked unfazed by the blow they'd just delivered.

"We have to do something," Cal whispered.

Sloan raised his foot and cocked his ankle so that the heel of his hard-soled shoe was just above Frank's temple. This would be the killing blow.

Sloan focused on his target, still lying motionless, then he looked from Cal to Jake.

"Last chance," Sloan said. "What will it be?"

Jake had to say something to at least buy some time to save Frank, at least for now. Maybe an opportunity to escape with Frank would arise.

"Okay, stop," Jake said. "I'll give you the information you want. Just leave him alone."

Sloan slowly lowered his foot to the ground and stepped toward the cell, his eyes fixed on Jake with a glare that made Jake's skin crawl.

"If I think for a second that you're not giving me accurate information, I will kill him instantly," Sloan said. "Then I will tear the two of you apart, limb by limb."

Seeing the speed and power of Sloan up close, Jake knew he was capable of doing just that, so he said nothing.

Sloan turned toward the guards, looked down at Frank, and kicked him in the side. "Get him out of here." He motioned toward Cal and Jake. "Then bring these two to my room. I want their information input directly into my data system."

Sloan stepped over Frank and exited quickly through the steel door.

Jake and Cal each sat on a cot not saying a word. With the guards gone, the cell block was silent. Jake no longer cared about Earth or that he was locked in a prison. He had just watched Frank, the closest person to a father that he had left, be beaten to near death. Frank was the one person who had kept his life on track after he'd watched Uncle Ben's brutal death. His heart ached for him. He wanted to go to him, help him as he had helped Jake. He wanted Frank to not be alone. He had no idea where they took Frank or if they would give him any medical attention or just let him suffer and—probably—die. No, he couldn't think that. He wouldn't let himself think that. Frank was alive and he would stay alive.

Jake *would* find him and he *would* help him.

Right now, Jake was out of options. Based on the information Cal had obtained in the pirate meeting, and with the Permidiums in Sloan's pocket, he had no reason to disbelieve that Earth was now under Sloan's control. From his questioning, he knew that a not insubstantial portion of the Legion was still out there, but where were they? And did they know what was going on? Who was leading them? Were they organized at all? But his mind kept going back to Frank. What was he thinking? How badly was he hurt? Was he even alive? He and Cal needed to get out of there and find the Legion. But more important, they needed to get out and find Frank.

Jake figured their best opportunity to escape would come when the guards were taking them to Sloan. But it would have to happen fast. Sloan was too clever for them to easily get away from him.

Jake hated waiting for an opportunity. He wanted to be proactive, to have a plan. He stood and started to pace.

"Any ideas as to what we're going to tell Sloan?" Cal asked.

"Nothing but a lie," Jake said.

"It better be a pretty good one," Cal said. "You know Sloan. He seems to know everything."

"Everything except where the Legion is," Jake replied. "It doesn't matter anyway. We have to get away from the guards before we ever reach Sloan. That'll be our best opportunity to get out of here and to find Frank."

"I was thinking the same thing," Cal said. "Frank needs us."

The faint sound of plasma gunfire could be heard from somewhere. Jake generally could hear nothing inside the cell block, so it must have been coming from inside whatever structure they were in.

"Did you hear that?" Cal asked as he stood.

Jake walked toward the cell bars without responding. More gunfire, this time louder. It was definitely inside the structure and getting closer. Jake's adrenaline started to flow at the thought of combat. Whoever it was and whatever the purpose, it was a potential fight and a potential opportunity to escape. He hoped the fight would enter the cell block. But what if they blew up the cell block? He quickly dismissed that thought and stayed positive, hopeful for any opportunity to get out of there.

"Stand clear!" someone shouted from just outside the steel door.

Jake and Cal each took a step back from the bars. Jake could hear movement outside the door. At least five or six people.

The voice shouted again. "Clear!"

Jake felt the concussion of the explosion a half second before he heard the deafening sound. The steel door was hurled past the jail cell. Jake fought to maintain his balance, but the force of the blow and the vibrations running through the stone floor knocked him backward. One step, two steps—his upper body was already bent too far back. He went down on the hard damp floor, his head just missing the back wall. Rock debris rained down on his face. Dust stung his eyes. The smell of gunpowder, old-fashioned black powder, filled the air. Jake recognized the odor from the antique western guns that he used to shoot with Frank. He had heard that it was still used sometimes when someone needed to sneak an explosive into an area because no modern technology could detect it.

Cal lay on the floor to Jake's left. He looked to be okay. Jake strained to see through the smoke and dust that filled the corridor outside the jail cell as the silhouette of a large figure appeared where the steel door had hung just moments ago. The figure strolled through the door, the outline of a plasma rifle hanging from one hand. Four or five other large figures followed. As the first person moved out of the haze, Jake could see he was unmistakably a Craton male. His red-and-black military-style uniform protruded out in front of his large chest. The rest of the men spread out through the cell block. All were Cratonites, not pirates, wearing Craton military uniforms.

The lead Cratonite stepped over to Jake and Cal's cell. He looked familiar to Jake. His dark complexion was enhanced by the dirt and sweat covering his face. He flipped his head to swing his long black hair out of his eyes.

Jake slowly got his legs under him and stood.

"Jake Saunders and Cal Danielson?" the soldier asked.

When he spoke, Jake finally recognized him. Romalor's son. "Novak? What are you doing here? You picked a fine time to avenge your father's death."

Novak's face was stern and commanding. "I seek not revenge. I have come to free the two of you."

"Free us?" Cal said as he stood up. "We don't need rescuing."

Novak's gaze ventured from the stone walls to the steel cell bars, all still very much intact. "Really? So, you have a plan of escape?"

"Well, we don't need to be rescued by a Cratonite," Cal stammered. "And particularly not by the son of Romalor."

Jake hesitated before saying anything. Why would the son of the Cratonite ruler that Jake killed be helping him? Craton never was very public with the rest of the galaxy, and ever since the Battle of Craton, it had been even more secretive. But Earth intelligence had determined that Novak had become the new ruler. That was as much as Earth knew about him.

To Jake's knowledge, Novak hadn't been on the front lines during the Battle of Craton, and given that Craton's leadership succession generally involved killing your rivals rather than any type of election or inheritance, Jake assumed Novak's rise to power, like his father's, was through elimination of his opponents. So again, Jake wondered why Novak would be helping them. Maybe to take them captive himself. It was an opportune time, with the Legion on the run. But why now, in the middle of the pirate war? Craton had to have bigger issues than Jake and Cal at the moment.

Jake turned to Cal and held up his hand. "Wait, Cal."

He turned back to Novak. "Why are you helping us? And how did you find us? There's no way you could have known we were in a jail cell underneath a hill in Tortuga on Titan."

Novak's gaze shifted and he fidgeted uncomfortably. "Well, okay, I might as well come right out with it. I don't know for certain the reason I am helping you get out of here. But I understand it's for the good of Craton. For the good of the galaxy."

Cal interrupted. "Since when did Craton care about the galaxy?"

"Easy Cal. Let him talk," said Jake.

Cal raised an eyebrow. "You're buying his story? Have you forgotten who his father was? Have you forgotten what Craton has done to almost every planet in the galaxy?"

"I know," Jake said. "But I just remembered something the old man told me. He told me to not be afraid to accept the aid of someone I think is my foe." Jake pointed at Novak. "This could be what he was talking about. And he hasn't been wrong yet."

Novak came closer to the cell bars. "You have spoken to an old, dark-skinned man? Was he blind?"

Jake lowered his head once quickly, urging him to go on.

Novak continued. "And did he talk in riddles, yet something made you believe everything he said?"

Jake walked to the bars. "Yes. You talked to him too?"

A voice shouted from just outside the cell block. "General, we're running out of time. We need to move before they get reinforcements here."

"Understood," Novak said, turning toward the opening that used to be a door. "Tell the men to keep the pathway to the ship clear. We'll be ready for evacuation momentarily."

Jake was alarmed that the Craton general would let one of his men talk to him that way, basically giving him an order to hurry up. Romalor would have never stood for that, let alone respond in a submissive manner.

Novak turned back to Jake. "We can discuss later. Right now, I have to get you out of here. The old man said that the survival of Craton and the galaxy would depend on it."

Jake was puzzled. Why didn't the old man tell him that? And why did he just give them hints and clues? If he knew everything he seemed to know, and if he wanted to help, why wouldn't the old man just tell him? But regardless of why Novak was helping Cal and him, this was the opportunity to escape that Jake was looking for. Why not take it?

Jake could see in Cal's face that he didn't trust Novak. But then Cal hadn't been given fortune-telling riddles.

"Come on, Cal. Let's get out of here. Trust me. It'll be fine."

Novak raised his plasma rifle, aiming it at the lock on the cell door.

Jake and Cal moved out of the line of fire, turned around, and hunched over. Jake heard two blasts from the gun. When he turned, the cell door hung open.

"Let's move out!" Novak shouted. He motioned Jake and Cal forward. "My men have confiscated a pirate ship for you."

They darted out of the cell. Jake stopped beside Novak. "We have to get our commander. He's here too, and he's in bad shape."

"Do you know where they have him?" Novak asked.

Jake shook his head. "No."

Novak looked genuinely sympathetic. "I'm sorry, Jake Saunders. There's no time. We have to leave now, or we'll never be able to. And we wouldn't know where to begin searching anyway. The old man directed me only to your whereabouts."

Cal put a hand on Jake's shoulder. "He's right, Jake. If you're going to trust him and if we're going to escape, it has to be now, before Sloan finds out they're here and before the guards get reinforcements. We can regroup and come back for Frank with the Legion. We're no good to Frank or anyone as long as we're stuck in here."

Jake knew both Novak and Cal were right, but he couldn't leave without Frank. Chances were that he wouldn't be alive when they had the opportunity to come back.

Jake addressed Novak. "Where are your spacecraft and the pirate ship?"

Novak pointed. "Down that corridor. Come on."

Jake shook his head. "No, you get your men out of here." He turned to Cal. "Get the pirate ship fired up and ready to launch." He turned to one of the Cratonite guards and pointed to his weapon.

"Can I borrow that?" Taking the gun, he turned back to Cal. "I'm going to make one pass through the halls and see if I can find Frank. They couldn't have taken him far."

Cal reached for Jake's arm. "No, Jake." Then shaking his head, he said, "You're not going to listen to me anyway. Good luck and be quick."

No sooner had Cal finished speaking when shouts came from every corridor except the one leading to the spacecraft. They were unmistakably pirate voices. "Come on! This way!" "To the cell block!" "Lock down all corridors before they get out!"

Jake tensed. He tried to slow his breathing and relax using his training techniques to prepare for a fight. But his heart wasn't racing because of a pending battle with pirate guards. It was racing because his only opportunity to get to Frank had just vanished.

His heart would not slow. Rather, it broke.

11

ABIGOR

Jake stared intently at the rear viewing screen, trying to see if anyone was following them from Titan. According to what the old man had told Novak, Tortuga was the pirate headquarters. How had the Legion missed that? How had Frank missed that? But if it was the pirate headquarters, then there would be plenty of pirates available to follow them. He still couldn't get his mind off Frank, but he had to focus right now. His best chance of freeing Frank was to find the Legion and return to Tortuga. Frank would last that long. He could do it.

"It would have been nice if we could have taken Novak up on his offer to rendezvous on Craton," Cal said as he navigated the pirate spacecraft.

"Agreed," Jake replied. "But we need to find the Legion, and we can't contact them from there, or from anywhere for that matter, on our conventional coms. You heard what Novak said. The Permidiums have locked onto every Legion frequency and are monitoring all of them. How they managed that, I have no idea. So, the only safe way to contact the Legion is through the Legion's vector communications system. That's why we need to go to Earth now and make contact with the Legion. Then we rendezvous on Craton." Jake paused and checked the rear viewing screen again. Still clear. "The problem is the last thing Novak told us. That the Permidium ship orbiting Earth has jammed all long-range communications to and from Earth, so how can we even use vector-space transmissions? And any ship coming close enough to Earth to send or receive a shortwave signal will be targeted by the Permidium ship if it doesn't emit the Permidium beacon, whatever that is. So, we're going to have a difficult time even getting close enough to contact someone on Earth once we get there."

"The long-range jam won't matter," Cal said, "if we can get to Earth. Whatever they're using to jam long-range communications won't jam vector-space transmissions. I won't bore you with the details, but vector transmissions are completely different."

Jake swiveled in his chair. "So, you're saying that if we can get close enough to Earth to have someone activate the vector system, we can reach the Legion?"

"Right," Cal replied, "but we have to get by the Permidium ship in order to communicate with Earth. Remember, only shortwave transmissions will work."

Jake smiled. "No worries. I have a solution for the beacon problem."

Cal raised a doubtful eyebrow. "Please, do tell what it is."

"Hey, I can come up with high-tech solutions too, you know," Jake said. "It's simple. We're in a pirate ship. Most likely every pirate ship is equipped with the beacon since it might have to go to Earth. So, we should be fine."

Cal raised both eyebrows. "Most likely . . . ? Should be . . . ? We're betting our lives on your assumptions?"

Jake wasn't very confident in this solution, but he didn't want Cal to know that.

"Sure," Jake said, "I'm certain one of those flashing lights means the beacon is turned on." He pointed to a series of red lights on the control panel that were each flashing at different intervals.

Cal shook his head. "I don't know, buddy. I haven't been able to figure out what those lights are for. But I guess it's a better plan than I have right now."

Jake continued to work the controls of the unfamiliar ship. It was very similar in structural design and instrumentation to a quantum light fighter, but it seemed to lack the speed and fire power of a light fighter. Jake wondered where the pirates had stolen the ship from.

A plasma blast sounded just to their right. The ship jerked and tipped hard to the left. Jake grabbed the control panel to keep from falling out of his seat. Cal fell against the side of the ship, slamming his head.

"What was that?" Jake said as he righted himself.

Cal pulled himself back into his chair, rubbing the side of his head with one hand and bringing the ship level with the other. He pointed at the viewing screen, still showing the rear view. "You stopped watching for followers from Tortuga. Looks like we have one. And that's a pretty fancy pirate ship."

Jake slid the lever to put shields at maximum. Cal was right. The sleek black-and-red spacecraft looked a little too fancy to be a typical pirate vessel.

A second later another blast hit even closer, again sending the spaceship into a dive to the left. This time Jake and Cal were braced for it and managed to remain in their seats. Cal quickly righted the ship.

"Enough of this," Jake said, bringing the rear firing arc online.

"Wait," Cal said, "they're hailing us."

Jake didn't want to wait. He wanted to fire before whoever it was found its target. But he locked on to the enemy ship and didn't fire. "All right, let's find out what they want," he said.

"Or what *it* wants," Cal said. "Sensors show only one life-form on board."

Cal opened the audio com. "This is Abigor. You have stolen this vessel from the Tortuga base. I'm giving you one chance to surrender yourselves and the ship or die. The first two were warning shots. The next one will not be. And I don't miss."

Jake shook his head.

Cal returned a quick nod, and Jake fired. A direct hit. Abigor's ship was close enough that they felt the vibrations from the concussion of the blast. Cal looked at the screen. Abigor's ship was seemingly unaffected by the blast.

"Sensors say we didn't do a lick of damage to his screens. What type of shields does he have on that thing?"

"Let me have the controls," Jake said. "You take over weapons. I'll get behind him. Maybe the forward arcs in this ship are more powerful than the rear."

Cal flipped the control switch to the copilot and turned on his weapons array.

"Hang on," Jake said.

Jake immediately put the spaceship into a barrel roll. While rolling, he moved the navigation lever toward himself hard, steering the ship into a reverse somersault. This was an exercise Jake had practiced for hours, one that very few pilots could pull off. Jake did it perfectly, falling in behind Abigor's ship as Jake and Cal came out of the maneuver.

"Lock on target," Jake said.

"Locked," Cal replied.

Jake looked up at the forward viewing screen. A blinking red circle surrounded Abigor's ship. "Fire!"

Before Cal could do so, the rear of Abigor's spaceship flashed and a second later the viewing screen lit up in a red-and-orange eruption that rocked their ship violently. Jake was knocked out of his seat as the ship jolted and rolled onto its side. A sharp pain shot through the side of his head as it smacked the wall. Cal was barely in his seat, hanging on to the control panel with one hand and reaching for the thruster control with the other.

The ship's plasma circuits sparked and smoked, and its lights blinked off and on.

"Our shields are completely down," Cal shouted.

"His firepower and shields are too much for this piece-of-junk ship," Jake shouted. "We have to get out of here."

Jake no longer had a "fight to the death" mentality. Now that he had Diane, he had something to live for. Or, more important, he had someone counting on him to return. He hated to lose any fight, but he now knew that sometimes you have to give up on a battle in order to win the war.

But how could he and Cal safely retreat? They were in a very inferior fighting machine that was badly damaged with no shields. And their weapons didn't seem to faze Abigor's ship. While their "borrowed" ship flew much like a quantum light fighter, it sure didn't fight like one.

Cal reached the thruster control with his fingertips and with a groan and final stretch of his arm, he worked the control. The ship slowly leveled off.

Jake pulled himself upright, then stood rubbing the side of his head. He felt blood on his fingers, but knew he had no time to assess the extent of his injury. He quickly scanned the instruments.

"Weapons are offline," Jake said. "Not that they were doing us any good anyway." He paused. "The engines are off too, except for thrusters and subluminal."

"We're a sitting duck," Cal said. "I'm trying to divert all remaining power except life support to our shields."

"Is it working?"

"No, not yet."

Absent a miracle, Abigor would finish them off or demand they be taken prisoner, again. Jake didn't like the idea of either.

Abigor had turned and was heading straight toward their lifeless ship.

"Better hurry," Jake said. "Abigor is coming around. This is going to be it."

Jake watched the viewing screen helplessly.

Abigor drew within range to take the final shot, when suddenly, plasma blasts came from behind, missing their ship and erupting against Abigor's shields.

Abigor didn't return fire. He simply turned and jumped to light speed.

A now familiar voice came over Jake and Cal's open audio com. "That's twice I've had to save you two in one day."

Jake flipped on the com to video. There was Novak.

"I guess that's two we owe you," Jake said. "Thanks."

Jake turned the screen to external rear view. Novak was in the lead ship, flanked by his escort.

"You sure you don't want to return to Craton with us?"

Jake studied Cal, expecting to see some gesture that said they should go with Novak. Cal just shook his head.

Jake gave Cal an affirming nod as he started to speak into the com. "Thanks, but not right now. We really need to see what things are like on Earth and try to reach the Legion from there." Rescuing Frank was still foremost on Jake's mind.

"Understood," Novak said. "Good luck."

12

EARTH

Jake dropped the pirate ship out of light speed as they approached sensor range of Earth. He didn't know what to expect, just the second day after the attack.

Jake and Cal exchanged glances, then Jake tilted his head toward the flashing red lights on the control panel. "I guess we're about to test out my beacon theory."

"Yeah," Cal said. "And either you're right or we die. Pretty simple."

"I'm not seeing anything on the sensors yet," Jake said.

"Let's move in at subluminal speed," Cal said. "We should pick up Earth and the Permidium vessel at about the same time. We'll know pretty quickly if this ship is putting out a beacon or not."

Jake, still with the controls, slowly throttled the subluminal engines toward Earth. "Here we go. We'll need to get close enough for anyone listening to pick up our shortwave com."

"Right," Cal said. "I'm assuming the Permidium ship is blocking the signals from its orbit, rather than someone obstructing them on

Earth. That's why shortwave signals aren't blocked. So, we need to be between Earth and the Permidium ship in order to communicate with anyone listening on Earth. And it should be harder for the Permidiums to detect our shortwave frequency than if we were using long-range, so that buys us a little time, assuming we get past them in the first place." He glanced at Jake.

They kept their eyes on the sensor scan. Earth looked like a small blue-and-white ball in the forward viewing screen. It was a familiar sight to Jake, from his travels back and forth to Vernius. But this time, looking at the ball he knew as his home, it felt different. Things on Earth had changed drastically, for the worse. Just how bad things were now, he could only speculate. Had everything been destroyed? Was anyone still alive? How was Aunt Jane? Had the Sector Four countryside where she lived been attacked or just the cities? If she was alive, she had to be worried sick about him. He wanted to find her or get word to her that he was fine, but that wasn't their mission. The Legion, and Frank, had to come first. Aunt Jane, of all people, would understand that. Besides, why should he get the privilege of contacting family, when the rest of the Legion could not?

––– ••• ••• –––

Sam was exhausted from climbing over, under, and through the rubble for the past two days, searching for any building still intact or any other survivors. She felt useless, hopeless, and frustrated all at the same time. The entire headquarters campus seemed to be a pile of debris. Smoke billowed from every pile of building remains. The air smelled of burning rubber, molten metal, and death. The black smoke left a metallic taste in her mouth. Her Legion uniform stuck to her sweaty skin from the extremely warm weather, made even hotter by the multiple fires. And every cry, moan, or shout for help that she followed ended in a lifeless body or a silent buried corpse by the time she reached the source of the sound.

All but one. She had managed to pull a private from the destruction. She should be thankful for that one small glimmer of hope. One was better than none.

The private had been trapped under a beam that had fallen on his leg, but he was otherwise uninjured. Sam thought his shin was fractured, but Yakov, a big burly man with a Russian accent said, scratching his thick beard, "I am fine. Whoever they are, they'll have to try harder than that to eliminate Yakov Petrov."

Fractured or not, the injured leg left him walking with a noticeable limp. He supported himself with a makeshift wooden cane made from a piece of debris. Sam had wrapped the wound as best she could.

Sam cleared debris from in front of Yakov so he could make his way through more easily, as they headed toward the residential section of the headquarters. Sam was hoping that area wasn't hit as hard. They had found scraps of food and bottles of water here and there, but they needed to find a more sustainable source of rations, along with shelter and a working com. The only underground bunker that contained supplies was the large bunker that housed the Dark Forty project, but it had been targeted and destroyed when the quantum light fighters emerged.

"Any idea who did this?" Yakov asked between breaths as he continued to limp along.

Sam shook her head. "No, but I think they took out our defense station first, then invaded. They knew what they were doing."

"They probably did the same thing to every sector headquarters," Yakov said. "Otherwise, the Legion from those sectors would be here by now to help."

"That was my thought too," Sam said as she continued to clear debris. "I wonder if they attacked outside the headquarters. And what about the Presidential Sector?"

Yakov stumbled but Sam grabbed his arm just in time to prevent him from falling. Pain shot through her arms and legs as the weight of his massive frame was almost too much for her to bear.

"Thank you," he said as he quickly got his feet underneath him, taking his weight off of her. "I saw them hit the Presidential Mansion with the big ships. Everyone there has to be dead. They destroyed everything, even the bunker. As for outside the headquarters, no, they didn't attack there. At least not here in Sector One. I was over the southern part of the sector before I was shot down. It seems they wanted the civilians alive and their homes intact. And that's where they were landing ground units. I don't think we want to venture outside the rubble of the headquarters. It's probably swarming with whoever attacked us."

***

"Earth just popped up on our sensors," Cal said. "And now I see the Permidium ship on there too. Man, that thing is big."

"All right," Jake said looking at the flashing red lights. "It's 'do or die' time." He had never bet his life before on a few flashing lights.

The Permidium ship hadn't come into view on the screen yet, so he watched its outline on the sensor. Cal was right. It was almost the size of a large asteroid. Jake held his breath, watching for any sign of a weapon being fired from it. It had to have detected Cal's and his ship by now.

Jake felt a bead of perspiration form on his upper lip and he wiped his sweaty palms on his pants. He was actually nervous. He never got nervous. But this was completely out of his control, and he was relying on an educated guess at best.

Jake eased the subluminal throttle faster, not taking his eyes off of the sensor. He expected to see the Permidium ship fire. And when it did, he knew there would be nothing Cal and he could do to avoid such a destructive weapon. But as they drew closer to Earth, nothing happened. Earth grew larger in the viewing screen and eventually the Permidium ship appeared as well. It just sat there in orbit. No sign at all of it powering up its weapons.

Jake let out his breath, which he didn't realize he had been holding. Cal's pale face stared at the screen.

"I think we made it, buddy," Jake said. "Now let's see if we can find someone."

Cal opened the com. "Let's listen for outgoing messages or distress signals first. The sooner we start trying to communicate, the quicker the Permidiums or pirates on the planet will find our frequency and then find us."

The first shortwave frequency on the com was full of chatter. Jake didn't recognize the voices or any of the call letters. Probably all pirates. Cal continued to change frequencies, but each frequency either had pirate ships talking or silence.

Sam recognized the remains of a small office once connected to a hangar just outside the residential section. Sam sensed a flare of hope, but she didn't let herself get too excited. She didn't want to be let down again.

She had already had enough go wrong. All hangar offices had coms equipment, so Sam figured that was a good place to try to reach help before moving deeper into the residential area. That was, assuming there was any help out there.

Sam pointed to the small structure. "Let's try that hangar office. Maybe it'll have a working com."

"Agreed," Yakov said.

As they continued through the debris, covering the short distance to the office, Yakov's limp got noticeably worse.

The computer in the small office was broken into pieces and lying on the cracked and pitted concrete floor. The com equipment was also on the floor but appeared to be in one piece. Sam and Yakov began picking it up and reconnecting the wires.

Its power cells read fully charged when Sam flipped it on.

"Mayday, mayday," Sam said into the com as she stood over the desk that they had turned upright. "This is Sector One. We've been attacked. Is there any Legion out there listening? We are two survivors. I can't give my coordinates. This isn't a secure channel. We need medical attention and assistance. If there are any Legion hearing this, please give me a signal." Sam didn't want to say that they were Legion or that they were in the headquarters. Based on Yakov's information, the pirates may be leaving civilians outside of the headquarters alone.

Sam released the com and listened. Nothing except some slight static.

She changed the channel and pressed the com again. "Is anyone out there? Legion, civilians, anyone? We need assistance." She paused. "Anyone at all that can provide assistance?"

She released the com again. Still just static.

Sam continued one by one through the channels that the Legion generally used, that she thought might be the least likely to be used by whoever attacked them.

Jake kept maneuvering their spaceship in and out of the atmosphere. He figured the Permidiums would be less likely to suspect something different about them if they were in motion rather than in orbit. And he didn't want to drop down to the planet, as he assumed it was covered with pirates.

"I'm about through all the frequencies," Cal said. "I'll need to either start over or start sending a message. Which do you think? Sending could be risky, but we knew that before we came here."

Before Jake could answer, the com crackled and a woman's voice came through. She didn't sound like a pirate. "We need assistance. Please respond if you can hear me."

Jake gave Cal a nod, and Cal pressed the com and spoke. "We are Captains Cal Danielson and Jake Saunders of the Earth Legion. To whom am I speaking?"

The voice responded immediately. "I'm Private Samantha Simons, also of the Legion. Your voice sure is a sound for sore ears. I didn't even know if there were any other Legion alive."

"What's your condition?" Cal asked. "Are there any other survivors?"

"I'm fine but for a few bumps and bruises. I have Private Yakov Petrov with me. His leg is pretty banged up. We haven't been able to find any other survivors."

"Are you on the planet?" Jake added, careful not to request her location or divulge his and Cal's over the com.

"Yes, I'm on Earth," Sam responded. "It's horrible down here. It looks like hell on Earth. What happened? Who did this?"

Was the entire planet wiped out? Neither Jake nor Cal spoke. Jake felt a lump form in his throat at Sam's description of Earth, his home.

The com crackled again with Sam's voice. "Sir, are you still there? Can you give me an idea of your twenty?"

Cal blinked several times rapidly. "Yes, Private, I'm here. Negative on the twenty. Too risky. But we're in a secure location. Can we extract you?"

"Negative," Sam said. "No place to touch down in the headquarters, and the countryside is full of the attackers. Do you know who did this?"

Oddly, Jake felt relieved when he heard that the attackers were in the country. Maybe they didn't destroy those homes.

Jake pressed the com. "You said the countryside is full of the attackers? Does that mean they didn't destroy it?"

"Affirmative, sir," Sam replied. "That's our understanding."

Jake and Cal each let out a sigh.

Sam continued. "But sir, they destroyed the Presidential Mansion. The bunker and everything. The president likely is dead."

Neither Cal nor Jake said anything. What was there to say?

Cal pressed the com. "It was pirates with help from the Permidiums."

"Permidiums? Aren't they from the Andromeda galaxy?"

"It's a long story," Cal retorted. "For now, we need to secure you and try to reach the rest of the Legion."

"There isn't much you can do for us right now," Sam said. "We'll find shelter and other necessities. Just knowing friendlies are still out there does more for us than you can imagine. Can we help with contacting the Legion?"

Cal turned off the com. "What do you think? Should we task them with finding and sending the Legion vector-space transmission?"

Jake thought for a moment. They needed to access a transmitter module in order to send the vector transmission. The easiest place to locate a module would be in a sector headquarters, but it didn't sound like they would be able to touch down in or near there, if they could even get through to the surface at all.

"I think it's our best shot at this point," Jake said. "Let's do it. But it'll be tricky telling them where to find a transmitter without giving their location away if the pirates or Permidiums are eavesdropping."

"I have an idea for that." Cal opened the com. "If you're up for it, yes, we could use your help."

Jake heard more perk in Sam's voice. "You bet. It'll feel good to be useful after everything that happened here. Tell us what we need to do."

"You wouldn't happen to be a techy or a gamer, would you?" Cal asked.

Jake heard even more perk in Sam's voice. "Are you kidding, sir? I play every video and holographic game there is. And I just completed the Legion future officer training by writing my thesis on past, present, and future technologies. I called it 'Domination through Techno-Might.' I aced it."

Cal's eyes lit up. "Are you serious? You wrote that paper? Professor Jessy Hetzel sent it to me. She thought I might find it interesting. I loved it!"

"Captain Hetzel was my professor. So, you're into tech and games too? Wait! You said you're Cal Danielson. I thought that name sounded familiar. You shut down Craton's superweapon using a video game, and you were the first person to successfully jump to quantum drive from a stationary position. Oh my gosh. I've read all of your works. You're awesome . . . sir."

Jake raised his eyebrows at Cal and made a rolling motion with his hand. Cal seemed to ignore him as he spoke into the com again. "You can call me Cal."

"And please call me Sam. All my friends do. If you think that's appropriate, sir . . . I mean, Cal."

"Yes, of course it's appropriate, Sam."

Jake cleared his throat loudly. "Can we get on with this before we're shot out of the sky? The two of you can go on a geek date after we save Earth."

"Um, yes, of course," Cal stammered.

"And for the record, I piloted the stationary jump to quantum drive," Jake added.

Cal spoke into the com again. "Okay, you've played Earth Conquest on the holograph?"

"Of course, I love the game."

"Great. You know on the final level in champion mode there is only one way to defeat the gargoyle king and save Earth?"

"Yes, sure. I've done it multiple times."

"Good, then you had to call in your underworld allies for the final battle."

"Yes! I think I know where you're going with this."

Jake could hear the recognition in Sam's voice. He had to admit, this was pretty brilliant on Cal's part, but that didn't surprise him. While Jake had never played that game, he had heard about it. There was some controversy over how much it mimicked Legion procedures. In the final level, you had to contact your allies through a vector-space transmission so that only your allies could detect it. And the transmitters were located only in the huts of your four warrior champions. This was almost identical to the Legion's procedure. The Legion's vector-space transmissions could only be received and sent on small, portable vector-space transmitters given to all Legion officers, the president, and the president's cabinet members, but only after activated by a transmission sent from a larger transmitter module located in the homes of all Legion officers and the Presidential Mansion. The idea was to make the system as nonmilitary as possible to avoid discovery by the enemy, and it was to be used only as a last resort.

"Excellent," Cal said. "You need to contact your underworld allies. Warriors are officers."

"Got it, Cal," Sam replied with confidence in her voice.

"If you run into trouble, contact us on this frequency. We may have to depart for a while, but we'll be back."

"Okay, but we don't have a portable com. We'll contact you if and when we can, or you'll hear from the warrior."

"Understood," Cal said. He paused. "Please be careful, Sam."

"I will, Cal. Thanks for being there for us."

Jake thought he heard a tear in Sam's voice.

13

DIANE

"The Imperial Majesty won't be returning for another hour," Patha said. "I don't know if you should wait in her office. You know she doesn't like that."

Diane was hoping that the Imperial Majesty hadn't told her trusted assistant that the ambassador was on a short leash and not allowed near the Imperial Majesty's office, let alone allowed in it. Otherwise, her plan would be doomed from the start.

"It's okay, Patha," Diane said. "I have a lot of reading to do to prepare for this meeting anyway." Diane held up her data pod. "I need a quiet place where I won't be disturbed. The Imperial Majesty's office is perfect."

Patha frowned. "All right, I suppose it's okay this one time, given the circumstances."

Whew, Diane thought. She had cleared that hurdle, but she still had more hurdles to go.

Now if she could remember how Cal had explained the new data-to-audio transfer technology. She wished she had paid better attention, but she'd figured Cal was just being Cal, and she would never need to use it. But now, with the orbiting Permidium ship blocking all long-range audio, video, and data transmissions from Vernius, it was the only way she could think of to get a message out to Cal, Jake, or anyone in the Legion. She needed to tell them how Sloan was using Cal's transponder to control the Permidiums, and more important, that it might possibly tell them how to destroy the Permidium ships.

Diane shut the door, hurried to the Imperial Majesty's desk, sat down, and turned on her computer. She closed her eyes and thought back just a short time ago to the demonstration by Cal.

Cal was seated at one of the engineer's computers in the tech development center. "This is brand-new technology that only Vernius possesses," Cal said. "A data message disappears as it leaves Vernius and then reappears to the recipient as an audio message. Brilliant! I should have thought of it."

Diane, looking over Cal's shoulder, rolled her eyes. "Hurry up, Cal, I have a lot to do."

"Okay, okay. Here's the one-minute summary. Unlike other means of long-range communication, data-to-audio transfer messages can't be blocked. The designers haven't figured out how to convert the messages back into data, but I'll figure that out, now that they've showed it to me." Cal looked up from the computer and smiled.

"I'm sure you will, brother. Now, can we finish this little demonstration of yours?"

"Yes, but first there are two limitations you should know about."

"As if I'm going to be using this technology by myself?"

"You never know, sis. Always better to be prepared. The first limitation is that since it's so new, they are only installing it on the Imperial Majesty's computer until she's able to test it."

"Makes sense," Diane said. "And the second limitation?"

"You have to know the recipient's data inscription," Cal said. "The data message has to be sent to the recipient's inscription in order for it to find its target when

it reappears as an audio message over the recipient's com. Here's my inscription."
He pointed to the screen. "Jake can give you his."

"Okay, nice, good, are we finished?"

"Yep. Let's send a message to me to watch it work."

· · · · · · · · · ·

Diane opened her eyes. So, according to Cal, this should get a message past the Permidiums. She opened the data-to-audio transfer program and typed in the message she wanted to send. Now she just needed a recipient. She closed her eyes tight and rubbed her temple. *What was Cal's data inscription?* She couldn't remember. And she had never asked Jake for his. She didn't know anyone's data inscription.

She thought for a moment. She did know Jake's computer access codes, which would enable her to retrieve his inscription. She never accessed Jake's computer without his permission, but they had each given the other their access codes. That was prohibited except between married Legion couples.

Diane thought that was a big step toward marriage, but she had thought wrong. Jake seemed more distant than ever from her lately. She couldn't understand why, but it was making her distance herself from him as well. And she didn't like that. It hurt just thinking about it. She had to keep those thoughts out of her mind. She had much bigger issues right now. Vernius, Earth, and the entire galaxy had much bigger issues right now. She had to stay focused on the task at hand.

She pulled up Jake's profile, entered the various codes when prompted, and remotely accessed Jake's computer. Jake might be in a cell, but sending him the message was the best she could do. If Jake was free, he could act on the message. If he wasn't, maybe he could get the message out to someone else.

As she searched for Jake's data inscription, a message popped onto the screen from a couple days earlier.

Confirmation of luxury cruise: Jake and Debbie.

Diane knew she shouldn't read it, but she opened the confirmation anyway. Her heart sank as she read. A weeklong romantic space cruise . . . with someone else. No, Jake wouldn't do that. Maybe the name was just a mistake. She looked at the dates. It was the same week she was to be away helping her dad. And Jake knew that. He had planned this for when she would be gone. That's why he had been so distant from her and not wanting to discuss marriage. Who was Debbie, and how long had he been seeing her? She felt her heart breaking. She wiped a tear from her cheek with her fingertips. She knew something like this was a possibility because of the way he had been acting, but now that it was a reality, it hurt so bad.

Diane no longer cared about sending the message or saving Earth. Her world had just been crushed. She put her head in the palms of her hands and felt a lump form in her throat. She wanted to burst into tears. No! She would not cry. She was Legion. There was a duty she had to her planet and its people. A duty to Vernius and its people. She would send the message and she would see this through. She could sulk in her own self-pity later. She wasn't angry at Jake, just hurt. Hurt that he no longer loved her. But more important, hurt that he lied and went behind her back.

"Hello, Your Majesty," Diane heard Patha say outside the door.

She had to hurry. She had very little time. She quickly found Jake's data inscription and entered it into the message.

Diane heard footsteps getting close to the door, then heard Patha again. "The ambassador is already in your office waiting for you for your meeting."

Diane added a few more sentences to the message.

Jake, I know all about Debbie and your cruise. I'm not angry with you. I'm just so hurt that you lied to me. I hope you're okay wherever you are. I wish the best for you as I still love you more than life itself, but you have truly hurt me. I'm not sure if I can ever look at you again.

"What meeting?" the Imperial Majesty asked in a stern voice as the door started to open.

Diane hit send and looked up to meet the glare of the Imperial Majesty and face the consequences. She didn't have time to erase her tracks or the sent message, so she knew there was no use lying or trying to talk her way out of it. She'd accomplished her mission. Now she would pay the price, whatever that might be. But she didn't care, especially now that her world had ended.

14

TOO CLOSE FOR COMFORT

"I'm picking up something odd being emitted from the Permidium ship," Cal said.

Jake, still maneuvering the pirate ship in and out of Earth's atmosphere, hadn't checked the sensors in a while. He glanced at the viewing screen. The Permidium ship wasn't in sight given their current vantage point.

"Does it look like they've detected us?" Jake asked.

"No," Cal replied as he monitored the sensors again. "Whatever it is, it isn't directed toward us. It looks like it's directed toward the planet. Some type of broad scan."

Jake peered at the viewing screen again. Cal and he had been so caught up in what the Permidium ship was doing, they missed the three pirate ships approaching them.

"Uh-oh," Jake said. This can't be good.

Cal watched the screen as the com buzzed. "They're hailing us."

Jake flipped on the audio.

A squeaky voice came over the com. "You, in that vessel, what squadron are you from? And what is your assignment? The call numbers on your hull don't match any of the ships assigned to Earth. And your movements have been . . . let's say, erratic."

Jake turned off the com. "What do you think? Do we try to talk our way out of this or run for it?"

Cal raised an eyebrow. "Since we have no idea what their squadrons are and have no explanation for why we're here, I say we run. Head to Craton and wait to hear from Sam."

Jake didn't want to leave. He wanted to stay until Sam was able to send a transmission to the Legion. He wanted it to happen quickly so they could round up the Legion and get back to Frank. He could still see Frank's broken and bloodied face. He could still hear the crunch of Sloan's fist against Frank's flesh. But remaining near Earth wouldn't make Sam move any faster. She could only do what she could do. And he needed to stay alive to lead the Legion to Frank.

"Agreed," Jake said, increasing their subluminal speed and turning away from the three ships.

They both ignored the buzzing com as Jake increased velocity, preparing to jump to light speed.

"What did all that mean?" Yakov asked.

"It's hard to explain," Sam said. "But we need to move into the residential section and find an officer's quarters. Then we need to locate the officer's vector-space transmitter module and send a message to the Legion. That will activate the system, and then all Legion officers can communicate without the pirates or anyone else blocking or hearing them."

"I knew we had such a system but didn't know how it worked."

"Are you good to walk?" Sam asked. "We need to get moving."

Yakov nodded and began limping toward the residences.

Just as Sam thought, after getting through the demolished houses, they found a few streets where the houses were mostly intact.

Sam stopped.

Yakov held up as well, taking the opportunity to rub his injured thigh. "What's wrong?"

Sam scanned the surroundings. "How do we know which house belongs to an officer? We have to search house to house. Even then, there isn't really anything to distinguish an officer's residence from anyone else's unless we find some credentials or a uniform."

"That could take forever," Yakov replied, leaning heavily on his crutch.

"We'd better get started then," Sam said.

Yakov took a step, then started to collapse in front of Sam.

Sam reached quickly and grabbed his arm, but as his momentum carried him downward, she lost her grip and he hit the pavement. His weight was too much for her. The makeshift wrap on his leg was turning dark red. Sweat dripped from his dirty face.

Sam bent over him and helped him sit up. He leaned back against an overturned hover car.

"Let me rewrap your leg," Sam said.

"No!" Yakov commanded. "You need to find a transmitter. Leave me here. I'll be fine. Find the transmitter and send a message. That's the only way we'll get help."

Sam knew he was right. She needed to get a message out to the Legion, but she hated leaving a fallen comrade. "Okay, but as soon as I send the message, I'll be back with food and water." She hoped for both of their sakes that she could find some.

Yakov leaned back and closed his eyes.

Jake braced himself out of habit as he punched the light speed control. He waited for the slight g-force jerk of his head that always accompanied a jump. He felt nothing. He surveyed the instrument panel. It showed they were still at subluminal speed.

"Anytime, buddy," Cal said. "They're powering weapons."

"It didn't jump," Jake said as he worked the controls. "Trying again."

Jake hit the light speed control once more. Again, he felt nothing, and the instrument panel still showed they were on subluminal power. Jake's armpits were getting damp and a bead of sweat dropped from his forehead. He was nervous again. They couldn't go to light speed with their shields up, so if the pirates started firing, they would be forced to raise their shields and fight. Three against one, and they were in a pirate ship. And no doubt the three would multiply very quickly.

"Give me control," Cal said. "Let me try."

As Jake hit the pilot control to transfer the helm to Cal, the spacecraft jolted violently. Jake reached for something to grab hold of but caught only air as he tumbled out of his seat. Pain shot up his shoulder as it was driven into the floor.

"That was a glancing hit without shields," Cal said, hanging onto the instrument panel to stay in his seat. "A direct hit and we're dead."

Jake's nervousness was pushed away by determination. He had been nervous before because they were running. Now it was time to fight. That's what he was best at. He would give Cal one shot at getting to light speed and that would be it. He wasn't going to wait and hope they could get the light speed working while they took a direct hit. He would try to take out these three ships, and hopefully, more wouldn't follow.

Still lying on the floor, Jake looked up at Cal and shouted, "Now!"

Cal hit his light speed control. Jake felt nothing. He jumped up, and without even checking the instrument panel, he reached over Cal's shoulder with both arms, simultaneously transferring the helm back to him and raising the shields. Just as he did, the ship jolted hard. Jake grabbed Cal's chair to maintain his balance, twisted his body, and fell into his seat.

"That was close," Cal said. "A direct hit, but you got the shields up just in time."

Jake didn't answer. He didn't even really hear Cal. He was focused on the battle now. As soon as he fell into his chair, he pushed the spacecraft to full throttle, turned, and headed straight for the three ships.

Disappointment and impatience started to overtake Sam. *Where are an officer's quarters?* she thought. She had been down two streets and nothing. No sign of an officer in any of the houses.

The entire neighborhood was eerily quiet. Not a single person anywhere outside and all the houses so far were empty. All the Legion would have been fighting either off the planet or, unfortunately for them, on the planet. And the pirates must have moved all the civilians to the countryside.

As Sam started to enter another house, she heard a slurry voice from behind her. "You there. Stop."

Sam's heart raced. She had been so cautious, checking around every corner before moving forward. How did she miss whoever this was?

She slowly turned around to see two disheveled men. Their clothes were torn, and sweat soaked the first man's shaggy beard. The second man was cleanly shaven and less disgusting-looking, but they were unmistakably human pirates.

The first man pointed a new-looking plasma rifle at her, showing his yellow-stained teeth in a smile. "I thought we killed off all the Legion. Looks like we missed one."

The second man raised a sepder, but he clearly didn't know how to use it. He aimed it at Sam, but it was still in sword mode. Sam wondered how many Legion sepders had been taken by the pirates.

"And a pretty one at that," the second pirate said.

Sam slowly raised her hands to shoulder level. "I'm just trying to find some food and water. That's all. You've already defeated us. Just let me go. I won't cause any problems."

She highly doubted that they would just let her go, but it was worth a try.

Both men moved toward her slowly. The first spoke. "Now we can't just let you go, missy. But I tell you what. You give us what we want, and we just might be on our way and never mention you to anyone." His smile grew.

"Yeah, I like that idea," the second pirate chimed in, but without a smile. "Shouldn't we wait for Shorty to catch up, though?"

"Shorty will find us," the first pirate replied, not taking his eyes off of Sam. "Besides, we won't be going anywhere for a while."

Even though Sam had a pretty good idea as to what they wanted, she had to ask. "And just what do you want?"

They came closer to Sam, who was standing in the open doorway to the house. The first pirate let out an exaggerated laugh that made her skin crawl. As she felt a bead of sweat running down her back, she hoped they couldn't see her arms shaking. She had hand-to-hand combat training required of all Legion cadets, but that was it. And there were two of them, each twice her size. She really didn't know what to do. She wanted to kick herself for not looking for a weapon earlier. She just figured she would eventually come across one. And she was with Yakov, who had a plasma gun on his waist.

The second pirate stepped toward Sam, dropping the sepder. When he was close enough for her to see past the dirt on his face, she could tell that he was younger than he looked from a distance. His face was expressionless as he reached out and stroked her hair.

Sam's stomach churned. It was all she could do to not vomit. With her hands still raised, she finally decided to do the only thing she could think of. In one motion she grabbed the man's shoulders and pulled him toward her. At the same time, she raised her knee sharply into his groin.

Sam thought her ears would pop at the man's shout as he doubled over.

Through clenched teeth and drool he turned his red face toward the first man. "Kill her!"

Sam had no plan to deal with the other man. She had nowhere to run. He was too far away for her to jump him, even if she was strong enough to do so. And it was too late to hide. She knew this was the end. But at least she would die fighting, not while being molested.

The first man's smile turned to a snarl as he aimed his rifle at Sam. Sam stared him directly in the eyes. She was scared to death, but she wasn't going to make it easy for him.

The second pirate shouted again. "Shoot her!"

Sam could see the first pirate's finger start to squeeze the trigger. She braced herself for the impact and flinched at the distinct sound of a plasma blast. But she felt nothing.

Is there no pain when you die?

Everything looked the same, yet seemingly in slow motion. The pirate's rifle was still aimed at her.

Then the pirate slowly fell forward until he smacked the ground face first, his rifle dropping to the side. Yakov was standing behind him, one hand leaning on his crutch, the other hand holding his plasma gun, which was now pointed at Sam.

Sam let out a deep breath just as the second pirate grabbed the sepder, jumped to his feet, wrapped an arm around Sam's neck and held the sepder blade at her throat.

She immediately felt every muscle in her body stiffen. She had to tell herself to breathe, as she was afraid to make even the slightest movement. The cold, sharp edge of the blade touched her throat slightly enough that if she swallowed, her neck would expand just enough for it to break her skin.

Her mind raced. The Legion had trained her for this exact situation. There was a technique that, if properly performed, would free her and reverse the weapon on her attacker. But it was no use. She was too overwhelmed to think. All the training in the world hadn't mentally prepared her for when a situation like this actually happened. She could recall nothing.

"Drop the gun," the pirate said looking at Yakov, "or I'll cut her throat."

Yakov started limping toward them, his gun now aimed at the pirate's head.

Yakov had just saved her life, and now she had put him in an impossible situation. He could save her again, let her die, or accidentally kill her himself. She should have been more alert and moved more quickly away from the pirate. After all, he wasn't dead. She had merely kicked him.

"You drop your weapon," Yakov said in his Russian accent, "or as my Commander Cantor says, you'll make my day."

The pirate firmed his grip on the sepder and growled, "Last warn—"

Blood splattered Sam's face. She instinctively flinched and the pirate and sepder dropped.

Sam quickly took inventory of herself. She was fine. She felt her throat. No cuts. She let out a sigh and relaxed. Yakov did it again. He saved her life twice in a matter of minutes.

"Thank you."

As the last syllable left her mouth, another plasma blast rang from the roof above her out of her field of vision. Yakov's chest opened up in a bloody burn, and he crumpled over.

"No!" Sam shouted, but this time she didn't think. The sight of her fallen comrade triggered her instincts. She immediately dropped to the ground, grabbed the sepder, flipped it into gun mode, and in one continuous motion rolled out from the doorway giving her a line of sight to the roof behind her. She saw the wide-eyed look on another ragged-clothed pirate's face as she fired. She even surprised herself with such a quick action. The pirate's rather small, lifeless body dropped at her feet.

Hanging on to the sepder, she pulled herself up, ran to Yakov, and knelt beside him. Tears blurred her vision as she checked for a pulse that she knew she wouldn't find. She had barely gotten to know him, but he felt like a lifelong friend. He was her only ally. The only thing keeping her sanity together. What would she have done without his companionship these past two days, without him to share her grief? What would she do now? And he was gone because of her. She'd put herself in the position she was in. She'd failed to be cautious enough. And he had to save her life twice because of that, and then lost his own. She had never even asked him about his family. Was he married? Did he have children? He had become her lifeline, yet she knew nothing about him. As she wiped tears from her face, she decided that she had to continue on. She had to find a transmitter and contact the Legion, or Yakov's death would be for nothing.

Sam looked around. Yakov at least deserved a proper burial, but there was no place to dig, nothing to dig with, and no time. The best that she could come up with was a blanket she plundered from the rubble. Laying it over his body, she said a short prayer, then turned toward the house.

Upon entering, she felt a weight lift off her shoulders.

"Thank you," she whispered.

A picture of a man with his family was displayed on the table. A picture of the same man with Commander Cantor pinning Superior-Guard officer stripes to his Legion uniform hung on the wall.

"Power up the plasma guns or whatever weapons this thing has," Jake said. "But wait until I tell you to fire. I want to hit them hard at close range."

He kept a steady course in a direct line with the three ships. He assumed they would break formation any second and spread out for an attack. That's what he would do if he were them. But he hoped they wouldn't. Otherwise, his idea wouldn't work. His plan was risky though. If all three fired on Cal and him at once, he doubted their shields would hold. But he wanted to get close enough to penetrate their shields in one shot.

"Target the center ship," Jake said.

"We're getting awfully close," Cal said. "They're increasing speed. You're playing a dangerous game of chicken, buddy."

Jake took a deep breath. He felt calm. He was always calmest when he was in combat and on the attack.

"They aren't changing course," Cal said.

"Steady," Jake replied. "Steady."

The pirates hadn't fired yet either, probably waiting to see what Jake would do, or, as Jake was hoping, too confused about what Jake was doing. Nobody in their right mind would fly head-on into a pack of three heavily armed vessels.

"Five seconds until impact with the center ship," Cal said in an overly loud tone. "All three of them have weapons locked on."

"Brace yourself," Jake replied.

The three pirate ships continued to fly in a tight formation, not slowing at all.

"Five, four, three," Cal said.

"Fire!" Jake shouted as he pulled back fast and hard on the navigation lever.

Cal fired, then grabbed the control panel to keep himself in his seat.

Jake, hanging on tight himself as the ship started a reverse somersault, watched the sensors. The three pirate ships had fired as well, but a couple seconds later. Their shots missed.

Jake watched the middle ship disappear from the sensor and a couple seconds later both of the other ships vanished.

"Direct hit," Cal said.

That's what Jake had hoped for. But that cut it too close, even for him.

As they came out of the somersault, there was nothing but space debris showing on the viewing screen.

Jake rechecked the sensors. They weren't showing any other ships outside the atmosphere except the Permidium vessel, which wasn't moving. *Good,* Jake thought. Maybe they would have time to fix the light speed drive and get away from Earth before they were detected by any other pirates.

15

HOPE

Aretha collapsed in the sparse shade of a lone sumac tree, the first shade she had come to since abandoning her hover car. She crawled on all fours, dragging herself through the sand and rocks to the trunk of the tree and sat up, leaning against it. She pulled her last bottle of water out of her handbag. The cool, clear liquid was like a balm for her cracked lips. The water numbed her parched throat, soothing the burning discomfort. Never had she been so thirsty. She had been rationing the bottles. She didn't know when she would find more. It had been two days since she witnessed the attack on her planet, a day and a half since she'd left her vehicle. After seeing the overwhelming attack of the enemy ships, she knew nobody would be passing her way anytime soon.

She should be to the outskirts of Sector One's countryside by now. Had she gotten lost? Was she walking in circles? Her eyes had strained against the brightness of the day trying to keep the sun positioned so that she walked east. She had become so lightheaded she wasn't sure which direction she had traveled the last six hours or so.

She tried to will herself to get up, to keep going, but her legs would not obey her commands. She could only sit there, barely even able to raise her water bottle to her lips. If she didn't keep moving, she would die. Nobody knew she was out there. With the attack she'd seen, she figured there were probably thousands of people missing. And was there even anyone alive to search for them? Was anyone alive at all, besides her?

She swallowed the last precious gulp of water, the bottle sliding from her motionless hand, and closed her eyes.

Cal was in the hold working on the drive when Jake felt a vibration on his belt. It took a few seconds for the vibration to register. It was from a device he had been issued but had never used. A portable vector-space transmitter.

Jakes eyes widened and he jumped out of his seat. "Cal, I'm getting a vector-space message."

"My transmitter is buzzing too," Cal said as he quickly climbed out of the hold.

Jake plugged his transmitter into the ship's com system so that the audio would be amplified. He opened the com.

It was Sam's voice. They caught her in mid-sentence: ". . . on Earth in Sector One headquarters. The damage is extensive, and casualties are extremely heavy. I have found no other survivors in the headquarters. I don't believe the countryside was hit hard, but pirates are in control there."

Jake wondered what happened to Yakov if there are no other survivors. Sam had said that he was injured, but Jake didn't think the injuries were that severe from what he had heard.

Sam continued. "This vector-space message should be received by all surviving Legion officers. Please reply back to me if you are out there. We need to rendezvous and organize."

Cal sat down and quickly pressed the com with a smile on his face. "Sam! You're all right! You did it!"

"Cal, is that you?" Sam replied. "Are you guys okay? Where are you? Now it's safe to tell me."

"Yes, we're fine. We're orbiting Earth. I was so worried about you. Can we pick you up?"

Jake raised his eyebrow at Cal. "You do know that every Legion officer listening can hear you, right?"

Cal gritted his teeth and blushed.

"I didn't think you were thinking straight," Jake said with a slight grin.

Sam's voice came over the com again. "No, it's still not safe down here and there's no place to land. Besides, my understanding is that one main transmitter module must remain open for the vector-space transmission system to operate. I'll stay here and make sure this or another one stays open. Now that I'm in the residences, I should be fine."

"Great, Private," Jake said before Cal could respond. "We'll need eyes on the ground anyway."

"But what about the portable transmitter of any officer the pirates have captured?" Sam asked. "Won't the pirates be able to listen in on it?"

"Negative," Cal said. "Each transmitter is synced to the specific officer's touch. Only he or she can activate it."

"Are we clear for the transmission?" Jake asked Cal.

"Go ahead."

Jake took a deep breath and pressed the com. "Legion officers, we are Captains Jake Saunders and Cal Danielson. I'm sure you all know by now that Earth has been attacked and is under the control of pirates and the Permidiums. All Legion will rendezvous on the planet Craton. Yes, I said Craton. It's the only safe, unoccupied planet that we know of. We'll have access to their military hangars. If you can't get there or need help, send us a message."

Jake turned off the com. "Anything else we need to add?"

Cal pressed the com. "This is the only secure communication. Use only vector-space transmissions." He paused. "Sam, can you repeat this message every fifteen minutes?"

"Yes, sure, Cal," Sam replied.

"And Sam," Cal said, "please be safe."

Cal released the com and stood up. "I should have the light speed drive fixed shortly, and we can head to Craton ourselves."

A glimmer of hope at just the possibility of saving Frank flooded Jake's thoughts. Contacting the Legion was the first step in getting back to Tortuga. Now they just needed to organize the troops and prepare for a prisoner evacuation.

Aretha felt a vibration on her hip. But it didn't matter. She was just imagining it. She didn't care. She just wanted to sleep. She knew if she fell asleep, she would never wake up. But still, that was all she wanted to do. Her throat and lips burned. There was desert in every direction for miles. She had no more water, no transportation, and no communication. The president and the rest of the cabinet was likely gone. She didn't even have the energy to open her eyes. She would just rest here in the only shade around. She would just rest for a little while, and if she fell asleep? Well, at least the pain would be gone.

The vibration on her hip continued. She felt aggravated. How could she rest with that? She wanted it to stop, but it wouldn't.

"Stop," she barely got out through her parched lips. Trying to talk burned her throat even more. She tried to swallow, but there was nothing to swallow except dry air.

The vibrations continued. With her eyes still closed, she moved her hand to the vibration. She felt the same sensation on her fingertips. *Maybe it's real*, she thought. She peered down at the vibrating device through slitted eyelids, her mind still in a semiconscious state. What was the device? She couldn't think. She had to wake up. But she just wanted to drift off forever. No, she needed to focus. She needed to force her mind back to consciousness.

She opened her eyes wider and became aware of her surroundings. She remembered her hover car breaking down, the aircraft attacking Earth, the bright explosion in the Presidential Sector. She examined the device again. It was her portable vector-space transmitter attached to her belt. She took it everywhere but had never used it.

She pressed the com button to activate the transmitter and heard an unfamiliar female voice. "It's the only safe unoccupied planet that we know of. We'll have access to their military hangars. If you can't get there or need help, send us a message. This message will repeat every fifteen minutes."

Aretha's mind jumped back to full consciousness. There was Legion out there. They were organizing. There was hope.

She pulled the transmitter from her belt to speak, but nothing came out of her mouth. She tried again. Her throat burned. Her tongue wouldn't work. But she had to speak. There was hope that she could be rescued.

Again, she tried, with all the effort she could muster. "Help me."

She heard only silence. She moved the transmitter closer to her mouth, took a deep breath, and ignoring the pain in her throat and her bleeding lips, she shouted as loud as her spent lungs would allow her. "Please, I need help." She dropped the transmitter and hung her head.

There was another long moment of disappointing silence before the transmitter crackled. "We are Captains Saunders and Danielson. We have your location. Leave your transmitter on. We're on our way."

Aretha laid her head back against the trunk of the tree and closed her eyes again. But it wasn't so she could fall asleep forever. This time it was to say a simple prayer. "Thank you."

16

GOOD NEWS, BAD NEWS

A groan came from behind Jake. He turned to see Aretha Brown stirring on the portable cot Cal had found in the pirate spaceship.

"Where am I?" Aretha said in a groggy voice. She started to sit up, then grabbed her head and fell back onto the cot.

"Take it easy," Jake said. "You're on a pirate spaceship."

Aretha raised an eyebrow.

"Well, not a pirate spaceship," Jake said. "I meant, yes it's a pirate spaceship, but we aren't pirates."

"My head is killing me," Aretha said.

Cal turned around in his seat and interrupted. "Mine is too, after that explanation." He looked at Jake. "Nice job welcoming the lead senator, Jake."

Jake turned to completely face Aretha. "We're Legion Captains Jake Saunders and Cal Danielson. We picked you up in the desert between Sector One and the Presidential Sector. It's a long story how we ended up in a pirate spaceship, so we'll save that for later.

We're on our way to rendezvous on Craton with whatever's left of the Legion."

"You were in pretty bad shape," Cal said. "Extremely dehydrated. I gave you several intravenous liquid drips. You'll have a headache for a while, but you'll be fine." He handed her a bottle of water. "Here, keep drinking."

Jake went on to inform her of the status of things on Earth; who was behind the attack, including Sloan; and how Craton became involved. He left out the old man in the bar.

"Our next order of business needs to be reconstructing our government," Jake said.

Aretha sat on the edge of the cot and raised an eyebrow at Jake. "What?"

Jake continued. "If we're going to organize the Legion, develop a counterattack, and retake Earth, we need a leader. With the president and the rest of the cabinet either dead or missing, like it or not, you're next in line."

Aretha sighed. "I don't like it, but you're right. We need to remain a planet and keep our government and military structure intact. We may not have a home at the moment, but our system can still function."

Cal turned from the controls. "Typically, the outgoing president—or in his or her absence, one of his or her cabinet members—swears in the new president. After that, it's the highest-ranking Legion officer. Since we can't locate anyone higher than a Captain at the moment, looks like Jake and I can swear you in."

Putting a hand to her forehead, Aretha began to stand up.

"Easy there," Jake said. "You don't have to stand for this."

Aretha straightened her body. Her swollen lips, dry face, and windblown hair made her look much older than her mid-fifties.

"Yes," Aretha said, her voice deeper and more commanding than before, "I do have to stand for this. Out of respect for my planet and the presidents who have come before me. And as a symbol, if only to the three of us, that Earth is standing up after being knocked to the canvas and will fight back." She gazed seriously at the two men. "I can only imagine what the two of you have gone through to get to Earth and rescue me." She took in the well-worn pirate ship. "My sincerest gratitude goes out to you. Thank you. You saved my life and have given Earth a fighting chance."

"We really appreciate that, Ms. Brown," Cal said. "But don't thank us too quickly. We've barely scratched the surface of what needs to be done to retake Earth."

Jake proceeded to swear in Aretha using words that he could recall from watching presidential inaugurations. He figured the Legion officers and Sam listening over a vector-space device were proper witnesses.

Cal smiled. "Congratulations. Sorry, but the best we have for the president of Earth United's inauguration celebration is bottled water and some dried rations we found."

Aretha started to answer when the com on Jake's belt buzzed. Jake and Cal exchanged glances. It wasn't a vector-space transmission signal or a normal communication hail.

"I know that sound," Cal said. "It's from Vernius's new data-to-audio transfer technology. It's a way to get a message out when transmissions are blocked."

"Like the Legion's vector-space transmissions?" Jake asked.

"Yeah," Cal said. "But you don't need a special system or devices in place to use it. The downside is that you need to know the recipient's data inscription and it's received on a delay, which can be lengthy. It could be Diane."

A million thoughts went through Jake's head. Was Diane in trouble? Had Vernius been attacked like Earth? If the transmission was on a delay, how long ago did she send it? Would it be too late to help her? He had become so consumed with thoughts of Frank that he hadn't thought that Vernius and Diane might be in trouble. He felt an adrenaline rush. He needed to hear the message, but he was too afraid to listen.

"Jake, are you going to listen to the message?" Cal prompted.

"Yeah, yes, of course." Jake pressed the com on his belt. Sure enough, it was Diane's voice.

The three of them listened intently as Diane explained the Permidium ship's blockade of Vernius and the Imperial Majesty's siding with Sloan. She went on to say that Sloan had Cal's transponder and was using it against the Permidiums, which Jake and Cal already knew. Jake and Cal listened wide-eyed as Diane explained that the transponder might contain information on how to destroy the Permidium ships.

"So that's how Sloan got them to play his game—he's holding that transponder over the Permidiums," Cal said.

"Wait," Jake said. "There's more."

Diane's voice continued, "Jake, I know all about Debbie and your cruise. I'm not angry with you. I'm just so hurt that you lied to me. I hope you're okay, wherever you are. I wish the best for you as I still love you more than life itself, but you have truly hurt me. I'm not sure if I can ever look at you again."

Jake's eyes widened further. "We have to contact Diane, now!"

"We can't," said Cal. "I can't send a data-to-audio transmission in reverse. The Legion didn't equip ambassadors with vector-space transmitters, and you heard Diane: the Permidiums are blocking transmissions to and from Vernius."

"And the only Legion officers on Vernius were you two," Aretha added.

Jake's heart sank. A lump started to form in his throat and his eyes teared up. He tried to talk but couldn't. He waited for Cal to say, "I told you so," but it never came.

Aretha placed a hand on Jake's shoulder. "I'm sorry, Jake."

Cal eyed Jake with an expression of sincere sympathy. "It's okay, buddy. You know it's just a huge misunderstanding. You'll get it straightened out, give her the ring, and be married in no time."

"Thanks. I know. But what if Vernius was attacked? What if something happened to her? This is her last thought of me."

17

EZEKIEL

Deep in thought, Ezekiel shifted on the cold stone he used as a seat. Maybe Diabolus wouldn't show up deep inside a cave on Titan, or maybe he couldn't find the place. It definitely wasn't a lavish setting, but he figured that since he couldn't see, he might as well meet in as dark a place as possible to help even the odds.

How did Diabolus know he had been watching him? And how long had he known? He thought about the message the young boy had brought him: *A tall man said to tell you that Diabolus knows you are watching him, and he would like to talk to you. You name the place.*

Ezekiel had sat quietly for a while, thinking about how to respond or whether to respond at all, while the boy waited for an answer.

"Sir, what should I tell the man?" the boy had asked. "He promised me a coin, but only if I return with an answer."

Ezekiel had told the boy, "Tell the man I will meet him in the Sepulchral Caverns on Titan."

And here he sat, waiting for Diabolus.

The element of surprise was obviously gone.

But this would give him a chance to warn Diabolus one last time, as he promised the Chamber he would do. And it was a one-on-one opportunity to sedate Diabolus if he didn't heed the warning, which is the response Ezekiel suspected.

But being blind, how would he be able to inject Diabolus in the neck by himself when they came face-to-face?

Ezekiel took some deep, calming breaths. He couldn't let Diabolus know he was uncertain, and he couldn't let him know he was afraid. He tried to foresee the outcome of their meeting, but he could not. Why couldn't he foresee anything that involved Diabolus?

The quietness was broken by footsteps on the rocky cave floor.

Ezekiel's blindness heightened his other senses. The footsteps sounded louder than they probably were. The musty smell of the cave permeated his nostrils.

"Why did you have to pick a filthy, dank-smelling place like this to meet?" came Sloan's voice.

Ezekiel kept his head about level with Sloan's waist. "The boy said it was my choice. And I like the solitude, Diabolus. Or should I call you Sloan?"

"You always were the quiet type, Ezekiel." Sloan sat down facing Ezekiel on a rock to his right. "And you can call me anything you like."

"So, why this meeting?"

"I think I should be asking you the questions, old man," Sloan replied. "Why have you been watching me?"

Ezekiel wasn't sure how to respond. He contemplated the question for a moment, hoping for some foresight.

"What's the matter? Can't think of anything to say? Or should I say, can't you foresee anything?" Sloan chuckled. "That's right, your one so-called gift doesn't work on me, does it? That's because I'm more powerful in every way than anyone from Lotox, ever. You and the *Chamber* should be glad I left the planet. Why follow me around the galaxy? What business am I of yours now? I'm not bothering Lotox any longer."

"What you do reflects on Lotox. We can't have our people going around trying to take over planets and galaxies."

"Why not?" Sloan paused. "Because it's not in your precious ancestral code? And what about that code? I thought you weren't allowed to interfere. You interfered a year ago and you did it again the other day." Sloan leaned back and stretched out his legs. "That code of yours is holding Lotox back. The planet would be much stronger without it."

"Stronger how?" Ezekiel replied. "Stronger like you? Causing havoc throughout the universe for your own selfish gain and pride? I think not."

Sloan shook his head. "Ezekiel, my old foe. Return to Lotox. Tell the Chamber you couldn't find me, or whatever you want. The Chamber will be none the wiser. You can live out your final days in peace. You're old and weak and powerless against me."

Ezekiel wanted to reason with this man called Sloan. "Diabolus, why do you seek money, power, and authority over these people? We both know you are a more powerful being. Wouldn't it be more challenging to seek those things on Lotox, where your competition is more equal?"

Sloan shook his head. "There is no competition for me on Lotox. You all are inferior to me. At least here there are armies fighting me."

"Yes, but you have armies fighting *for* you too. You can't do it alone. And they don't fight for you because they respect you. They fight for you because they fear you or you've tricked them."

Ezekiel sensed Sloan narrowing his eyes. "It matters not, the reason they fight for me. The fact that I am able to get them to do so is my victory. And when I lead them to victory over the rest of the galaxy, that will be another win for me."

"But who's counting besides you? Nobody respects you. Nobody wants you around. Nobody on Lotox, not your enemies here. Not even your allies want to be with you. Everything you do is simply for you."

Ezekiel could sense a fire burning in Sloan's eyes as he spoke. "But I do not care about any of that. What I care about is ruling a galaxy and having a galaxy worship me. Whether it's out of fear, or hate, or whatever reason. It does not matter, as long as I reign over them."

Ezekiel conceded that there was no reasoning with Sloan. "You truly are mad. There is nothing you won't do to achieve your selfish ambitions."

"Ezekiel, old man," Sloan said straightening his back, his tone becoming sterner. "I am giving you one last warning to leave this galaxy. Because if you stay here and get in my way, this time you'll lose much more than your eyesight."

"No!" Ezekiel shouted slapping the rock with his hand. He was getting warm, not from fear, but from the anger starting to well up inside him at Sloan's threat. "It is you who are being warned. Stop what you are doing right now, or your days of roaming the galaxy will be over."

Sloan tilted his head back and laughed confidently. "And just who is going to stop me? You think I don't know about that syringe in your pocket and the serum the Chamber developed?"

That caught Ezekiel completely off guard. How could Sloan possibly know about that?

Sloan simpered and continued. "What's the matter, old man? Are you now blind *and* mute?" Sloan stood. "That's right. I might not have your gift of foresight, but I know things. In fact, I know everything. And you can't foresee what I know. So don't try to play games with me, old man. You're not even close to being in the same league as I am. I will crush you."

"These people are stronger and more resourceful than you give them credit for," Ezekiel said. He knew he was grasping at straws. He wasn't confident that anyone could stand up against Sloan. "You underestimate them."

Sloan chuckled again as he turned to leave. "Who, the humans? Earth was the most powerful planet in the galaxy, and it crumbled in less than a day. I'm taking over this galaxy planet by planet, and there's not a thing you or anyone can do about it." Sloan started walking toward the mouth of the cavern, continuing to talk without looking back. "When I'm finished here, maybe I will just return to Lotox." He paused. "And take it over."

18

CRATON

C hills went up Jake's spine as he walked into Craton's central command center, which sat high atop a mountain range with West Craton on one side and East Craton and Craton City on the other. The retractable dome roof was closed. The last time he was in this space, he had fought Novak's father, Romalor, to the death.

He left Cal and Aretha standing by the door and walked to the west side of the room to look out the window. Rocks filled the Pit, where he and Cal had battled Hargar to escape.

Novak got up from his seat behind his desk and went up to Jake. Cleaned up, he appeared handsome, like his father. But unlike his father, Jake could tell, Novak cared about his people and his planet. And further, he cared about the galaxy and others in it.

"I had the Pit filled in," Novak said. "It was the first thing I did when I took over. We're still working out the kinks, but I'm trying to install a judicial process not unlike what you have on Earth."

Jake was still unable to fully grasp the fact that he was safe in that building.

He couldn't let down his guard. "That's good," was all he could say.

Novak continued speaking, hands clasped behind his back in an unaggressive stance. "The second thing I did was blast a tunnel through the mountain, allowing free passage between West and East Craton. The people in the West are no longer forced to live in poverty in the middle of a desert. And the people in the East can help develop the West.

Jake was still looking out the window. "That's good," he said again.

Jake had thought he had lost Diane on Craton. He had been so foolish in his quest for revenge against Romalor that he almost ran her off. He said he would never let that happen again. Yet here he was. He had done the same thing all over, trying to be clever. And he was losing her again.

Novak put a hand on Jake's shoulder. "I know it must be difficult for you to be here, Jake. I completely understand. This place holds some horrible memories for you. But know that it does for me as well. I hated the way my father ruled, and the manner of all rulers before him. But we have a lot of work to do and not much time to get it done. For all we know, the Permidium ships are on their way here right now, to wipe out Craton."

Jake forced his mind to return to the issue at hand and his new enemy, Sloan. Novak was right: they had to figure out how to defeat the Permidiums and Sloan.

Jake closed his eyes and focused. He opened them, and still looking out the window, he replied, "No, Sloan won't attack Craton."

"How can you know that?" Novak asked.

Jake turned to face Novak. "Because he doesn't think Craton is enough of a challenge. He only attacks the strong, and he thinks Craton is weak. He doesn't know that you were able to rebuild in just a year. Earth didn't even know that, and we watch you daily."

Novak went back to his desk and sat down. "I hope you're right." Then he saw Cal and Aretha standing in the entryway. "My apologies. Please come in." He gestured with his hand. "Cal Danielson, right?"

"Yes," Cal said.

Novak turned his attention to Aretha. "And you are?"

Aretha stepped forward and stuck out her hand. "Senator Aretha Brown."

Cal cleared his throat. "You mean President Aretha Brown."

"Unfortunately, that's correct. I guess I'm not used to it yet," she said to Cal. Turning back to Novak, she added, "Thank you for your hospitality and assistance. Earth will never forget this."

Novak stood and shook Aretha's hand. "Nice to meet you, Madam President. I'm sorry about your planet and the loss of so many lives. They hit you pretty hard."

For the first time, Jake saw a flare of fire in Aretha's eyes as she spoke. "They kicked us in the butt when we weren't looking. But if you kick a tiger in the rear, you better have a plan to deal with its teeth."

Novak smiled approvingly. "That's the attitude we need around here. Let's hope we all can overlook the past, and never forget our new alliance," he said to Jake. He waved a hand toward a couch and arrangement of chairs as he sat back down behind his desk. "Please, sit."

Aretha, Cal, and Jake each took a seat.

The only other person in the room was an older, plump Cratonite sitting behind a computer facing a floor-to-ceiling video screen behind Novak's desk: the same screen that Jake had watched Sloan and Romalor talk on a year ago. But that didn't bother him. He was now focused on the task at hand.

Novak motioned toward the other Cratonite. "This is Lannick, one of my officers."

Lannick turned and acknowledged the guests.

Novak continued. "He's the only officer of my father's that I kept on. His military knowledge and tactics are unsurpassed. And he survived my father's regime even though he secretly opposed him."

Jake heard what Novak was saying, but his mind kept wandering off to Diane. Was she okay? Was she safe? He needed to tell her that this was all a big misunderstanding. His heart ached for her. But he had to focus. He couldn't contact her or get to her with the Permidium ship's blockade and signal jam. He needed to help develop a plan for Craton. It was the only way to rescue Frank, retake Earth, and get to Diane.

The giant screen showed a diagram of all the solar systems in the galaxy, scaled down, with red dots on most of the systems.

"So, what do the red dots on the screen represent?" Cal asked.

Lannick responded in a husky voice. "We have dots by the planets that we believe the pirates already control—or I should say, the Permidiums control—and zooming in, you can see that those planets occur in almost every system in this galaxy."

"The Permidiums and Sloan," Jake added.

"It might have been easier to mark the planets that haven't been taken over," Cal said.

"Yes," Lannick responded, zooming in on Vernius's solar system. "As you can see, as an example, that virtually every inhabited planet in this system is controlled, either through a hostile takeover or succumbing to fear and handing over the reins."

Jake noticed the dot on Vernius.

Aretha leaned forward. "We need a plan to start taking back key planets."

Lannick swiveled in his chair to face the rest of them. "We've been working through every possible scenario. We have readings from the attack on Earth. And Craton's warships combined with what's left of your Legion can't mount an attack even close to what Earth had as defenses. Every scenario fails miserably. The Permidium ships are just too powerful."

"Yes, but there's only four Permidium ships, right?" Aretha asked. "What if we strike where they aren't?"

Lannick turned to address Aretha. "Yes, only four that we know of. But even if it is only four, one is blockading Earth because of its military prowess and one is blockading Vernius because of its technology. We believe the other two are mobile, and anywhere we strike, they will either arrive to defend or retake. So that'll just cause more death and damage without accomplishing anything."

"And we have a bigger problem," Novak said. "From what we're detecting, the Permidium ships at Earth and Vernius are constructing some type of hilaetite containment field. Once it's constructed, we believe there will be no way into or out of those planets, and no communications whatsoever. From what we're detecting, even your vector-space communications, as you explained them, will be blocked."

"That's what Jake and I detected," Cal confirmed.

Jake asked Novak, "How much time do we have?"

Novak looked at Lannick, who responded: "Good question. Our readings are weak from this distance, but our best guess is we have maybe twenty-four hours at the current rate of construction. And it looks like once completed, the Permidium ship will be inside the containment field, so we'll have no way to get at it, let alone get to Earth. The same for Vernius."

Jake's shoulders drooped. He suddenly felt fatigued. He didn't know when he last had a decent night's sleep or halfway nutritious meal. And this news just killed what hope he had left. Everything was going wrong. Everything was out of his control. They had just one day for their mission, and they still had no idea of how to accomplish it.

Cal sat up, his voice optimistic. "Okay, one problem at a time. Diane . . ." He acknowledged Novak, then Lannick. "Earth's Ambassador to Vernius sent Jake an encrypted message that a portable transponder, *my* transponder that is now in Sloan's hands, may contain data that can be used to figure out how to destroy the Permidium ships."

"But what good is that when Sloan has it?" Jake asked sarcastically. He knew there was no way to get the transponder from Sloan. They didn't know where Sloan was, let alone where he had stashed the transponder. And how could they get close to him anyway?

Cal stood up. "Sloan has the transponder, but I backed it up on my computer."

That lifted Jake's spirits slightly. There was some hope, but very little, because Cal's computer was on Vernius. "But we can't contact anyone on Vernius, and I doubt our trick will get us past the Permidium ship again."

Cal sidled up to Jake and leaned down. "Not that computer. My old computer before we moved to Vernius. It's at my dad's."

"In the country in Sector One?" Jake asked.

"Exactly," Cal said spinning around toward the others. "We may not be able to get past the Permidium ship, but we have Sam on the ground."

Aretha raised an eyebrow.

"Um," Cal said. "I mean Private Simons."

Aretha tilted her head. "You're in contact with this Private Simons?"

"Yes," Cal said. "She's the one who located a vector-space transmitter module and activated it."

Aretha continued with some doubt in her voice. "But you said that the countryside is occupied by pirates. Can one lone Legion private make it through?"

"I can talk her through to my dad's," Cal said.

"And in an occupied territory," Lannick added, "a lone person stands a better chance of sneaking through than a group."

Jake was starting to like the plan. "Then we figure out how to defeat the Permidium ship, assemble the Legion along with Craton's fighters, attack the Permidium ships at Vernius and Earth, and take out the pirates. And they'll probably have reinforcements from Tortuga that we'll have to eliminate. We can do that while freeing Frank . . . I mean Commander Cantor."

Cal shook his head, but it was Novak who responded. "No, there's not enough time to do all that in sequence. We only have a day, remember?"

"He's right," Aretha said.

"It all has to happen simultaneously," Lannick said. "It's going to take precise planning."

"And a lot of luck," said Cal.

"But we won't know how to take out the Permidiums until we retrieve Cal's backup data," Jake said.

"Right, but we have a good idea," Cal replied.

Cal had everyone's attention. Lannick said what Jake figured they all were thinking. "We do?"

"Of course," Cal said as he began to pace. "Whatever data my transponder picked up during our brief encounter with the Permidiums last year, it's not going to be directions on how to build a hilaetite-destroying bomb or anything like that, and it's not going to tell us where on the ship to shoot a plasma missile." Cal's voice slowly grew louder, and his words came faster. "It's going to be something to do with the design of the ship. A flaw, or a built-in fail-safe if one of their ships goes rogue. So, all we need is to get someone inside the two Permidium ships. Once I get the data from Sam . . . I mean Private Simons . . . I can figure out what to do and relay that to the people on the inside. I would be one of them on the inside, but I'm likely going to need something stronger than a portable transponder or data pod to do the analysis. I'll need to be at a console."

"And at the same time, we can assemble the Legion and Craton's military to take out the pirates on Earth, Vernius, and Tortuga," Jake put in. "We have to go after Tortuga. They'll have reinforcements there, and Frank is being held there. I imagine they have other prisoners too. We have to make their rescue a priority."

Jake felt a burst of adrenaline. They might be able to do it all.

Lannick shook his head.

"We've run the numbers: even with our highest estimate of the number of Legion spacecraft still out there, we will need them all if we're going to have a large-enough fleet of Legion and Cratonites to attack the pirates at just two of the three locations, and that's stretching it. With pretty much every other planet with a military already giving in to the Permidiums and Mr. Sloan, we have lost all our allies in the war."

Aretha stood up. "Leave the Legion to me. Jake, we will free all prisoners and we will make sure Vernius is safe, but keep in mind, freeing Earth is our first and only priority right now."

Jake stood as well. "But the Permidiums are constructing containment fields around both Earth and Vernius. There has to be a way to stop both ships."

"Jake, I appreciate everything you've done, and I wouldn't even be here right now if not for you. We desperately need you for our plan. But you have to trust Mr. Leximer and I. We will do everything possible to free and protect people throughout the galaxy, but we have to make priorities. The decisions will be made by Mr. Leximer"—her head bobbed toward Novak—"and me."

Jake closed his eyes and sighed. She was right. She was the president. And what Earth needed more than anything right now was a strong leader. That was Aretha Brown. He had trouble trusting anyone apart from his comrades in battle, but this was one decision he couldn't control. He had to trust the president.

Aretha continued, "Jake, I know you're concerned about Diane and Commander Cantor, but our first focus has to be Earth. We need to free it first. If that means we have to throw all our resources at Earth, we will. Once it's free, then we can turn to Vernius, Titan, and the rest of the galaxy."

Cal regarded Jake. "She's my sister, buddy, but the president is right. And you and I both know it."

Jake did know it, and a part of him had expected it to come to that when this whole plan started to formulate, but deep down, he was hoping the Vernius mission could take priority. He knew his first duty was to the Legion and he had to do what was best for Earth.

Lannick spoke before Jake could respond. "But don't forget about the wild card in all this. The other two Permidium ships. We don't know where they are, so we can't get anyone on them even if we had the resources. We have to hope they withdraw when their other ships are destroyed rather than come to their aid."

Novak stood. "Even if some of us don't like it, are we all in agreement with the plan then?"

Everyone gestured or said yes in one way or another, including Jake. They were well beyond any type of formal vote.

"Good," Novak said. "We're now on a twenty-four-hour timetable. The clock is ticking." He addressed Aretha. "Madam President, you need to get your Legion here." He turned toward Cal. "Mr. Danielson, you need to get your Sam up to speed and on the move."

Lannick swiveled back to the video screen and his computer. "And I have to figure out how to get someone on the Permidium ships. But I have an idea. And I'll need you, Captain Saunders."

19

WITCH TRIAL

Locked in her room in the palace with two guards posted outside her door, Diane had never felt more frightened and alone. The love of her life no longer loved her, and she had been caught defying the Imperial Majesty's orders. Even though she was a citizen of Earth and a member of the Legion, this was a matter under Vernius's jurisdiction. And on Vernius, there was no impartial judge and jury. The law was whatever the Imperial Majesty said it was. She was the judge, jury, and executioner. Diane didn't want to even think about that last word, but it was definitely a possibility.

She sat in a throne-like chair in a corner of the room, where she liked to think. She felt so insignificant in the massive room and even more so in the expansive galaxy. Who would even care that she was gone? Cal and her dad would.

But were either of them still alive? She had no way of contacting them even if she could get out of her room.

She tried to make herself want to fight. Stand up for herself. Not wallow in self-pity. But she had no will to do so anymore. Jake had taken everything from her. But still she kept saying to herself, "I am Legion. I am a Danielson. I can't give up. I won't give up."

One of the guards opened the door, and the Imperial Majesty stepped inside, followed by Sloan. Sloan's giant frame towered over the Vernition ruler.

Diane stood, whether out of habit when the Imperial Majesty entered the room, or to maybe try for a quick escape—she wasn't sure.

The Imperial Majesty pointed at Diane. "This is the one who sent the message."

Sloan slowly walked up to Diane with his hands folded behind his back. In a low, stern tone he said, "I know you. You, along with the Saunders and Danielson boys always seem to be trying to thwart my plans." He turned and paced back toward the Imperial Majesty, looking straight ahead, his hands still behind his back. "I am a very reasonable man. I keep trying over and over to give the three of you the benefit of the doubt. I even made Mr. Saunders an offer to join me. Yet you three continue to repay me with these attacks."

"Reasonable?" Diane blurted. "Ha, so now you're a comedian. You're nothing but a pathetic weakling who's too insecure and inept to do anything. You just try to make others fear you because it's the only way you can get any attention." Diane felt her blood start to boil the more she talked. Maybe she really was angry at Jake, angry at Sloan, angry at the world for what it was doing to her. And she was taking it all out on Sloan. Maybe not her smartest move, but she didn't care. "What's the matter, the other little boys wouldn't play with you on the playground? Why don't you go back to wherever you came from? But they probably don't want you either."

Sloan remained with his back to Diane and looked over his shoulder with his trademark evil grin.

"Are you finished? You can rant and rave all you want. I don't care, because I hold all the cards. You hold nothing." He turned toward the Imperial Majesty. "Your Majesty here thinks you should be banished from Vernius and that is punishment enough for your actions." He turned toward Diane. "What do you think your punishment should be?"

Diane didn't know what to say. She was caught off guard by what Sloan had just said. She hadn't thought the Imperial Majesty would let her off so easily. She stared deep into the ruler's eyes. What she saw both pleased and frightened her. Sloan was telling the truth: Diane sensed true compassion for her in those eyes. But she also saw fear. Fear that she had no control over what Sloan would do. Fear for her people. Whatever the Imperial Majesty said and whatever Diane would say wouldn't matter. Sloan would do whatever he wanted to do. And he was right; he held all the cards, at least for now.

"Do you have nothing to say for yourself?" Sloan asked.

Diane went to the window overlooking the courtyard. The flowers were in full bloom. She stared down at the people going about their business. Maybe she could play on the Imperial Majesty's compassion and get her to change her mind about Sloan. It would be too late for Vernius to do anything now, but Vernius could be helpful if the Legion was able to determine how to stop the Permidiums.

"It doesn't matter what I say, and it doesn't matter what the Imperial Majesty says." She waved a palm at the Imperial Majesty. "You're going to do whatever you want to do. You're just using her, just like you use everyone. You're not going to make her your number two. You'll throw her away when you're finished with her, just like you do everyone else."

"Diane!" the Imperial Majesty gasped. "Your life is in Mr. Sloan's hands, and he gave me his word that he wouldn't do anything to Vernius or its people if we follow his plans."

"Follow his plans? You mean his orders. And I've witnessed first-hand what this man is capable of. He'll break his word as easily as you crack an egg for breakfast."

The subtle approach wasn't working. Diane would have to try the direct approach one last time. It was her final move to save herself, and Vernius, from Sloan's control. She walked past Sloan to the Imperial

Majesty and looked her in the eye. "Your Majesty, I implore you one last time. Whatever the consequences, do not follow this man." She pointed to Sloan. "He is evil. I'm begging you. Not for me. I don't care what happens to me. I'm pleading with you for your people, the Vernitions. And I'm pleading for you. You will be far better off opposing Sloan than siding with him." Diane turned toward Sloan and glared deep into his eyes. "Even if it means dying."

She walked back to the window and looked out. She knew she had just sentenced herself to death.

The answer came immediately. "I am sorry, Diane. But I believe that what is best for the people of Vernius is to place the planet in the hands of Mr. Sloan."

"Well, this is a pleasant discussion," Sloan said. "But I have a lot of work to do."

Diane turned around.

"Mr. Sloan," the Imperial Majesty said, "please have some compassion for her. She was just looking out for her friends. She meant no real harm to you."

Diane appreciated the Imperial Majesty's attempt to buy her some leniency, but she was certain that it would do no good.

Sloan steepled his fingers and pressed his lips together before speaking. "My typical punishment for actions such as yours is execution, immediately." He narrowed his eyes.

Diane folded her arms so Sloan wouldn't see her hands shake. She was prepared to die, but the thought of the process of dying scared her. She had done all she could do and had said all she had to say. She would not plead or give Sloan the satisfaction of knowing she was scared. She straightened her back, preparing for the death sentence.

Sloan addressed the Imperial Majesty. "But to show my gratitude for your loyalty, Your Majesty, I will spare this young woman's life, or at least I won't be the cause of her death."

Diane's hopes rose for a second, but then she realized the trickery in his words. Sloan would just have someone else kill her.

"Thank you, Mr. Sloan," the Imperial Majesty said, taking his arm in her hands.

Sloan pulled away immediately. "My Permidium friends have developed a neat little device perfect for instances like this. They have found it quite a useful tool on their planet. It serves as an excellent deterrent, it keeps them from overcrowding their prisons, and it's not capital punishment."

Diane felt even more scared. At least a quick execution by Sloan would be relatively painless. This sounded like a torture device.

Sloan went to the door, then stopped and turned back. "The Permidiums have developed a capsule, just big enough for one person to sit in. It has enough food, water, and oxygen for thirty days. It is shot into space at light speed. It has no engine and no means of stopping, but it is quite solid. It travels until it collides with an immoveable object. If the occupant is lucky, it runs into an inhabitable planet, the capsule lands without too much damage, and the occupant finds a food and water source and lives out his or her days."

Sloan opened the door and addressed the guards. "Fetch me Abigor."

He grinned at Diane and the Imperial Majesty. "But if the capsule stops on an uninhabitable planet, the occupant dies. If the capsule stops on anything else, like an asteroid, or hits a star, the occupant dies." Sloan gritted his teeth. "Burning up can't be fun. And if the occupant stops nowhere in thirty days, the occupant dies. Again, not a fun way to go." He glared at Diane. "But at least I'm not executing you."

Diane turned and looked out the window so Sloan wouldn't see the tears welling up in her eyes. Tears of fear at the painful way she would likely die, and tears of sorrow at the realization that she would never see Jake again. No matter how angry she was at him or what she had said, she thought, or hoped, she would at least see him again. Somewhere, somehow.

"Oh," Sloan added, "one more thing. Depending on the severity of the crime, the sentence can be to launch the capsule in a direction where there are known habitable planets to give the criminal a better chance. The direction is programmed directly into the capsule by the administrator of justice so there is no trace of where the capsule is heading and no way for anyone to find out. Only the administrator knows." He paused for effect. "And I plan on being your administrator."

Diane swore she could see fire in Sloan's eyes.

Sloan made a fist and spoke through gritted teeth. "And I plan on launching you in a direction that as far as anybody has been able to chart, there isn't a single planet!"

The Imperial Majesty grabbed Sloan's arm again. "But Mr. Sloan . . ."

Sloan shoved her to the floor with one quick jerk of his arm and looked down at her, still gritting his teeth. "Forgive me if I don't trust you, but I will have my men watch her until the capsule is prepared." Sloan turned and quickly exited the room.

Diane sank into her chair, her heart throbbing, her breathing labored. Everything she was holding back since she found the note on Jake's computer was about to come out. The betrayal by her only love and the reality of a horrifying death to come were too much. She put her face in her hands and let the tears flow.

20

CALLING IN THE CAVALRY

Cal and Aretha were seated at separate stations in the coms room on one of the lower levels in the Craton mountainside military complex. The room was bustling with Craton personnel.

"Hello," the female towering over Cal said in a deep voice. "My name is Freya. What do they call you on Earth?" Easily over six feet, Freya was the Craton coms officer assigned to Cal.

Cal's eyes met her waist from where he sat. Her lower uniform consisted of metal shin guards and tight, metallic shorts. He moved his gaze up to her bare stomach and then to the metal chest plate that covered her to her neck and out to her shoulders. He wondered if she wore more in battle. Cal gulped. She was very attractive.

"What's the matter? Cat got your tongue?" Freya laughed a bit overdramatically. "I've been studying Earth's language. So you not need translator chip. Do you like?"

Cal's eyes widened. "Um, yes, very good." He had never met anyone from another planet who actually tried to speak an Earth language. Everyone relied on translator chips.

"I thought you like it." She slapped him on the back.

Cal immediately arched his back at the sting. He would hate to be on the receiving end of a *nonfriendly* smack from her.

"You have back problem?" She asked.

"Um, no, I was . . . I was just stretching."

"Good." She sat down next to him. "You not say your name."

Cal was still staring at her breastplate. "Um, it's, um, Cal."

Freya's eyes followed Cal's stare. "Is something wrong with my plate?"

Cal shook his head. "Um, no, no I was just . . . just admiring your uniform."

Freya raised an eyebrow. "I see." She turned to the computer table. "Is 'um' used a lot on Earth? I notice you like to say it."

Cal forced himself to focus. "No, no, I was . . . well, you just caught me off guard."

"I see."

Cal swiveled his chair toward the computer table. "Okay, then, let's get started."

He felt like an idiot. He had never been that close to a Cratonite female, or any female, for that matter, who stood over six feet tall.

Cal started working the basic controls on the computer. He loved the modern design with the computer built into the clear glass table. EarthNX probably supplied Romalor with this technology along with the hilaetite weapon design. At least it was working out for him now. And he remembered some of the symbols on the controls from when he and Diane had shut down the hilaetite weapon using his transponder.

"You good with computers," Freya said. "I impressed."

"Thanks, but that's as far as I can get with the Craton symbols. You'll have to take it from here." Cal pointed at his vector-space transmitter, which was plugged in to the computer table. "When Private Simons responds to my hail, we want to be able to track her on the monitor," he said, indicating the computer screen, which showed a recent image of Sector One captured by a probe.

"Okay," Freya said. "That's easy enough." She scooted closer to Cal and leaned in front of him to type on the keyboard.

Cal's nose was touching her long dark hair. Surprisingly, it smelled of lavender. Not what he expected from a Cratonite warrior. He stretched his collar with one finger to try to let out some of the heat.

Freya turned her face toward Cal, her cheek practically touching his. "Is this the same thing we're doing for your president so she can track where your Legion is?"

Cal felt the dampness in his armpits. He took some deep breaths and tried thinking of anything besides the Cratonite female who was face-to-face with him. He had to focus. They were on a mission, and they didn't have much time. He was certain that Freya was not bothered in the least by their close proximity. It seemed to be something Cratonites were used to.

Cal needed to answer her questions. "Um, yes, yes, it is."

"You okay? You breathe hard."

"Um." Cal wasn't sure how to respond, so he made something up. "Yes, I'm okay. I'm just worried about everything. That's all."

"Um," Freya said, and then gave her forced laugh again. "Then I will open a separate link to the system." She continued typing.

"You're all set, Madam President," the Cratonite said as he backed away from the computer table. "You can open your vector-space-transmitter com and speak. The location of anyone that responds or simply opens his or her com to talk will light up on the table. I've set it for the expanse of the entire galaxy, but you can zoom in and out with two fingers. Spread them to zoom in and bring your fingers together to zoom out. Like this." He gave her a demonstration.

"Thank you," Aretha said. She was stunned by how hospitable the Cratonites were. All the stories she'd heard from the Romalor years had made her frightened to set foot on the planet. But it looked like

Romalor's son had changed things quite a lot in just a year. Yet Craton was fighting for survival as much as Earth was. Craton and Earth truly had a common enemy right now.

Aretha paused before pressing the transmitter com. She briefly ran what she wanted to say through her mind again, and then proceeded. "Legion officers, this is President Aretha Brown. I am safe and secure on the planet Craton. As was communicated to you earlier, this is the Legion's rendezvous point. Please proceed here immediately if you have not started. Cratonite ships will direct you into their hangars once you enter its atmosphere. We have developed a plan to retake Earth, but we have less than twenty-four hours before our window of opportunity closes. And we need every single Legion vessel if we are going to succeed. So, please set course for Craton immediately. This is both a request and an order from your President." She paused. She had just relayed the facts and given an order. Anyone in command could do that. What she really needed to do was motivate the Legion. Give them a reason to fight. They had to be dejected. Their planet had been invaded and captured in a matter of hours. They'd lost almost half their fellow Legion soldiers. She needed to give them hope. She needed to lead.

She looked down at the table. No lights yet. She pressed the transmitter com again. "If you're in a safe area, please broadcast your com so that your entire division can hear me." She waited a few minutes to give the officers a chance to gather people and broadcast. "Men and women of the Legion. I know you are all in pain, feeling defeated and ready to give up. I know because I was there myself. Ready to close my eyes forever on this nightmare. But people, this is not a nightmare. Earth was sucker punched. The people of Earth have been hit hard before, and we have always come back stronger—always." She raised her voice. "We aren't just in a fight for our individual lives. We're in a fight for the survival of our planet. And we can and will win this fight!" She lowered her voice again and leaned closer to the com. "We have a plan. We have the means to destroy the enemy's most potent weapon.

We will do what Earth does best: fight back." She raised her voice again. "For when they attacked Earth and wiped out half our Legion, they made one big mistake. They wiped out only half our Legion!"

Still not a single light on the table. Aretha hung her head. She was exhausted. She did her best to lead, but she wasn't Jack Buchanan. The officers would have shown up for Jack. But she couldn't blame them. After hearing how easily the Permidiums dispatched their fellow Legion soldiers, why would they want to go risk their lives in a battle they assumed was hopeless? Why not live out their days wherever they were holed up?

Aretha looked up at the Cratonite who had helped her. His face had a look of genuine compassion.

"Thank you for your assistance," Aretha said as she rose and started to walk away.

"Madam President," the Cratonite said from behind her. "Look."

Aretha stopped and turned around. Lights were coming on everywhere on the screen.

The transmitter com started humming with voices.

"Copy that, Madam President."

"On our way, Madam President."

"See you on Craton."

"Let's give them a taste of their own medicine."

Aretha's lips widened into a smile. She couldn't believe it. The Legion was coming. All of them.

Jake and Novak stood behind Lannick, looking at the large screen in the central command center. Lannick's fingers flew back and forth over the keys. Different formulas and shapes, like molecules and atoms, appeared on the screen, connecting, then some disconnecting, and some exploding. New formulas and slightly different shapes continually appeared.

This looks like something Cal would do, Jake thought.

"What is this?" Novak asked.

Lannick continued looking at the screen and typing while he replied. "I used to be a scientist. That was before I realized that on Craton, if you wanted a decent way of life, you needed to be in the military." He paused and turned toward Novak. "I mean, that was before you took over, sir."

"It's okay, Lannick, I understand," Novak replied as he clasped his hands behind his back. "You were saying?"

Lannick turned back to his work. "Anyway, as a scientist, I conducted a lot of studies on hilaetite. The Permidium ships are amazing. How do they keep the hilaetite crystals from detonating when they are in such close proximity to one another? You know how volatile they are."

"So, is that what you're doing?" Novak asked. "Trying to figure out how to combine crystals? The best scientists in the galaxy have been trying to do that forever. And how would that help us get a person onto the Permidium ship?"

Lannick shook his head, still working on the keyboard. "It wouldn't help with that. And that's not what I'm doing. I'm trying to determine if another spaceship carrying hilaetite, even if it doesn't have a beacon, could trick the Permidium ship so that it would open a hangar for the ship to dock inside, thinking the ship is a friendly."

"Clever idea," Jake said. "But what's with all the math and cartoon drawings?"

Lannick turned to look at Jake. "Cartoon drawings?"

"Never mind," Jake said. "I was trying to be funny."

"Oh, yes," Lannick replied. "Craton has no word for Earth's 'funny.' We never, as you say, 'joke around.'"

Novak chuckled. "Can we stay on point?"

"Yes," Lannick said. "As I was saying, I am running the calculations to determine the possible spacing of hilaetite crystals on a ship that, with shielding between them, will allow the maximum number of crystals aboard without adversely reacting. We have no idea how the Permidiums have constructed their vessels out of almost one-hundred-percent hilaetite. If the"—he turned to Jake—"*cartoon* drawings stay connected without exploding, then I have the right number of crystals with the correct spacing." He turned back to the computer. "But it's still very, very risky. Since we need the Permidium ship to detect the crystals as if our ship is made of them, we can only shield the sides of the crystals from one another, not fully enclose them. Therefore, the wrong jerk or jolt could cause them to go off."

"Explode?" Jake said. "That would cause—"

"—a very big boom," concluded Lannick. He watched Jake and Novak as if waiting for a response. When none came, he pointed out, with a straight face, "That was a funny."

Neither Jake nor Novak changed their expression. All Jake could think of was the explosion of just one crystal, let alone the number that would be on the ship.

Novak finally spoke. "It wouldn't be so funny for whoever is piloting the ship, or anyone in the area, for that matter."

Jake still had questions. "But how do we know the Permidiums will allow the ship to board and not shoot it for lack of a beacon?"

"We don't. That's another calculated risk," said Novak.

Jake rolled his eyes. "This plan sure has a lot of calculations and risks. I kind of like things simple." He started to pace. "Even if the Permidium ship thinks we're also Permidium, they're going to hail us. They'll want to talk."

"Yet another risk," Lannick said. "We've been studying the hilaetite ship with our sensors. They send probes, also made out of hilaetite, that come and go constantly. Automated. We believe they are looking for Captain Danielson's transponder. Anyway, the hope is that the automated system believes our ship is no different from a probe."

Jake stopped. "Wouldn't it be easier and safer to steal the transponder from Sloan and just give it to them? It seems that's all they want. Then, when they leave, it's just us versus the pirates."

"I'm not so sure about easier and safer when dealing directly with Sloan," Novak said. "But it doesn't matter. We have no idea where he's stashed the transponder and we don't have the time to search. He probably has it on Vernius, based on your ambassador's message, and so we would still have to get through a Permidium ship to get there."

"Good point," Jake said. "But I have one last question. Where do you plan on getting all these crystals to make our fake Permidium ship?"

Novak and Lannick exchanged glances. Neither spoke for a moment.

The answer popped into Jake's mind as he watched the two of them contemplate. "Romalor had a stash of crystals, didn't he?"

Novak grimaced. "I was in the process of making arrangements to send them to Pergan, but with trying to keep Craton intact, rebuild our society, and change our government, I've had a few other things on my plate."

Jake shook his head gently. "No need to explain. Earth suspected Romalor had crystals. And what you've done to change Craton in just a year is amazing. I have no doubt you intended to turn over the crystals. And now that you didn't, it's working out for us. Or at least it's working out for everyone except the pilot that has to fly Lannick's homemade Permidium ship."

Lannick grinned for the first time. "Another funny?"

Jake blinked and shook his head. "Not this time."

Cal was glad Freya had left him alone to talk to Sam. Finally, he could concentrate on what he was doing. He pressed the transmitter com.

"Sam, I mean Private Simons" —he had to assume that the Legion officers, as well as the president, were listening—"respond if you can hear me."

Silence.

Cal tried again. "Private Simons, please respond."

Everything that could have happened to her raced through his mind. Did the pirates find her? Had she been captured? Or worse?

Again, more silence. Then Cal saw the computer screen light up in the residential portion of Sector One headquarters moments before he heard Sam's voice. "Cal, is that you?"

Cal cleared his throat. "Yes, this is Captain Danielson." He tried to be assertive to fool the Legion officers. He knew he was failing miserably, but that didn't matter right now.

"Oh yes, of course. I meant Captain Danielson."

"What's your situation?"

"All still clear in the residential area. No friendlies or foes."

"Good. We have a plan to retake Earth, but it hinges on you getting to my computer at my dad's house in the country."

"That's the occupied area."

"I know," Cal said. "I wish there was another way." Why did he have to force Sam into what she was going to have to face? But she was Legion, and she would do it, no questions asked. He knew that.

He proceeded to fill Sam in on the plan, the location of his dad's house, and the critical timing.

"Leave the transmitter module where you are now open so we can still send vector transmissions and so I'll be able to track you from here," Cal said. "And we can stay in constant communication. If something happens where we lose communication through that module, my dad has an old one, as a retired officer. You can activate it when you get there and open up the vector transmissions again."

"Got it, Captain."

Cal liked it better when she called him Cal. It gave him a warm feeling all over. But what were these butterflies in his stomach? He had never felt those before with anyone, and he hadn't even met Sam in person.

"It'll take you a while to get to my dad's place on foot, so you'd better get moving now," Cal said. "But one more thing before you go:

In order for us to communicate and for me to track you, you're going to have to find a portable transmitter on a deceased officer."

Cal could hear the grief in her voice. "I don't think that'll be a problem."

21

SAM

C al watched the red dot indicating Sam's transmitter move ever so slowly along the table while he gave directions to his dad's house.

Sam's labored breathing came through the com as she spoke. "What's your dad's name? I don't think you told me."

"Bernard, but everyone calls him Bernie," Cal said. "What are you seeing down there?"

"I'm almost out of the headquarters. There isn't much still standing and not smoldering. Looks like the final level of Dota Underlords 2200."

Cal loved that ancient game, which Mikindo Corp brought back several years ago, redesigned, of course. Sam could be his perfect match.

"I get the picture," Cal said. "Let's just hope Kunkka isn't stalking around."

As soon as that came out, Cal regretted saying it. How could he joke about a Dota Underlords homing in on Sam, when there were real pirates there who probably weren't much less dangerous?

"That's okay. I would take him out with Snapfire."

As much as Sam may have been trying to cover, Cal could still hear the fear in her voice.

"All right, Captain," Sam said. "I'm out of the headquarters. I can see a pretty good distance ahead. Things aren't bad here. Looks like the farther out I get, the less destruction there is. But pirate ships fly over every now and then."

"Do you see anybody?"

"Nobody: no people or pirates. But I'm sticking to the trees, following the coordinates you gave me."

"Good." Cal wanted to try to keep her mind off things, but he needed a better topic than a violent video game. "Sam, tell me about yourself. Where are you from? Do you have family?"

"I was . . ."

Cal heard a thump.

"Ouch, crap, that hurt."

"You okay?"

"Yeah, stepped in a hole with one foot and tripped on a log with the other. I never was very good with the obstacle course in basic. Anyway, I was saying, I was born and raised here in Sector One. My parents were Legion. I'm an only child."

Cal listened as intently as if she were in the room. That was good. He had her talking. And they had similar backgrounds. They both came from Legion families.

"You said your parents *were* Legion?" Cal asked. "So, they're retired?"

Cal knew he asked the wrong question when there was a long silence. That was twice now. Could he be any more pathetic?

"No, they were both in Sector Four when Romalor attacked."

Cal didn't need to hear any more than that. Was there any topic that didn't lead back to death and violence? Probably not if you grew up Legion.

Jake didn't know what to expect as he walked into the hangar. He had received word to meet Novak and Lannick there immediately, that Lannick had determined the number and spacing of the hilaetite crystals that worked, at least in theory. Jake assumed the Cratonites were now assembling the hilaetite ship in order to test it out.

The hangar looked large enough to hold a hundred fighters, but it sat empty but for one fighter in the middle. The fighter had wires running from it to a number of computer tables set up on either side of it. Several Cratonites, including Lannick, were manning the workstations, while others were climbing in and on the fighter, performing various tasks. Still more were slowly and carefully removing small black boxes from a utility loader and handing them to the Cratonites on the fighter.

Jake watched closely as a relatively lanky Cratonite removed a crystal from one of the black boxes and started to attach it to the outside of the fighter as if he were welding it on, with a long thin device that looked hot to the touch. When the lanky fellow finished his "weld," he removed a four-sided box-like object from the loader and attached it to the fighter in the same manner, enclosing the crystal on four sides, leaving the top exposed. Others were doing the same thing all over the ship.

Footsteps to Jake's right echoed in the cavernous hangar. "Quite an operation, isn't it?" came Novak's voice.

Jake turned to face him. "Sure is. How safe is it to be in here anyway?"

Novak patted Jake on the back. "About as safe as anyplace these days."

Jake thought for a moment. "You have a good point." He paused. "So, Lannick figured out how to do it?"

"I hope," Novak replied. "We'll know soon enough." He gestured forward with his hand. "Let's walk."

The hangar smelled of some type of cleaning agent, and the air was dry and comfortable. Jake wondered if the humidity was controlled for the crystals or for the workers handling them.

Novak spoke as they continued toward the fighter. "Your president and I have decided on the final plan. You're not going to like it, but it's the best we could do."

Jake didn't like the sound of those words. He scratched the back of his head. "Let me have it."

"You heard Lannick. There aren't enough fighters to attack Earth, Tortuga, and Vernius at the same time. We have to focus on two of the three. And we only have enough hilaetite crystals to camouflage one ship. So, that means we attack Tortuga and—"

Jake interrupted before Novak could finish. "—and Earth."

"I'm afraid so, Jake. Vernius will have to wait."

"Even if we're successful in retaking Earth, if the other Permidium ship isn't scared off and it completes its containment field, we'll have no way to contact Vernius, let alone retake it," Jake said. "We don't have a store of hilaetite on Earth, even if we were able to get to the Permidium ship."

"One step at a time," Novak said. "First, we get your planet back. Then we can regroup and look at Vernius and the other planets."

While Jake ached to tell Diane the truth and clear up the misunderstanding, and he knew she must be feeling awful, at least she wasn't in any immediate danger. He had time to get to her. So, he had to focus on step one. And at least step one included Tortuga, which meant rescuing Frank. Given his condition, he was most in need of immediate assistance. Between his thoughts of what he was putting Diane through and the horrible beating Frank took, Jake was having trouble being patient and letting the pieces of the plan fall into place.

Novak continued. "The plan is for me to take my fighters and the few destroyers we have to Tortuga and take out the pirate reinforcements camped there and free your commander and any other prisoners. The president and I feel that if we are successful on Earth, the pirates, or Sloan, will execute any and all prisoners. So, Tortuga has to happen precisely at the same time as the Earth attack. Too soon, and we may tip off the pirates and Permidiums about the Earth attack. Too late, and the reinforcements might get off the planet and the prisoners might be killed."

"Got it, agreed," Jake said. "Who's leading the Earth attack?"

"One of your Superior Guards. A Captain Reynolds."

"Good choice," Jake said. "A good man. Saved my life once."

Jake thought back to the final battle against Craton. Captain Reynolds and his Charlie division had moved in just as Jake and Cal were about to take the final killing shot from a flurry of Craton fighters.

Novak and Jake stopped behind Lannick, at the computer table.

"But what exactly do you want me to do?" Jake asked. "Lannick said he needed me as part of his idea."

Novak motioned at the fighter. "Right, this is all yours."

Jake's eyes widened. It caught him a little by surprise. He figured he would be on the fighter crew, but he didn't think he would be leading it.

"I'm in charge of the crew?" Jake asked.

"No," Novak replied. "You *are* the crew."

"What? Why? Why just one person?"

Novak turned toward Jake. "Two reasons. First, since we're trying to make it look like a probe, we want as little chance as possible for the Permidiums to detect life on it. Their probes are unmanned. Second, for much the same reason, we feel it's safest for just one person to board the Permidium ship. Much less chance of being detected. And even if we sent more men, if you're detected, one man or a full crew, it won't matter." He paused. "I hate to be blunt, but if you're detected on the Permidium ship, with their advanced weapons, you won't have a chance."

The reality of that hit Jake. His only move, which he often used, was to deflect the reality with a joke. "Well, thanks for that encouragement. And you run this planet?"

Novak didn't respond to Jake's comment, but instead continued talking. "Lannick feels that you're the most qualified for the job since you know the most about the Permidiums, besides Cal. President Brown and I agree."

Jake figured as much.

Novak checked his timepiece, then shouted, "Let's get a move on. I know this is delicate work, but we only have twelve hours."

Twelve hours, Jake thought. And then they would lose all communication with Earth. If Cal couldn't talk to Sam, then he wouldn't be able to get the information to figure out how to destroy the Permidium ship.

Then they would have nothing. No Hope for Earth, no hope for Vernius, and worst of all, no hope of seeing Diane again.

Cal checked the computer clock. Sam had been on the move for twelve hours. She had to be exhausted.

"Cal, I hear someone," Sam's voice was a whisper. "Make that multiple someones."

"Good guys or bad?" Cal asked.

"I can't tell. I'm in some brush behind a tree. I can make out what looks like an old, abandoned house among the trees up ahead."

"Okay, lay low until they pass."

"They're coming out of the house. Definitely pirates, by the looks of them. I have no idea what they're doing out here in the middle of nowhere." Sam paused. "I think they're holed up in the house. They don't look like they're in any hurry to leave. I'm going to have to move around them."

Cal wondered what Sloan would do if he knew his pirate recruits were just hanging out on Earth with no purpose.

"Okay," Cal said. "But be very careful, and quiet."

"Thanks for stating the obvious, Mr. Dota Underlord Sand King."

Cal was quiet so Sam wouldn't have to talk as she circumvented the group. He couldn't hear a thing either. That was good. That meant Sam was being reticent, and nobody was after her.

The silence was broken by a bark.

Oh great, Cal thought, *they have a dog.*

The barking grew faster and louder.

"Sam, what's going on?"

"A dog. They have a dog. And I think it knows I'm here. At least it's on a leash."

The yapping sounded like it was moving closer to Sam. Then Cal could faintly hear one of the pirates talking. Oh no, were they nearing Sam too?

"Sam, you have to get out of there!"

Sam's voice came as a panicked whisper. "They'll see me. They're looking toward where the dog is barking, straight at my hiding place. The dog is leading them this way."

"Do you have a weapon?"

"I picked up a plasma handgun. But there are so many pirates."

"Okay, Sam. Stay calm. I'm thinking."

How could Cal expect her to stay calm when he was terrified for her? He rubbed his sweaty palms on his pant legs. He couldn't remember when he had been so nervous.

"They're coming this way. The man is unleashing the dog. What do I do?"

Cal's mind was spinning. He had to think of something. But what? He had no idea.

Cal jumped backward in his seat as a blood-curdling growl came through the com followed by barking. Through the snarling, he could hear multiple voices, more clearly now.

"There's someone over there."

"Grab the guns. We're going hunting."

"Let's go."

Then the voices were drowned out by the growling dog.

It was the sound a dog makes when clenching something in its teeth, tugging and shaking its head back and forth.

Cal faintly heard Sam's voice. "No, no. Help!"

A plasma gun fired, then there was nothing but static before the com went silent. The red dot on the computer table was gone. Sam's transmitter was shut down.

"NO!" Cal shouted into the com. "Sam!"

There was nothing but dead air.

22

TROJAN HORSE

An incoming call crackled through Jake's vector-space transmitter. "This is where we drop off, Captain," Reynolds said.

"Reynolds, I'm glad it's you that has my back again," Jake replied.

He wished he had the Legion fighters with him all the way to Earth, but they had to stop outside the Permidium ship's range. Until Jake could destroy the Permidium ship, he was on his own. If Sam was unsuccessful in locating Cal's father's house or Cal's transponder computer backup, or if Cal was unable to decipher whatever was in the transponder, or if he was unable to gain access to the Permidium ship, then he was likely a goner, and Earth would be forever in the hands of Sloan and the pirates. A lot of "ifs."

Jake stopped along with his fighter escort and double-checked his sensors. All readings looked good. The hilaetite crystals were stable. He had plenty of fuel. He had plenty of ammo, although that wouldn't do much good against the Permidiums. He checked his timepiece, synchronized with the rest of the Legion and Cratonite military. Four hours remaining.

He pressed the com. "Cal, any word from Sam?"

"Negative." Jake could hear the dejection in Cal's voice.

He was at the critical point.

If he didn't move forward, there wouldn't be enough time to board the Permidium ship, find and tap into its computer, and do whatever he needed to do in order to destroy the ship before the containment field was completed. And once completed, he wouldn't be able to board. But if he moved now and Sam or Cal were unsuccessful, he had no escape plan. It would be a one-way trip. He either would be successful or dead.

And nobody even talked of the possibility that the destruction sequence might be immediate. In that case, even if Sam, Cal, and he were successful, it still might be a one-way trip.

Jake spoke into the com again. "Madam President, are you on com?"

"I am, Jake. I'm here with Lannick. Mr. Leximer is on route to Tortuga."

"How much closer can we push it?"

Lannick replied. "Captain, there are too many variables and unknowns to be able to estimate with much certainty. You could cruise right in, set up shop, and be waiting on your Private Simons and Captain Danielson. Or, more likely, you'll face some roadblocks. So, we're trying to give you as much time as possible. Based on my computer simulations, you're at the critical departure point for the worst-case scenario."

Jake pretty much assumed it would be the latter, if he was even able to get into the ship at all. "I think you mean the second to worst-case scenario," he replied.

"Jake," Aretha said. "I think we have to assume Private Simons didn't make it. And we have not had any contact with anyone else on the planet. So, it would be a suicide mission for you to board the Permidium ship now. I think we need to abort the mission. I can't ask you to proceed when the stakes for you are so high."

"But the stakes are just as high for Earth if I don't go." Jake paused. "If there's even the slightest chance that Private Simons made it, I have to try."

Aretha sighed. "Jake, I had a feeling you would say that. Like I said, I won't order you to proceed. But we have little hope other than this plan, so I won't stop you either."

Jake made one final systems check, then proceeded at subluminal speed. "I have to do this."

"Good luck," Aretha said.

"We'll see you on the planet, Captain Saunders," Reynolds said.

Jake punched the Craton fighter into light speed.

Novak and his squadron dropped out of light speed outside Titan.

Novak swiveled his captain's chair toward his first officer, Dak. "Can you confirm the coordinates of the pirate fighters? I don't want us blowing up civilian buildings, even if they are mostly full of drunken pirates. Most of them aren't part of the war."

"Yes," Dak replied as he sat at the helm. "It appears your intel is accurate. The fighters are all hidden in makeshift hangars here." He pointed to an area on the viewing screen. "The planet isn't equipped as a military base, so these hangars aren't near any civilians. In fact, my readings don't show any life-forms at all near the hangars. I don't think they expect a thing. We should be able to take them out with few, if any, casualties."

Novak felt that if he correctly figured out the old man's riddles regarding the location of the fighters, then he likely had an accurate location of the prisoners as well.

"I doubt they even know that we know they're here," Novak said.

Then he hesitated. If the pirates weren't with their ships, they were either drunk somewhere or waiting for orders. He didn't like the thought of the latter. That would make Novak's ground attack to find and release the prisoners much more difficult. But their first priority was to take out the fighters so that reinforcements couldn't make it to Earth, assuming things were going successfully there.

Novak glanced at his timepiece. Four hours left. "Let's proceed."

Dak was correct: they had no resistance taking out the grounded fighters, and there were no casualties on either side. The fact that no pirates were at the hangars meant that Novak would have to change his ground tactics. He didn't like that. The original plan was to land with a small group to locate the prisoners, assuming they would be taking out a lot of the pirate resistance with the fighter attack. Now Novak had to improvise. He had to assume they would meet heavy resistance on the ground. Yet he had to protect their flank by leaving enough fighters in the air in case the pirates did anticipate them coming and had fighters hidden elsewhere. He had to account for all contingencies.

This was the type of decision Novak hated making the most. He had to make it now, without any advisors' input. If he made the wrong choice, it could cost his entire squadron their lives.

He rubbed his forehead, then stood and faced Dak. "Direct half the fighters to land and leave the rest with the destroyers in the air. That'll give us a lethal ground force."

But he wondered if it would be enough. He didn't know how many pirates were on Titan. Of course, it would help if most of them were inebriated.

"General, are you sure we need to land half the fighters to have enough footmen?" the navigation officer asked Novak. "These are just pirates after all."

For a brief moment Novak felt his father's blood course through his veins as he clenched his fists. Romalor would have killed the officer on the spot for questioning his orders. But Novak wasn't his father, and he had worked hard to move Craton away from his father's ways. Novak wanted advice and counsel. However, he did have to draw the line.

This wasn't advice or counsel. This was reluctance to follow an order. But he wouldn't scold the officer. He would correct him.

He took a deep breath to calm himself. "First, never underestimate your opponent. You should know that, if you're an officer. Second, we call these people pirates, but they're species from planets all over the galaxy, many of which planets produce formidable enemies. Let's not make the mistake of taking this mission lightly."

The officer cowered in his chair. "Yes, sir. I wasn't thinking."

Novak said to Dak, "Once you've notified the others, take us down."

As the Permidium ship came into sensor range, Jake watched his monitors for any type of projectile coming from it toward him. Even at this distance, however, he figured he would see the flash of light if the Permidiums fired at him. Slower moving objects moved to and from the Permidium vessel, but none seemed to be directed at him. *Those must be the probes Lannick mentioned.* He could also detect the containment field that he and Cal had picked up earlier.

One factor that Lannick hadn't accounted for was velocity. How fast did the probes travel? He would have to improvise and try to calculate their speed based on his sensor readings. That was a Cal job, but Cal wasn't there. That was okay, though. Running the calculations would keep his mind from reminding him that he could die at any second.

He moved closer to the Permidium ship at subluminal while gathering sensor data on the probes and determining their speed. They all moved at the same velocity, which made it easier to calculate. But if he was off in his calculations, it would cause his ship to stand out more.

He continued forward at the calculated rate of speed. Still no sign that the Permidiums thought of him as anything other than one of their probes. Fooling the Permidiums' automated system was one thing, but he wasn't as convinced as Lannick that the Permidiums wouldn't look at him when he came into visual range. His ship clearly didn't look like a probe.

Jake punched the com, still connected to the vector-space transmitter. "Any word from Private Simons?"

Anyone with a transmitter could have answered, but it was Cal who responded. "Still nothing, Jake. How are things going on your end?"

"So far so good. The disguise is working. I'm coming into visual range of the Permidium ship now."

Jake thought that he should feel nervous or just a bit scared. He had narrowly escaped death on more than one occasion, but never had he intentionally and so meticulously driven himself into the belly of the beast on what was most likely a one-way mission, whether successful or not. But he wasn't the least bit worried. He was in his comfort zone, the heat of battle, the risk of death around every corner. It was still what truly drove him.

But he did have one regret that he couldn't push out of his mind. That he would die without Diane knowing the truth of how much he loved her and how he wanted to make her his wife and spend the rest of his life with her. Cal would tell her everything and she would believe Cal. But Jake would go to his grave without being able to say how sorry he was for putting her through that.

He had to shove those thoughts to the side. He had a mission to accomplish, and he couldn't afford to be distracted.

He put the Permidium ship on his viewing screen. He could now get a good look at the probes moving in and out. They were definitely made of hilaetite. His ship was covered with hilaetite, but that's where the similarities stopped. He truly hoped that the Permidiums didn't look at him in their viewing screen, assuming they had one.

He moved closer still. No sign of anything unusual.

He was about one hundred yards from the ship when he noticed something on his sensors moving quickly toward him from behind. He flipped the screen to rear view. It was a spacecraft about the size of his, probably a pirate ship, since the Permidiums hadn't shot it down.

Jake was directly between the pirate ship and the Permidium vessel. *Is it targeting me or is it heading toward the Permidiums?* Jake asked himself. How could the pirate ship not see that he wasn't really a probe?

Jake wasn't equipped for a dogfight, another contingency they didn't have time to account for. The Craton fighter had shields, but if Jake raised them, it would block the Permidiums' automated probe system from detecting the hilaetite crystals on his ship.

Jake maintained his course toward the open probe hatch on the Permidium ship. If he altered course to see if the pirate ship would follow him or simply fly by, the probe system could detect the anomaly and signal a malfunctioning probe, triggering a series of events likely culminating with the Permidium ship blowing him up. And he couldn't try to contact the pirate ship. Probes don't talk.

If the pirate ship hit him or shot at him without shields and with all the hilaetite on his hull, it would be good-bye Jake and pirate ship, but whatever was stabilizing the Permidium ship's hilaetite would probably shield it from the blast.

The pirate ship was closing fast, still not firing. Jake's only thought was that it was on autopilot and the autopilot detected him as a probe. They probably had their shields up and probes just bounced off the shields with no damage to either one. But the hilaetite on Jake's ship wasn't stabilized. He wouldn't simply bounce off.

Jake was thirty yards from the hatch. The pirate ship was twenty yards from Jake. It must be aiming to enter the Permidium ship for some reason. Why it would enter through the probe hatch, Jake couldn't determine. At Jake's current rate of speed, the pirate ship would impact him at ten yards from the hatch. With the hatch open, that just might be enough to detonate the Permidium ship from the inside, destroying it. Jake would give his life if he knew that would happen. But he couldn't risk it. If it didn't work, their plan would be over.

Jake had to take yet another risk in order to avoid the impact. Since he couldn't change course or raise shields, his only other option was to speed up and hope that he would be able to change direction once inside. He also had to hope the last-minute speed variation wouldn't be material enough to set off an alarm.

Jake increased his speed slightly. Twenty yards away. The pirate ship was still gaining. He increased again. Fifteen yards. The pirate ship was five yards away. He increased speed a third time. Ten yards. The pirate ship edged up to a few feet from Jake's hull and their velocities matched. They both eased through the hatch, just a few feet between them. Jake let out his breath that he didn't realize he had been holding. *That was close*, he thought.

The hatch opened on the inside into a cavernous room. That single room could hold every ship in the Craton and Earth fleet combined, when at full power. There was no floor. The whole room was round with docking bays covering every part of the walls, all the way around, except where various-sized robotic arms were attached.

As soon as Jake's fighter entered, his engine and all systems except life support immediately shut down. Jake recalled that happening a year ago when Cal, Diane, and he had encountered the Permidiums. One of the medium-sized arms quickly locked on to Jake's vessel—while its forward momentum still kept it ahead of the pirate ship—and jerked the ship out of the entranceway.

The arm took Jake up and to the right, toward one of the docking bays—a very efficient way to dock ships. The arms moved spacecraft and probes in every direction, never colliding. *So that's why the pirate ship entered that hatch. It isn't a probe hatch. It's a hatch for everything.* The size of the vessel or probe or whatever object dictated which size arm would be used and which docking bay the object would be placed in. *What technology*, Jake thought. And the arms must not detect hilaetite crystal, just the object's size.

Having passed any detection barriers outside, once Jake's vessel entered the hatch, the arm docked it as the spacecraft that it was.

Jake held his breath again as the arm settled his hilaetite-covered ship not so gently into the bay. A door opened in the wall next to the front of his fighter, and a short walkway jetted out. Jake put his vector-space transmitter back on his belt, grabbed his bag of necessities, opened the fighter's hatch, climbed onto the walkway, and passed through the door.

Jake pressed the com on the transmitter. "I'm in."

23

NEVER GIVE UP

Cal stared at the computer clock, willing time to move more slow-ly. Only two hours remained until the shield would seal off Earth.

"You should take a break." Aretha's voice came from behind him. "You haven't gotten up from that computer since we started. I'll relieve you and listen for Sam."

It barely registered to him that the president of Earth United was telling him to take a break. That she would do his job.

Cal swiveled his chair to face Aretha. "It's all right. Thanks, but I'm fine. I need to see this through, for better or for worse." He paused. "Did you hear that Jake made it in?"

"Yes," Aretha said. "Good news travels just as fast on Craton as on Earth."

Despite the good news, hopelessness flooded Cal. "It doesn't look very promising, does it?" He glanced at the computer table. No sign of Sam's red dot. "I've thought through every possible way to save Earth, both with technology and with force, and none of them work without my transponder information. The pirate spacecraft now outnumber us even with the Cratonites, and we have no answer for the Permidium ships and their hilaetite weapons, not to mention that Sloan is always one step ahead of us. They've wiped out over half the Legion and our entire government except for you. Sam is probably dead. Jake is going to be dead. Who knows what Novak is going to run into on Titan? This is one equation, no matter how many times I try, I cannot solve. There is no answer."

Aretha pulled up a chair and sat facing Cal. "Cal, you're one of the most intelligent people I have ever met. The cadets and prospective officers study your work." Aretha leaned back in her chair. "You're famous in the Legion. Even if this plan fails, if anyone can come up with another plan, it's you."

There was a time when Cal would have believed that. In fact, he would have told people that, whether out of confidence or arrogance. But not anymore. He was growing more and more despondent by the minute. "I don't know. If Sam and Jake aren't able to come through, I give up. Pirates win."

"Cal, I know Sam and Jake mean a lot to you, but you can't give up." Aretha leaned forward, putting her elbows on her knees. "I'm sure you know this, but all of our technology today, from the defense shield to quantum drive, and even the sepder, come from a single source, a single invention over three hundred years ago."

"The incandescent lightbulb," Cal said.

"Invented by Thomas Edison," Aretha continued. "Did you know that he failed thousands of times before he was successful? He said our greatest weakness lies in giving up. The most certain way to succeed is always to try just one more time." She paused. "You can't quit, I can't quit, the Legion can't quit. We have to keep trying."

Cal was starting to process what the president had said when a red dot caught his attention out of the corner of his eye. He swiveled to better see the computer table. "Sam!" he shouted to anyone who was listening. He could feel the blood surge through his veins. Sam must be alive.

That meant Jake could make it. And their plan still had a chance. One little red dot changed everything.

Sam's voice crackled over the speaker. "Cal, you there?"

Cal pressed the com. "You bet I am. What happened? I thought I lost you. For good." He paused, thinking about that. Sam, dead. He barely knew Sam, but the thought of her being gone forever had made him want to give up. "Where are you?"

"I'm at your dad's. We're booting up your old computer now. I'm talking on your dad's transmitter module. That dog had a meal of mine. I'll fill you in on the rest when we have more time."

"I'm just glad you're okay."

The com was silent for a moment. "It's good to hear your voice, Cal."

Cal could detect a hint of tears of joy in Sam's tone. That warmed his heart.

"I'm glad to hear your voice too, son," Bernie said.

"Hey, Dad," Cal replied. "Glad you're okay. Thanks for helping out."

"I'll do anything you guys need. Sam filled me in on what's been happening. We figured it was pirates after we had an encounter with one, but we had no idea how they got through the defense shield or who else was behind it. We've been organizing down here, waiting for some type of opportunity. I've got a small fleet of retired Legion and other pilots with small armed aircraft. I'm certain the other sectors have organized as well. We're ready to go when you guys break through."

Cal turned his head toward Aretha, now standing behind him.

Aretha nodded once.

"Got it, Dad. We'll need all the help we can get when we strike. But we have a more immediate concern."

"Right," Bernie said before Cal could go on. "Sam explained. Looks like she has your computer up and running. I'll give the com back to her."

"Cal, what exactly am I looking for?" Sam asked.

Cal gave Sam his passwords and told her where his transponder backup was located. Before he could explain how to get there, Sam found it.

She's amazing, Cal thought. *Who else could have done that?* "Okay, great. Can you send me the data through my dad's transmitter module?"

"We're connecting it to your computer now," Sam said. "And we'll transmit in just a few seconds." She paused for a moment. "Now."

Cal looked down at the glass table and flipped the screen from tracking to data mode.

"It's coming through. This could take a while. I have to weed through the information until we find the correct date a year ago, when we encountered the ship."

Cal checked the clock. One hour, twenty-seven minutes remaining.

Despite Dak's persistent objections, Novak was out in front of the ground forces. Generals rarely even participate in away missions on enemy planets, let alone take the lead, but this was one trait he and his father had in common. Romalor always led the way for his troops. Of course, things were much different then. If a general showed any sign of weakness, he was ripe to be overthrown. Nevertheless, this mission was too important. Novak wanted it done correctly. It wasn't that he was too prideful to stay behind. At least that's what he told himself.

Novak led his infantry through the dark of night from what was left of the hangars into Tortuga. He had been to Tortuga once before with his father, and the city was just as filthy as he remembered. Novak's stomach lurched at the stench of garbage, alcohol, and urine permeating the warm air.

As they entered the city proper, they saw people moving about inside the lighted buildings, but the streets were eerily quiet. Not even the occasional drunk stumbling along the sidewalk. Novak motioned for his squad to spread out. If they were walking into an ambush, he at least didn't want his entire ground force to be in one spot.

He held up his fisted right hand without turning around, the back of it to his troops. Everyone halted immediately. He surveyed the empty streets and sidewalks. The rooftops seemed undisturbed as well. Everything was motionless. Not even a breeze to ruffle the papers littering the ground. Still looking forward, he made a circling motion with his raised hand and then pointed to the right, signaling Dak to take his company and move to the right flank. He had a bad feeling. He wanted his two companies to be completely separated.

No sooner had Dak moved off to the next line of buildings than a barrage of plasma fire came at Novak from both sides and the rooftops above.

Even though Novak was anticipating that possibility, he jumped at the first few blasts, startled and disoriented. He had overanticipated the attack, making him that much more tense when it happened.

His instincts immediately took over. Dropping to his knees, he swiveled his own plasma rifle, looking for targets and barking orders. "Take cover! Get to the buildings? Off the streets! Move! Move! Move!"

The Cratonite infantry scattered quickly. Not in a hasty manner running for their lives, but rather in an organized, coherent structure. A sense of pride welled up inside Novak, not for himself, but for how his squad was reacting. A large part of his military had never seen combat. He had to dismiss a large portion of his father's forces who survived the war with Earth and were loyal to his father and his ways. The remaining infantry and pilots were all he had to start with. All the others were newly trained recruits.

Novak hadn't seen a lot of frontline action himself, and probably should have been very afraid, considering his current position. But he wasn't. Maybe fighting was in his blood or maybe he just didn't have the time to think about it. He now was focused only on completing his mission and keeping his people alive.

Novak moved toward the cover of the buildings as well. The dirt streets were exploding as plasma blasts burned holes in the ground. He squinted to keep the soil and debris out of his eyes. That, along with the darkness, made it difficult for him to determine his heading. He wasn't far from the buildings on one side of the street, but the shots seemed to be coming from every direction. For all he knew, he could be running right toward some pirates.

He wiped the sweat and grime from his face with his sleeve as he continued to move and shout orders. He pushed through the broken wood-plank door of an adobe building and rolled, coming up on one knee, his weapon at the ready.

Nobody was inside.

Four other Cratonites followed him through the door and immediately took up defensive postures by the windows. Novak saw a slight twinge of fear in each of their faces, but that didn't bother him. They were well trained. And a little fear was good. It kept a body alert and lessened the chances of making a careless mistake.

The building looked like it had been a general merchandise store in its better days. Many of the shelves were toppled over. What merchandise remained was strewn across the floor and either broken or partially opened. Novak was behind his contingent as they tried to work the beat-up auto controls on the windows. Finally, they gave up and broke through the blinds and frames with the butts of their guns, shards of metal and glass flying outward.

The four soldiers with him, Zeph, Mic, Dru, and Freya, started firing through the now glassless windows, aiming at the rooftops across the street. Beads of sweat formed on their faces.

Novak breathed slowly, forcing himself to stay calm. He was warm, but he wasn't sweating, at least not like the other four. He wanted to talk to them, try to calm their nerves, but this wasn't the right time. They were holding their positions. They might be scared, but they were doing their jobs exactly as they had been trained to do.

"Officer," Novak said. "What do you see?"

Freya, the only officer among them besides Novak, spoke quickly, her voice shaky, as she continued to aim and fire. "Looks like they've all moved to the rooftops. It's difficult getting an angle on them. But the same is true for them trying to hit us."

"But they have us pinned in," Zeph said with a bit of panic in his voice, as he continued to fire.

Novak pressed his com. "Dak, what's your position?"

Novak's com crackled with Dak's voice. "We circled wide, but it looks like the pirates are concentrated on your street. We're moving toward you to assist."

"Negative!" Novak replied quickly. "You've given me the intel I need. Stay clear of my location."

"But General—" Dak objected.

"That's an order."

Mic turned toward Novak and raised an eyebrow.

Novak didn't have time to explain his plan, but he wanted to ease Mic's mind.

Before he could say a word, there was a blast.

Right before Novak's eyes, Mic's head opened up, blood splattering everywhere as he slumped forward and hit the floor.

"No! Mic!" Novak immediately began chest compressions, ignoring the fact that half of Mic's face was gone. He knew death was a part of being in the military, but he never got used to losing soldiers. He pressed harder and faster. He couldn't let Mic die. He couldn't.

He continued frantically with the compressions until he felt Freya's hand on his shoulder.

"General, he's gone."

He stopped, his crossed hands still on Mic's chest, head bowed. He was winded. He needed to catch his breath. *Inhale, exhale,* he thought. *Inhale, exhale.* He straightened up and looked from Freya to Zeph to Dru. All three were watching him. He could see in their faces the compassion for the loss of a comrade, the fear for the situation in which they remained, and the question of what they should do next. He was their leader, their general. He had to get them out of harm's way. He had to get his entire company to safety. He didn't want to lose any more soldiers on this mission. And they had to finish what they came here to do.

He stood and looked down at Mic. The entry and exit wound came from a conventional weapon. The pirates must not have enough plasma guns to go around. He stored that bit of information away for later.

"What's the plan, General?" Freya asked.

Novak didn't look at her and didn't respond. Instead, he pressed his com again, opening it up to his entire company. "This is your general. Continue to lay down fire, but find a rear exit in whatever building you're in. On my command, cease firing and run for those exits as fast as you can."

Freya gave him a puzzled look, then the corners of her mouth turned up in understanding.

Novak addressed Dru, who had resumed his position at the makeshift embrasure. "Go find us an exit out the back."

He pressed the com one more time. "Lannick, any sign of pirate resistance in the air?"

"Negative, General."

He had trouble hearing Lannick over the plasma blasts and chunks of buildings crumbling. He moved up and peered out the window over Freya's shoulder. There was enough plasma fire from both sides to light up the street.

He stepped back and spoke into the com again. "Bring the fighters to my coordinates. Notify me when you're thirty seconds out. Then target all buildings on this street, both sides."

"Affirmative."

"Brilliant, General," Freya said.

"Don't say that until we're out of this mess. If we stop firing too soon, it'll tip off the pirates that something is up. But if we wait too long to evacuate, then we'll go down with the pirates."

"How did you arrive at thirty seconds, sir?" Freya asked.

One side of Novak's mouth turned up. "I guessed."

Moments later, Novak's com crackled. "Lannick here. We're thirty seconds out, General."

Novak pressed his com. "Everyone, clear out, now! Get to your exits!"

Novak, Freya, Dru, and Zeph raced toward theirs, Dru leading the way.

Novak felt the tension of being on the clock. They now had less than thirty seconds to get out of the building. He could see the tensity in the others too as they continued to run.

They burst through a back door into a dingy alley. Novak always had trouble running with all the military gear, but he sprinted as fast as he could, knowing what was about to happen. He heard the fighter engines first, followed a few seconds later by deafening explosions as the plasma missiles hit their targets. The concussion from the blasts forced Novak to the ground, his face planting into the dirt alley, his gun flying forward out of his hand. Freya, Zeph, and Dru went down as well. Novak turned to see the building they were just in engulfed in flames, as were all the other buildings on that street as far as he could see from his vantage point. The heat singed his hair.

Novak rolled into a sitting position as the fighters made a second pass in the opposite direction. But they didn't fire.

Lannick's voice came over the com. "All clear, General."

His com crackled again, this time with Dak's voice. "General, we found what we're looking for. Your intel was accurate once again. We're in a building full of prisoners, unguarded. A few prisoners are in pretty bad shape. We'd better get a few ships down here to get them out of here.

Freya sat up beside Novak, wiping the blackened dirt and sweat from her face. "Like I said General, brilliant."

24

TIGHT SQUEEZE

Jake pulled his data pod from his bag and flipped it to atmospheric mode. The readings showed an atmosphere content similar to Earth's. He slowly removed his mask and took a deep breath, ready to put the mask back on if needed. He stood motionless, as if that would help him determine if the air was breathable. It was. He checked his timepiece. Two hours remaining. He dropped the mask into the bag and moved on, checking around each corner before proceeding.

The inside of the ship was nothing like he had expected. It wasn't made of hilaetite. The walls, floor, doors, and ceiling were all made of a hard, shiny substance that felt a lot like steel but gave off a glow. The pinkish-orange color of everything was almost hypnotizing. Jake shook his head and tried not to think about it. He had to move.

Jake didn't know what he was looking for. Nobody knew what was needed to destroy the ship, or if destruction data even existed on Cal's transponder. They just assumed that if it existed, the destruction would be technologically based. And that it would have to do with a ship's system, accessed by the ship's computer. So, Cal had told him to look for an access point to the computer. Cal said that the closer a computer was to the ship's bridge, the more likely it would provide deep access. They were also counting on the transponder telling them how to access the computer and even how to read the Permidium language. Now that Jake was beyond the point of no return, he realized exactly how many "ifs" and "hopes" were in this plan.

He had no idea where to begin looking, and not much more of an idea as to what direction or on what floor the bridge was. The ship was gigantic, comprising hallway after hallway of doors, all requiring some type of scanning device to open.

He stopped to think. From the outside, it looked like the hatch was in the rear of the ship, on a lower level. Perhaps even the bottom level. The bridge is generally at the top front of a ship. So, he would move in that direction and go up wherever he could.

As he approached the next corner, he heard two similar voices talking. They sounded like they were computer generated. They must have translator chips and be in the Legion database because he could understand them.

"Why did the conciliator want us to go to the vessel room?" one Permidium asked.

"She said that a slight speed and size variation in an onboarding probe was detected," said the second Permidium. "She wants us to check it out, and then discuss our findings with her. I have already downloaded the data from the detection timeframe on my device."

Their voices were coming closer. Jake looked around. There was not a single open door or even a crack to wedge into. He drew his sepder, flattened his back against the wall near the corner, held his breath, and closed his eyes for a moment, hoping they would continue down the hall they were on and not turn the corner. He didn't want to have to use his sepder. He had no idea how strong Permidiums were or what handheld weapons they had, let alone the risk of attracting attention.

He opened his eyes as they passed, not turning the corner. He almost gasped at the sight of their translucent bodies seemingly floating on the floor, not walking. Their feet were slightly shuffling, but they weren't taking steps and were making no noise other than talking. Yet, they moved swiftly. Except for that, they looked like women on Earth, each with her hair pulled tight in a bun.

He let out his breath slowly. *That was close*, he thought. But the bad news was that they had detected his ship. That might mean he now had even less time.

Every hallway looked the same and every door was locked. He finally came to what appeared to be an enclosed vertical transportation unit. He guessed that he was about in the middle of the ship by now, but still on the lower level.

Jake studied the closed door. It was operated by a scan pad that looked different from the others he had seen. *Why not give it a try?* he thought. He moved the palm of his hand across the pad without touching it. Nothing happened. He placed his palm on the pad. Still nothing. *This is impossible*, he thought as he pressed the pad in frustration. The doors began to hum and then opened. "No way," he whispered to himself.

Fortunately, the unit was empty. He stepped inside. It, like the rest of the ship, smelled very clean. Not like a disinfectant, but more like a room after the house robot wiped down the furniture with a fresh-smelling cleaner. Jake could make nothing of the lights and writing on the wall panel inside the unit. He guessed that the top light was for the bridge, so he pressed the light below it. He knew this was a risky move. The doors could open in front of any number of Permidiums, and he would have no place to run. But he had to find a centrally located computer, and soon.

Jake drew his sepder again, really hoping he wouldn't have to use it. The unit paused for a moment, then the doors started to hum again. Jake readied himself with his sepder drawn back above his shoulder, his knees bent. The doors slowly opened. He expected to see a few surprised Permidiums. At least he would have the jump on them.

But there was nobody.

The vertical transportation unit opened into an empty hallway. Jake took a deep breath and exhaled slowly. He wiggled his shoulders to loosen his sweaty shirt from his back. He hadn't noticed before, but the air felt warmer in the Permidium ship than elsewhere. Or maybe it was just nerves.

He looked in both directions and then stepped out, still holding his sepder. He heard faint voices to his right. He started to move away from them, but then had an idea. Maybe he could follow them and somehow get into a room. If he was lucky, it would have a computer. He wasn't going to enter a room otherwise.

He moved to the right. The voices were moving away from him, so he continued in that direction. Peeking around a corner, he saw two Permidiums standing outside a door. Both females again. He stayed back and listened.

"They haven't found anything abnormal in the vessel room yet," one Permidium said. "The conciliator wants me to check the computer readings again during the detection timeframe on the master computer. I need access."

"Yes, I understand," the other Permidium said. "Here."

Jake saw the second Permidium scan a pad outside the door. The door clicked open. He had hit the jackpot.

He had found a primary computer room, but how would he get in? And if he did, he wouldn't be alone. He had to think quickly. Clear one obstacle at a time, which meant first, get inside the room. He watched as the auto door slid open and the first Permidium entered. How long until it would close? The second Permidium left immediately in the opposite direction. As soon as she turned the corner, Jake took off at a sprint down the hallway toward the still open door, his boots surprisingly quiet on the floor.

What is this material? he thought as he ran.

Jake was halfway to the door when it started to slide shut. He gave it everything he had. Ten yards away, and it was halfway closed. Five yards, and three quarters closed. Jake dove headfirst on his stomach with his sepder in his outstretched arm pointed at the quickly dwindling opening. His shirt and leather jacket slid smoothly along the floor. He stretched his arm as far as he could, the tip of the sepder crossing the threshold just as the door closed on the blade. The door gave off a hum, but the sepder held, giving Jake a two-inch opening to work with. Jake noticed his timepiece as he lay there. One hour, twenty-seven minutes remaining.

Cal scrolled through the data as fast as he could until he came close to their encounter with the Permidium ship. He slowed down, reading everything the transponder had collected. He found where Diane and he had used the transponder to disarm Romalor's weapon. He was close now. He went a little further. It was recording information from Marco Veneto's fighter as he was trying to escape.

"Here! Got it," Cal said to Aretha, still sitting behind him. "This is where it started picking up information from the hilaetite ship. Freya showed me how to use the Cratonite translator program. She pointed me to a language that should be similar enough to Permidium to make out the data."

Cal fed the data stream into the program. It came out in broken English, but it was good enough for him to read.

"What are you seeing?" Aretha asked.

"I'm not sure. Wow, the transponder picked up a lot of information. It must have connected deep in their system. It's difficult since I don't know exactly what I'm looking for."

Cal continued to read. "That's odd," he said.

"What is?" Aretha replied.

"The Permidium data isn't organized chronologically. It seems all jumbled. I need to figure out how it's organized in order to figure out where the destruction data might be. This is going to be harder than I thought."

Something buzzed in Aretha's jacket pocket.

"What's that?" Cal asked as he continued to read through the data.

"A com the general gave me for intra-planet calls here on Craton."

Cal listened as Aretha pulled the com from her pocket and spoke. "Senator . . . I mean President Brown here."

"It's Novak. We just returned. You might want to get down here, to hangar two. We've recovered a lot of your Legion. A couple are in pretty bad shape. I believe one of them is your commander. We're evacuating them to our military hospital now, but I don't think your commander is going to make it."

Cal's heart sank. Not Frank. He always seemed so indestructible. But with the beating Cal had watched Sloan give him, anyone else would already be dead. He wanted to see him, but he knew he couldn't. There was no time. He would likely never see Frank alive again. Even worse, Jake would never be able to talk to Frank again. *That will be heart-wrenching for Jake,* Cal thought. He should tell him about Frank. Jake would want to know, but now wasn't the right time. Jake needed to concentrate on his task.

Hearing this news would cripple him.

But what if Jake doesn't make it? Then he would never know about Frank. No. Cal couldn't think that way.

Jake would succeed.

Cal turned around. "Go, I have this."

"Yeah, I'm not much help here," Aretha said.

Cal paused for a moment, then spoke in a more subdued tone. "Tell Frank we all love him."

Aretha stared at Cal for a moment, her eyes tearing, then she bowed her head and left.

Cal's vector-space transmitter buzzed, then he heard Jake's voice. "Cal, you there?"

Cal checked the clock. One hour.

Jake crawled forward quickly, careful not to pull his sepder out of the doorway. He hoped the Permidium inside couldn't hear the buzz of the frozen door. He pulled himself up using the crack in the door. He wedged his back against the door frame and wall the best he could, slipped the toe of his boot into the crack as well as a hand, and pushed. He pushed harder and harder. His biceps began to burn. The veins in his neck swelled. His toes and fingers ached. He wanted to grunt loudly but just gritted his teeth instead, so he wouldn't make noise. The door started to give. As it did, he could wedge more of his body between the frame and the edge of the door, and then two hands on the door. Shortly, he had the opening wide enough to slip through. As he brought his left leg through, he used it to swipe at his sepder on the floor, pulling it along.

He grabbed his sepder and turned quickly. A floor-to-ceiling unit of server racks blocked his view of the rest of the room, and fortunately, blocked the rest of the room's view of him. He paused for a moment, taking deep breaths, before making his way to the edge of the shelving. As he looked around, he saw that the Permidium was standing, or rather hovering, at the back wall of the room. The entire wall illuminated a monitor screen. The wall wasn't the screen, rather the screen lit up in the air in front of the wall. The keyboard was simply another illuminated image, floating in front of the Permidium.

Now, how to subdue the Permidium quickly and quietly. Jake stepped back behind the shelving unit and slipped his bag off his back. He pulled out a small crossbow: one of Frank's specialties, designed with the same material and technology as his longbow. He loaded a tranquilizer dart. He had no idea if it would work on Permidiums, or if it would even stick into their translucent bodies. But it was his best shot at doing this quietly. He couldn't miss, or she was liable to sound some sort of alarm. Jake flattened his back against the shelving, held the crossbow to his chest, took a deep breath, and then slowly exhaled.

He had to nail it in one shot. In one smooth motion, he spun, stepping out from behind the shelving, raised the crossbow, aimed for the middle of her upper back, and fired.

A perfect shot. The Permidium arched her back and let out a slight squeak, then dropped to the floor without making another sound. Jake moved forward and stopped to check for a pulse in case he had overdosed her. Assuming her organs were in the same place as human organs, he reached down to touch her neck. His fingers went partway through her skin as if passing through a movie projector image, but then stopped as he felt a skin surface and a pulse.

Jake moved to the computer. He examined the wafting keyboard and then the floating screen. He felt helpless. He touched the keyboard. Just as with the Permidium's skin, his finger slowly moved into the keyboard before it struck the solid keys. If he moved too quickly or too hard, his finger went right through the keys.

He did a time check. One hour. He pressed his transmitter com. "Cal, you there?"

25

FORTNITE

C al, still focused on the computer but talking to any of the Cratonites in the room who cared to listen, slapped the table. "Got
it! The Permidiums organize their data by topic, rather than time. So
all events related to a single event or a single person are stored together, regardless of the period of time in which the events occurred or the
person lived. And they are cross categorized, so you might find the
same data in two or three places."

Cal was excited now. That made it easier to search. He could
simply search for hilaetite ship destruction or design flaws. Now for the
hard part, figuring out just what Jake needed to do.

Cal lost his train of thought when the vector-space transmitter
buzzed. "Jake, Cal, it's Captain Reynolds here. We're under a heavy
assault from Earth's pirate ships. And we're getting picked apart. They
know we can't go within range of the Permidium vessel, so they come
at us with a wave of fighters, then immediately retreat to the protection of the Permidiums. The Permidiums are going to wonder if something's up."

Jake replied, "Yeah, the Permidiums already suspect an intruder. They're searching their hangar for my ship."

"We still haven't figured out the destruction sequence," Cal added.

"Should we retreat to Craton until you guys have the Permidiums disabled?" Reynolds asked.

"Negative," Jake said. "We need you to move in and retake Earth immediately, once the Permidium ship is down, before any of the others arrive. I don't know if they can, but they may be able to pick up and complete the containment field."

Cal thought, *If they ever take down the Permidium ship.*

Jake continued, "You're going to have to hold them off the best you can until we can get rid of the Permidium protection. Sorry, Captain."

"Roger that," Reynolds replied in a confident tone.

Cal pressed the com. "Lannick, have you rerun the calculations of your original time estimate for the Permidiums to complete the containment field?"

There was a pause before Lannick responded, "Affirmative."

"And . . . ?"

"I was dead on."

Cal lowered his chin and rubbed his forehead, then glanced at the clock. Thirty minutes.

———

Cal had talked quickly in order to get back to his work, but it was enough for Jake to figure out how to get into the system and be ready for Cal's specific instructions, which Jake hoped would come before it was too late.

In the meantime, Jake started scrolling through the Permidiums' data. It looked like he had access to everything. Thankfully, the portable translator device that the Cratonites had given him worked. It was a wireless connection and translated everything into English, or at least good enough English for him to understand, and even provided a translated keyboard on the monitor that he could match up with the actual keyboard.

As Jake scrolled through the data, something caught his attention: the word *Sloan*. Jake stopped and started reading. The Permidiums had an entire file on Sloan, all in one place. And it dated back to at least 2185, the year Jake was born. It looked like they'd recorded every transmission they picked up about someone or something, not just Permidium interactions. Jake started to skim the file, but he froze when he read the word *Saunders*. He was reading from the year 2187. He knew that year as well. The year his father had died. He started reading again, this time slowly. It was an entire account of his dad's encounter with a Permidium vessel. Jake didn't know what type of ship or ships had killed his father. Nobody knew. His heart started to ache for his dad. It said that he had tried to communicate with the vessel, but the Permidiums didn't have translator chips until Mr. Sloan finally provided them just over a year ago. The report went on to say that after listening to the translated recordings, they now knew that Alec Saunders and Olga Vetrov were trying to communicate peacefully, and that they meant no harm.

Jake's eyes began to tear. Was his father's death just a big misunderstanding? *But the Permidiums were aggressive. Look what they did to Earth.*

As he continued to read, his tears dried, and he began to feel his old enemy start to boil up inside him—anger. The report said that a Mr. Sloan had warned them about the Milky Way galaxy. That it was aggressive and would invade the Permidiums' Andromeda galaxy as soon as it was able, in order to harvest the abundant hilaetite crystals there. He promised to help the Permidiums with a strategy against the Milky Way galaxy. The first step was to send scouts into the Milky Way and destroy any ships getting too close to their galaxy. As part of step one, Mr. Sloan warned them that the inhabitants of the Milky Way would attempt to communicate, but to ignore them and destroy them. Communication was just a ploy by the inhabitants. Jake could feel his anger growing. Sloan had started to plan all of this over twenty years ago.

He paused and took a deep breath, trying to calm himself. He knew he should stop reading and stay focused on the current mission, but he couldn't. He had to know everything. This explained why the Permidiums were in the far edges of the Milky Way galaxy back in 2187 and again when Cal, Diane, and he had encountered them last year. They probably entered the galaxy at other times but never encountered any ships, or none that Earth was aware of. And by the time of last year's encounter, the Permidiums had translator chips. Cal, Diane, and Jake could hear them. But the Permidiums still didn't communicate, other than to give a succinct warning. And why did they give them and Veneto a warning anyway? Maybe they were starting to question Sloan. In any event, they weren't questioning Sloan now.

So, it was Sloan who was responsible for his dad's death. A dad he never had a chance to know. Sloan had snatched that away from him. But Jake stayed calm. That was a long time ago, and this was now. He had to concentrate.

He started to close out of Sloan's file when another name caught his attention: *Diane Danielson.*

Jake's heart started to race. What could they have on Diane? He read on. The only entries were current. There was an interaction with the Imperial Majesty. The Permidiums must be monitoring the planet from the ship at Vernius. It sounded like Diane and the Imperial Majesty weren't getting along. He continued. The next entry was an interaction among Diane, the Imperial Majesty, and Sloan. Jake felt his heart race even faster at the sight of Sloan's name. That couldn't be good.

Jake's eyes grew wide and beads of sweat formed on his forehead as he read on. Diane was caught sending the transmission to him. The Imperial Majesty saved her from execution. That was too close. Jake took a breath he hadn't realized he was holding.

He froze as he read the final entry. Sloan had sentenced her to exile at the ends of the universe. Jake's chest tightened as he read how the capsule worked. He couldn't breathe. He put his hands out to lean on the keyboard but fell forward through the hovering image. His legs quivered as he lost his balance and hit the floor.

Jake lay there, his head buried in his hands, emotions running rampant. First sorrow for Diane, then sorrow for himself, for making Diane think he didn't love her, then anxiousness and panic over needing to get to Vernius to save Diane, and finally anger again. Not just any anger, but the same anger he felt toward Romalor for killing his Uncle Ben. An anger that had controlled his life for eight years, and which he'd sworn to never let return.

But Sloan was behind the events that had led to his uncle's death. Sloan had caused his dad's death, and he had beaten Frank to near death. He had destroyed Earth and now, given how the capsule worked, Sloan was about to execute Diane. Hate was too soft a word to describe how he felt about Sloan.

Jake clenched his fists and slammed them on the floor. He had to pull himself together. He had to focus on the task at hand, one step at a time. He had to get the containment field stopped and destroy the Permidium ship, then he could go to Vernius. He had to stay alive to help Diane. And they needed to hurry. Time was running out for Earth, and time was running out for Diane. Jake's eyes moved to his timepiece. Thirty minutes.

Cal pounded his fist on the table. Another dead end. He had performed all the typical search terms to try to figure out how to disable or even destroy Permidium spacecraft. Ship design flaws, vessel destruction, disable ship, spacecraft weaknesses, weapons flaws, weapons resistance. But he came up with nothing. He tried every other term he could think of and again, nothing. The Permidium vessels seemed indestructible. Was Sloan bluffing the Permidiums? He glanced at the clock. Twenty minutes remaining until he would lose the ability to communicate with Jake inside the containment field.

Cal put his face in his hands. *Think, Cal, think.*

The vector-space com buzzed. It was his dad. "How's it going up there? Anything we can do to help?"

Cal wanted to give them good news. He wanted to give everyone good news. Whatever he said would be heard by any Legion officer listening to a vector-space transmitter. But he only had bad news. "Not good. I can't figure it out. I can't find anything in their ships that we can exploit. I'm out of options, and we're almost out of time."

Captain Reynolds spoke next. "Better hurry it up. We're still getting hammered out here. We're completely on the defensive with that Permidium ship still able to gun us down."

"Cal, you have to do it," Jake said. Not just for us, but for Diane. Things are much worse for her than we thought."

Cal's head spun. He had never been this stumped, with so much pressure from so many people.

"Cal," Sam said in a soft, calm voice. "It's okay. Relax. Take your time. Let's think together."

How did Sam know exactly how he felt and what he needed to hear? She was wonderful. "Any ideas, Sam?"

The com was quiet for a moment until Sam broke the silence. "How do you win Fortnite, The Remake: Save the Universe? It's very similar to this situation. You have to take out the enemies' AI defense shield in order to advance. And in order to do so, you have to hack into the AI system and find its flaw. In the game, the flaw was the shield itself. You turn the shield into an offensive weapon against the AI. I'm just reaching, but does that give you any ideas here?"

Cal had played Fortnite many times since the remake came out, and he had won on more than one occasion. Sam was right: in the game, you use the weapon to destroy the weapon. *Use the weapon*, Cal thought.

"That's it!" Cal shouted into the com. "That has to be it! You're a genius, Sam."

Cal quickly searched for the data on hilaetite crystals. It was voluminous. He looked at the clock. Fifteen minutes. He narrowed the search down to stabilization of hilaetite. Bingo! There it was. The Permidiums were able to construct entire ships out of hilaetite crystals and use those combined crystals as a weapon because they developed an onboard system to stabilize the crystals.

Cal finished reading and then pressed the com. "Jake, I have it."

"Go," Jake said.

"The Permidiums have developed what they call a pulse emitter to stabilize the hilaetite crystals. It emits an ultra-wave that sort of lets the crystals 'talk' to each other. It stabilizes them as if all connected are one giant crystal. And we know that one crystal can be used alone, no matter how large it is. You just need to locate the pulse emitter in their system and shut it off. It looks like there's a backup, so you'll need to shut that down as well."

"I'm on it," Jake said in an upbeat tone.

"Wait," Cal said. "You'll need two things. The first is easy. The password to access the main pulse-emitter system. It means 'Armageddon' in English." Cal gave him the sequence of Permidium keyboard symbols that spelled *Armageddon* in Permidium.

"And the second thing?" Jake asked.

"I have no idea where or how, in the time we have left, you'll find this. It looks like you'll need some type of scanning device. A key card or something. There should be an electric eye on the keyboard to scan it. It's a final fail-safe. I imagine a pretty high ranked officer is going to be holding it."

The com was silent for a moment. Cal shook his head. He should have figured it wouldn't be that easy to shut down a system that was so vital. They needed more time. A lot more time. He started to feel hopeless again.

"Wait," Jake said.

The com went silent again before Jake spoke. "I think I have it. I'll get to it."

Cal perked up immediately. There wasn't time to ask what he'd found or where he'd found it. He would have to trust Jake. But his excitement didn't last long. He didn't want to tell Jake the last part, but he had to. He owed him the truth. "Jake, there's one more thing."

"What's that?" Jake asked, still upbeat.

Cal spoke solemnly. "The effect of disengaging the pulse emitter is instantaneous. That ship will blow and destroy everything for miles and beyond. And there's no way to disengage it remotely."

The com was quiet again. Not a single Legion said a word. Even the Cratonites diligently working around Cal must have overheard, as they all stopped and turned their attention to Cal. It seemed like forever. Cal checked the clock. Ten minutes.

Jake finally replied, this time in a calm voice. "Understood, buddy."

26

THE CONCILIATOR

J ake needed to tell Cal about Diane's situation so that Cal could head straight for Vernius as soon as the Permidium ship was destroyed. Hopefully, the other Permidiums would take notice and leave the galaxy. But first he had to locate the pulse-emitter system in the computer, as well as the backup.

He had only ten minutes. He could tell Cal about Diane right before taking those systems offline.

He was starting to search when the screen projection flashed and buzzed. A message scrolled across the screen overriding any command. It read, "Warning: The conciliator believes an intruder is on board. A non-Permidium spacecraft was found in the vessel room. If found, approach with caution. Assume the intruder is dangerous."

Now Jake really had to hurry. They were probably searching the computer system as well, looking for any anomalies.

Jake found it odd that the message didn't say to contact security if he was found. Maybe they had no security detail. Maybe they didn't need it, with the weapons they had.

Jake found the pulse-emitter system and backup quickly. Eight minutes. He heard voices in the hallway, but he continued to work the floating keyboard as quickly as his fingers would move. But he was trained for fighting, not typing.

Jake disengaged the backup system first. If they were looking, they might not detect that as easily as the main system going offline, which would give him time to disengage the other system.

The voices were right outside the door now, and they were not moving away.

Jake pulled up the main emitter system, typed in the Armageddon password, and then pulled out the card he had taken off the anesthetized Permidium. Like the keyboard, the card seemed to have no physical qualities, like a projection. After his fingers went a little way into the projection, they grasped something solid. He hoped he had the right card.

The door clicked, followed by a slight stream of light from the hallway, reflecting to the side of the server racks.

Jake checked the time. Four minutes. He quickly swiped the card in front of the blinking red eye and watched the projected monitor. It worked. The prompt read, "Bypass confirmed." And there was a prompt for "Disengage System" and a prompt for "Cancel."

Jake was out of time, but he hesitated. He still hadn't told Cal about the urgency in getting to Diane, and when he pressed the key for "Disengage System," he would be killed instantly. He wasn't afraid of dying, especially like this. It would be quick and painless. And he would die knowing that he saved Earth and, hopefully, the rest of the galaxy. But he would also die knowing that he was not able to save Diane.

"Don't touch that keyboard," a computer-like, feminine voice said from behind him. All Permidiums sounded the same to him, or at least all the females, who were all he had seen.

Jake squeezed his eyes shut, furrowing his brow. How stupid he was to hesitate. His hands were at his sides now. He was sure the

Permidiums had a weapon trained on his back. Any movement toward the keyboard, and he would be incapacitated or, more likely, dead. The Permidiums could see the monitor as well as he could, they knew what was happening. And he couldn't make a move toward them. There were at least two of them, maybe more. He had heard them talking. The clock showed only three minutes remaining, but he had a bigger problem now.

"You are a very resourceful young man," one of the Permidiums said in her monotone voice. "One more click, and we would all be deceased. You were willing to give up your life to destroy us. Why?"

Jake remained with his back to them, his hands at his side. "It's the only way to stop your containment field and destroy your ship so we can have our planet back. You killed a lot of good men and women and decimated our planet, just to recover a stupid transponder. I should be the one asking why. You could have just asked for it, and we would have given it to you."

The Permidiums were silent. His com buzzed. Cal. "Jake, we're almost out of time. What's going on?"

Jake's hands were close to the com, but he didn't want to move them, and he really wasn't in any position to talk to Cal anyway.

What are they doing anyway, Jake thought? *Are they even still behind me?* The Permidiums remained completely silent. He heard one of them talk earlier about discussing the situation. Maybe that's what they were doing here.

Finally, one of the Permidiums broke the silence. "We have discussed your response. We attacked your planet first, before you could attack us. That was the reason you stole our data, correct? In order to learn how to destroy us, correct?"

Jake was getting frustrated. He had only thirty seconds left on the clock, and the Permidiums were so far off the truth that he doubted he could convince them otherwise if he had thirty hours.

Jake shook his head slowly. "No, we had no intention of destroying you or attacking you. Heck, we didn't even know who you were or that we even had this data. We recorded it by accident. We only learned of it through Sloan."

"Mr. Sloan told you about the destruction data?"

Jake perked up. Maybe he had stumbled onto something. If he could show Sloan as a common enemy, maybe the Permidiums would turn on him.

"Yes, we heard about it from him." He wasn't lying. Diane had heard Sloan tell the Imperial Majesty.

"But Mr. Sloan has been preparing us for years for an attack from this galaxy. He showed us how you recorded the data from an encounter with one of our ships. He wouldn't also help you."

Jake's com buzzed again, and again it was Cal. "Jake, ten seconds until the containment field is complete. Give us a signal if you're still—" The communication cut off. The containment field was complete.

Lannick had been right on in his calculation. His only chance now, Earth's only chance now, was for him to talk the Permidiums down. But talking wasn't one of his strong suits.

It would be useless going for the final keyboard key at this point, so Jake slowly turned to face his accusers and likely executioners. There were indeed three Permidiums, all female, two with some type of gun he had never seen before aimed at him. The third had a hovering keyboard and a miniature floating screen in front of her, like the mainframe Jake was using but much smaller. That must be one of their portable computers.

"Do you have anything further to say, Jake Saunders?"

"How do you know who I am?"

"We have scanned you and run you through our data system. We have extensive records on you from Mr. Sloan." The Permidium who was speaking paused. "Mr. Saunders, we ask you again, why should we believe that Mr. Sloan would also assist you?"

Jake stared each Permidium in the eye, one at a time. "He wasn't assisting us. And he wasn't assisting you. Sloan doesn't assist anybody.

He uses people to get what he wants, whenever he wants it." Jake started to think about Sloan causing his dad's death, and about his plans for Diane. He felt the anger well up again. "Sloan doesn't care about Permidium, he doesn't care about Earth, and I doubt he cares about whatever planet he came from. He cares only about himself. He's been trying to take over this galaxy for some time now. And he's using you to do so. Once he no longer has a use for you, he'll get rid of Permidium, just like he does everyone else and everything else." Jake paused and took a deep breath, trying to calm himself. He didn't want to seem crazy to the Permidiums. He needed them to believe him. But he couldn't read them. They all just stood there listening, motionless. Their faces were as monotonal as their voices.

Jake continued. "Look, Sloan tried to take over the galaxy a year ago. He played Earth and Craton against each other. I'm sure you've accessed Earth's records searching for the transponder. Check it out for yourself. I'm telling you the truth."

Two of the Permidiums looked at the one who Jake thought had been doing all the talking. Maybe she was the conciliator. She spoke. "We will look for the data and then discuss." She gestured to the Permidium with the computer, who then started silently typing at an alarming speed.

While two weapons were still pointed at him, all three Permidiums were focused on the floating monitor. Jake wondered what Cal, the president, Novak, and the rest of the Legion were thinking. Had they given up since the containment field was complete? Did they think Jake was dead? He hoped the president would keep Captain Reynolds and the Legion in a position to strike the pirates for a little while longer if Jake was somehow successful.

The three Permidiums whispered among themselves. Jake could hear absolutely nothing. Finally, the lead Permidium spoke. "We see that you tell the truth about Mr. Sloan. We also find no record of your planet's knowledge of the contents of the transponder. Therefore, we have concluded that neither your planet nor your galaxy has any hostile intentions toward Permidium. If you can give us the transponder, we will be on our way."

"Just like that? One simple scan and you believe me? And no apologies or anything?" Jake wasn't sure why he was questioning them. He was very close to getting what he wanted. But he was still angry. They had attacked Earth and killed thousands of people without provocation.

"We don't understand your word, *apologies*."

Jake started to grit his teeth, then took a deep breath. "It's when you make a mistake, you feel sorry and express your regret to the person you hurt, or in this case, an entire galaxy."

The Permidiums all exchanged glances before the lead Permidium spoke again. "Permidiums do not make mistakes."

Jake rolled his eyes. "Of course not."

"Where is the transponder?" the Permidium asked.

Jake took a step forward without thinking, but the Permidiums quickly sharpened their aim.

Jake halted. "Thanks to you, Sloan now has it. And since you seem to have the only ship capable of standing up to Sloan"—Jake looked around—"why don't you go get it from him?" Jake knew he was getting an attitude, but he didn't care. He couldn't believe they could be so dismissive of everything they had done. And if they knew who he was, they had to know they'd killed his father. Yet no apologies for that either.

The Permidiums started talking among themselves again. How long had they been talking? He had hardly moved. His calf muscles and lower back were starting to ache.

After some time, the three of them focused on Jake again. "We believe you, Jake Saunders. We will deal with Mr. Sloan to retrieve the transponder. We will remove our energy field and all Permidium ships will depart your galaxy immediately."

The lead Permidium stepped closer to Jake, and for the first time, he saw a facial expression change. She narrowed her eyes and pursed her lips. "But note this, Jake Saunders, if you or anyone on Earth is in fact not telling the truth or hiding something, we will be back in a fury. Our first attack was designed to limit the loss of lives. If we attack again, there will be no more planet Earth."

Those words and her gaze sent a chill up Jake's spine. He had no doubt that she was telling the truth, nor that they had the capability of wiping out an entire planet.

Jake tried to make light of her comments and not show the fear they'd put in him. "So, you have the threat thing down pat." He paused. "I understand."

The lead Permidium motioned for the one with the computer, who then scurried behind Jake and reset the pulse-emitter systems.

Jake really didn't have a choice in the matter. He didn't try to stop her.

He had to trust that the Permidiums would leave the galaxy. From what he had seen, the Permidiums didn't joke and didn't lie. Despite all of their faults, they seemed to do everything they said they would. Besides, Earth's real enemy was the pirates, and the man who had orchestrated it all: Sloan.

Jake watched as the Permidium pulled up the containment-field system, or as the Permidiums had referred to it, the energy field. As long as it took to establish the field, it was removed with one click.

Jake turned his gaze to the lead Permidium and then down at his hands. He moved his hands slightly, then looked back at the Permidium. "May I?"

She nodded and lowered her weapon. The other Permidium followed suit.

Jake pressed the com. "Captain Reynolds, are you still in position to strike?"

"Jake, you're alive!" Cal shouted. "And the containment field just disappeared, what happened. What's going on?"

Jake wanted the com clear for Captain Reynolds to respond. "There's no time to explain. Reynolds, are you still in position?"

"Yes," Reynolds replied. "The president said she had a feeling that you weren't finished."

Jake was thankful for Aretha's confidence in him. "The Permidiums are no longer a problem," he said. "Engage the pirates."

The Permidium at the computer turned toward their leader. "Conciliator, I have contacted the other ships. They are departing."

Jake turned his attention to the conciliator. For a brief moment, Jake got a feeling from the old westerns he and Frank watched. This was the moment the bad guy said, "Got you," and shot you dead. But the conciliator simply turned to Jake. "You are free to go."

Jake started for the door, then stopped. He realized his only transportation was a hilaetite-covered ship, and he was going out into a pirate battle. One slight, glancing blow from anything would blow him to the next planet.

Jake turned back toward the conciliator. "Any chance I could trade spacecraft?"

———

The conciliator was right about the speed of the Permidium fighter. Jake felt the Gs in this thing. It easily eclipsed the light speed of a quantum light fighter, as well as the light fighter's maximum subluminal velocity. Jake would make the trip to Vernius in half the normal time. And with no hilaetite in the ship, he didn't have to worry about blowing up. Even the weapons system was conventional plasma, along with two pulse torpedoes. The conciliator had told him that it was their basic model.

He did notice, however, that it wasn't any more maneuverable than a light fighter. But that was okay. He was used to handling that type of ship, so he would rather this be the same if he did face any combat.

Jake pressed his com, still using the vector-space transmitter. "I'm clear. My target twenty is Vernius."

While Jake was being escorted out of the Permidium hangar in his new ship, he had explained Diane's situation to Cal, the president, and any other Legion listening on their transmitter. Not surprisingly, Cal sounded pretty distraught at the news. But what bothered Jake was that he couldn't get a clear answer about Frank's condition. All he was told was that Frank was rescued along with the rest of the prisoners, was on Craton, and was in good hands in the infirmary. That's all the information one gets when the person isn't doing well. If Frank was okay, Cal would have said as much. He needed to be mentally prepared for whatever resistance he was going to face on Vernius, which likely included facing off against Sloan. But he couldn't get Frank off his mind.

The president authorized him to go to Vernius but made it clear that Captain Reynolds couldn't spare any ships to assist him. With the beating the Legion took waiting for the Permidium ship to stand down, they were already severely outnumbered by the Earth pirates. And nobody from Craton could get to Vernius in time. Besides, the Craton fighters had already been dispatched to Earth to assist Captain Reynolds.

Even though the Legion was outnumbered, Jake was hopeful that they could retake Earth with the help of the Cratonite forces. But Jake was completely on his own. The Permidium ship blockading Vernius would have left. However, Jake had no idea how much pirate strength he would encounter, and Vernius had no fighters or other defense. It didn't matter though. Jake had to do everything he could to save Diane or die trying. Right now, she thought he didn't even love her, let alone that he would risk his life to save her.

27

DOGFIGHT

Diane stood in the tiny holding room in the spacecraft of one of Sloan's pirate lackeys, which had landed outside the Imperial Majesty's palace. The room had no windows and one metal door. She tried the door again, wincing at the pain in her wrists with every movement of her hands. The bands were cutting into her skin, and the raw flesh burned. She did her best to work her hands in unison so the bands wouldn't pull against each other. The door was still locked. Of course it was. Just like it was when she tried ten minutes ago.

She sat down on a small metal chair. A part of her wanted to break free, but there was no way to do so, and where would she go to escape Sloan? Besides, what did she have anymore? She lost the only person she would ever truly love. And even though she got the message out about the transponder, most likely her home planet was in the hands of Sloan and the pirates. So, the other part of her was fine with flying away in the capsule and dying. It was just the slow, suffering manner of this death that frightened her. But when the time came, she knew that she would handle it like a Legion soldier should.

The lock on the door clicked and it opened. Two well-dressed pirates stood outside. Neither one was the blond-haired, red-eyed pirate who cuffed her and locked her in there, but each looked just as physically fit. One was dark-skinned and appeared to be human. The other had to be from the planet Neptune, with his blue skin.

"It's time," the human pirate said.

Diane would look for a means of escape between there and the capsule, but she doubted that she would find an opportunity. Between her cuffed hands, the size of the two guards, and the plasma guns that each held, the situation looked pretty grim. Maybe, by some chance, the Imperial Majesty would stand up to Sloan and rescue her. But Diane doubted that would happen either. Even if the Imperial Majesty changed her stance, she lacked the resources on Vernius to make Sloan so much as flinch, let alone break Diane free.

If she didn't go along peacefully with the guards, she was certain they would enjoy dragging her to the capsule. So, she surrendered. Her legs quivered and her stomach started to churn as she rose from the chair. She moved very slowly so that her legs wouldn't fail her.

When it came down to it, she was frightened at what lay before her. She hated herself for feeling that way. And she hated herself even more for letting her fear show. That wasn't how a Legion soldier faced death. But then again, she was only Legion by her position, not by training.

"Move it," the blue-skinned pirate said with a snarl, "or we'll come in there and drag you out."

Diane's voice was soft and cracked. "I'm coming."

Again, she was angry with herself. She wanted to sound more forceful and unafraid.

As she exited the room, she caught a glimpse of the cockpit of the ship. It was empty. As they made their way to the exit, she noticed that the entire ship seemed empty: not a pirate or anyone else in sight, but for the two guards. If she was going to escape, this would be her chance. She was already on board her getaway horse, as Frank would say. She just had to subdue the two guards while her wrists were bound. *That's easy enough,* she thought sarcastically.

She could see the open exit door at the end of the hall. If she was going to make a move, it would have to be now. There was no time for any type of plan. The guards were on either side of her and slightly behind. She could smell their sweat. Each one had his plasma gun at his hip, trained on her.

She stopped suddenly so that their last strides put them even with her with their guns aimed slightly forward. She immediately lowered her right shoulder and drove it into the human's rib cage. He grunted and fell against the wall. She turned and grabbed the blue-skinned guard's hand with his weapon before he could correct his aim at her. She kicked him in the groin. He doubled over, releasing his grip. Diane rotated the gun in her still-cuffed hands. But the human guard had recovered before she could spin around to face him.

As she turned, she saw the butt of his gun coming toward her face. She instinctively turned her head and felt a striking pain. The butt caught her squarely in the temple. She dropped the plasma gun, bent forward, her vision blurry, and stumbled to the left. The blue-skinned guard growled as he brought his knee up into Diane's face. She felt her chin open up as more searing pain shot through her head. She keeled over.

She fought to regain her strength and stand up, but it was no use. Her stomach churned and her throat burned as bile came up in the back of her mouth. It was all she could do to keep from vomiting. Everything was spinning now. Her legs wobbled. She tried one last time to rise but fell forward as her world went dark.

Jake dropped out of light speed and kept an eye on his sensors as he came within range of Vernius. He wasn't sure what to expect. He didn't detect anything large enough to be a Permidium ship.

Good, Jake thought. *The Permidiums held up their end of the bargain.*

He saw several blips on the long-range sensors. They had to be pirates. He doubted Sloan would give up just because the Permidiums had left.

Jake's vector-space transmitter buzzed.

"Jake," Cal said. "The Craton fighters made it to Earth in time. There are heavy casualties, but Captain Reynolds is making it through to the planet. And according to Sam, there are major pockets of civilian resistance on the ground and in the air assisting the Legion that are landing. You did it, buddy. I thought you should know."

"Thanks Cal, but I think there are still pirates at Vernius."

"Yeah, that's the reports we're starting to get. With Novak taking out the reinforcements at Tortuga and the bulk of the rest of the pirates being at Earth, that just leaves a few scattered pockets of them around the galaxy. They've been defeated. They just don't know it."

Jake half smiled. "I wish someone would tell Sloan that."

"There aren't any Legion or Craton ships anywhere close enough to help you, Jake. So be careful." Cal paused. "And Jake."

"Yeah, buddy?"

"Bring my sister home."

Jake sat for a moment, wondering if he could beat the odds yet again. He really wasn't certain, but he wanted to give Cal reassurance.

"I will," Jake said.

At the same time that Vernius came into view on his screen, five pirate ships appeared as well, coming from the planet in attack formation, their shields up. From what the conciliator had said, the Permidiums had never used these fighters with the pirates. And it was obvious the pirate ships didn't mistake him for an ally. The pirates had no ships like this either.

Jake tried hailing them. No response.

He tried again, this time talking in case they were listening but not responding. "This is Jake Saunders of the Earth's Legion. Please stand down. The Legion has retaken Earth and Tortuga, and the

Permidiums have fled the galaxy. The war is over. I'm coming to Vernius in peace."

That last part wasn't true, but he was coming in peace with regard to the pirates. Jake's only beef now was with Sloan.

The pirates responded by firing long-range scatter blasts. He easily maneuvered around the spattering of plasma and raised his shields.

"Looks like they want to fight," Jake said out loud.

He kept his pace steady at the top light fighter speed. His heading was directly at the group of pirates. He liked the design of the Permidium fighter. It was better suited for one pilot than quantum light fighters. All controls were right at his fingertips.

"Wait for it, wait for it," Jake said to himself.

The two pirate ships on the outside of their formation broke off to flank him. That's what he expected.

"Wait," he told himself again. He wanted to fire, but he had a better plan if he could be patient enough to wait until they fired first. He wasn't nervous at all. He felt exhilarated. Sure, it was five on one, but they were five pirate ships. These were odds he liked. This was what he was used to. This type of combat was what he lived for.

When the two flanking ships were on either side of him, all five pirate ships fired their close-range plasma missiles.

"Now!" Jake shouted, only to himself.

He immediately punched the ship to full throttle while barrel diving below the three oncoming vessels. As he had hoped, the pirates didn't anticipate the speed of his Permidium ship. The two flanking pirates scored direct, close-range hits on each other, penetrating their shields. Each ship disappeared in a fireball. One of the other ships must have been distracted by the whole thing and veered too far right, hitting one of the fireballs and bursting into flames.

Jake immediately came up behind the remaining two ships and opened fire with his own plasma missiles. It all happened in a matter of seconds. With the speed of his ship, the pirates had no time to react. Jake landed multiple direct hits, destroying both ships.

There was no time to celebrate. He swung around toward the planet and opened the throttle again. There was still one ship showing on his scanner, coming from the right. He would intersect with it just before entering the planet's atmosphere. Jake kept on course, hoping his speed might just put him into the atmosphere before the ship intercepted him. But as the pirate ship came into view, he knew he wouldn't make it in time. He would have to fight. This time it would be better odds, one-on-one. But Jake didn't feel any exhilaration. This time, he felt the heat start to rise around him. Not nervous or scared, but knowing he was in for a battle. The last time he'd felt this way was when he raised his sepder to face Romalor. This time it wasn't Romalor's Goliath he faced. This time it was a sleek black-and-red fighter.

The first thing Diane felt was her toes dragging on the ground. Then her vision started to focus as she saw pavement slowly moving, speckled with drops of blood, her blood. She also felt blood trickling down her arm from her wrists where the bands had been. Her shoulders ached from being pulled and her head throbbed. She looked up to see the two guards dragging her, one by each arm. She wanted to break free and run, but she wasn't able to move. She tried to tell her legs to work, but they wouldn't obey. She looked forward. Sitting on the palace launchpad about thirty yards away was a round metallic object. The capsule.

The capsule was smaller than she expected. It was a perfectly round, giant gray ball with two boosters attached. As small as the boosters were, they were probably plasma powered and would drop off after the capsule exited the atmosphere.

Diane had neither the strength nor the will to fight the men as they half led and half dragged her up the portable metal steps to the capsule. The hatch door was open, awaiting her arrival. The human guard turned her, picked her up, and dropped her backward into the single seat, which was aimed upward like seats in rocket-style vessels. Diane's senses gradually returned, and her entire body ached. The blood was starting to crust on her face. Her split chin stung as beads of perspiration entered the open wound. Capsules couldn't be reused, but this one smelled like death, like disinfectant and medicine. Where did Sloan get the thing from anyway, in the middle of a war?

She looked around. There was no room to stand. What little space there was in the capsule apart from the seat was stuffed with rations, enough for thirty days, according to Sloan. There were a few lights in front of her on what would otherwise be a control panel, but no controls. There also was a sensor screen. Probably so she could tell what awaited her up ahead. And the hatch door had a small window. That was it. Diane had to look down in order to see straight out through the open hatch. As she did, Sloan appeared in the doorway with a smirk on his face.

"Comfortable?" he said.

Whatever fear Diane had now turned to anger at the sight of him. He was the person responsible for this, and the person to whom she would not show her fear. She tried to look away, but there was no place else to look, and she couldn't turn in the tight quarters.

"Not very talkative, I see," Sloan continued. "Well, no worries. You'll be on your way shortly. I just have to enter your trajectory."

Diane wanted to tell him everything she hated about him. How he would lose the war. How he would eventually pay for everything he had done. But what was the use? For all she knew, he had already won the war. And who would be around to make him pay? So, she said nothing.

Sloan opened a panel on the outside of the capsule just below the hatch. Diane could see his fingers working, probably on some sort of keypad. She had no idea what he was typing. No idea where she was heading.

She looked down again, past Sloan at the open launchpad. There were no spacecraft or aircraft in her line of sight. Only Vernitions bustling about. She was surprised at the lack of pirates. For a planet that was supposedly occupied, she saw very few of them. A lone figure caught her attention. A dark-skinned man standing perfectly still. He was a good distance away, and she just caught glimpses of him between the Vernitions moving around closer to her. He was elderly and unkempt with a shaggy gray beard and long hair. He was staring in her direction. In fact, if she didn't know any better, she could have sworn that he was staring right into the capsule, right at her. He was probably a pirate, although he looked too old to be engaged in much combat.

A larger group of Vernitions walked by, completely blocking her view for a few seconds. When the group had passed, the old man was gone.

Sloan stood straight, arching his back in a stretch. "There, that should do it. Your ride is all set now." He smiled. "Make sure you come back and visit us, although your Imperial Majesty won't be around to greet you. Her usefulness to me has nearly run its course." He winked and stepped down.

Diane felt a sudden surge of heat run through her body as she shouted. "No! Sloan! You can't!"

She reached for the corner of the open hatch to pull herself out of her seat just as the blue-skinned guard appeared in the doorway. She struggled against the incline of the seat but managed to pull herself to the edge. The guard raised his foot and with a quick thrust, planted his boot squarely into Diane's chest.

She tried to scream, but nothing came out as she felt her chest collapsing, crushing her lungs. She lost her grip on the hatch and fell backward into the seat. She bent forward, coughing and heaving for each breath, pain searing through her chest to add to the rest of her aches.

"Stay put," the guard commanded.

Diane willed herself to breathe slowly, to calm down. She fought back tears of pain, tears of sorrow, and tears of fear. This was it.

Whatever time she had left before they closed the hatch would be the last time that she would see the light of day.

———

Jake was thankful he still had his shields up as a long-range shot rocked his fighter.

"Where did that come from?" Jake said out loud. His sensors never picked up Abigor's shot. And what a precise shot it was at that range. Jake checked his shields. Down to 90 percent.

Jake wanted to turn and face Abigor head-on, but he didn't have time. Abigor continued to fire long range. Jake swung his fighter in the opposite direction and took evasive maneuvers. He managed to evade all shots. But Abigor was on his tail immediately.

That ship is fast, Jake thought. Could it keep up with his Permidium fighter? Jake punched the throttle as Abigor kept the pressure on with close-range plasma blasts. Jake maneuvered, but Abigor still landed a few shots. Shields at 60 percent.

Jake continued to speed up and evade, but Abigor matched his every throttle increase and move. *Why did it seem he was always running from Abigor?* Jake wondered. He pushed the Permidium ship to full subluminal throttle. Surely, he could open up some distance and give himself a little breathing room. He watched his sensors and his rear screen. He shook his head. Abigor seamlessly kept pace.

Jake didn't let it bother him. He focused. *Think Jake, think.* He had to do something different. Abigor would continue to whittle his shields down to nothing if he kept playing this cat-and-mouse game. He was yet to land a single shot on him. In fact, he hadn't even fired at the black-and-red fighter.

And all this maneuvering and fighting was time lost that he could be helping Diane. When would Sloan launch the capsule? Had he already launched it? According to the Permidiums' data, only Sloan would know where the capsule was headed. If he missed the capsule, he would have to find Sloan. But how much longer would Sloan be on the planet?

Jake's head and shoulders snapped forward and the fighter lurched out of control. *How stupid*, Jake thought. He'd lost focus and suffered a direct hit. He glanced at the shields: 20 percent. He couldn't gain control of the vessel. It kept wanting to spin right, so Jake went with the ship's momentum and rolled it in that direction in order to avoid another direct hit, which certainly would have come if he'd sat there spinning. Jake fought to bring the fighter under control, to bring it out of its roll. But the lack of gravity, the speed at which it was traveling, and Jake's temporary loss of control created a recipe that kept the ship rolling faster and faster with each turn.

Jake's head spun, and his vision started to blur. He fought to maintain consciousness as the ship accelerated. If he lost consciousness, three outcomes were possible, none of which had him surviving.

One, the ship would roll through the atmosphere and crash on the planet's surface.

Two, the ship would roll into outer space and continue to roll forever.

Or Three, Abigor would get a bead on the rolling ship and blow it up.

Jake could feel the g-force pushing him hard against his seat. The skin on his face felt like it was peeling off. His only idea was to jump to light speed, and he used every ounce of strength to reach for the control. It would either tear the ship apart or bring him out of the roll. If he jumped in the direction of Vernius, he would catapult directly into the planet's surface at light speed, but he didn't have the time or ability to chart a direction. He had no choice.

His hand was halfway to the control as his head was pressed further into the seat back. He fought against the force as his ears filled with mind-numbing pressure. His entire body ached. Then his vision went black. Drifting off, he started to relax. He saw Diane smiling at him, those beautiful dark eyes staring at him so lovingly. Those mesmerizing eyes that first drew him to her. She laughed with him and kissed him. He relaxed further. Then he saw Sloan. He was yelling at someone lying face down on the ground. He was standing over the person, threatening them. His face grew angrier and angrier.

Who was he yelling at? Who was he threatening? Whose life was he about to end? The person's head slowly turned. A face was coming into view ever so slowly.

It . . . was . . . Diane.

Jake's eyes popped open, and his hand lurched forward hitting the light speed control. The fighter shook violently. Jake fell forward. A sharp pain shot through his head as his face struck the instrument panel. Jake righted himself as the ship came to a dead stop. Jake was confused for a moment until the blood from a gash in his forehead trickled into his eye. He could taste the blood from his split lip. He slowly came to his senses. His head ached. He must have blown the light speed drive. But at least it stopped the roll. Nothing but space showed in the rear viewing screen. He flipped it to front view just in time to see Abigor slowing to a stop directly in front of him.

Jake looked at his shields. They were gone. His light speed move must have finished them off. But why wasn't Abigor firing? Jake was a sitting duck. Abigor could have destroyed him easily by now.

Jake thought for a moment. *That's it*, he thought. *Pride.* Abigor must want Jake to see what was coming, who was killing him. Abigor was looking for a sign of life. Jake slowly grinned, smeared the blood off his face with his hand, then turned the grin into a snarl. Pride would be Abigor's downfall. Jake knew all too well the damage that it could do to a person. He had been there himself.

Jake would play the oldest trick in the book. He saw the cowboys do it many times in the old west movies. He would play opossum.

Jake checked his systems. Besides the light drive, which he'd fried, and shields, which were already almost dissipated, everything else seemed to be working, including the weapons array. Jake wouldn't have time to lock on to a target; he would have to fire blindly. A target lock would take too long and the moment he showed a sign of life, Abigor would fire. Jake would have to time his shot exactly right and hit Abigor perfectly. Abigor had shields. Jake did not. He would have to penetrate Abigor's shields in one shot. If Abigor got off any type of counter at this range, he wouldn't miss. Without shields, Jake would be gone.

Jake had one chance. His sensor showed that Abigor already had a target lock on him. It would only take Abigor two seconds to fire. Jake would give a sign of life, wait one second, then fire. It would take one more second for his plasma burst to reach Abigor. Jake's target would be Abigor's forward firing arc. If he hit the arc at the same time Abigor fired, the two plasma shots would collide at the arc. The force should penetrate Abigor's shields, causing a chain reaction of internal ruptures that should detonate Abigor's entire ship. That was a lot of calculations without Cal's help and a big "if." And to top it off, he had to manually aim.

Jake wiped his forehead again, this time with his sleeve. He took a deep breath. He wasn't nervous and he wasn't afraid. He was in his comfort zone. He was finally, and for the first time against Abigor, on the attack. And Abigor didn't even know it.

Jake got everything ready to power up the engines. Then he took aim with his forward arc. "Steady," he whispered. "Steady." He hit the engine power and counted. "One." He fired. "Two."

A ball of flames erupted at Abigor's forward arc, followed by several consecutive eruptions from within Abigor's ship, before the entire black-and-red vessel was engulfed in a ball of fire.

Jake laid his head back and sighed.

Then he punched the ship to full throttle. "I'm coming, Diane."

28

THE CAPSULE

Jake's sensors showed a congregation of people at the Imperial Majesty's palace, so he made that his heading. He didn't detect any more pirate ships in the vicinity of the planet. Finally, a direct shot in. Jake's heart pounded, and his muscles tensed as every conceivable thought raced through his mind. Was he too late? Had the capsule already launched? If so, could he find Sloan? Could he get to Diane if she was still there? Sloan must have his own men, and Sloan was powerful enough alone.

Jake had experienced that firsthand. But his worst thought of all was knowing that Diane was being sent off to die, thinking that he didn't love her, when in reality, he loved her more than anything in the galaxy—more than life itself.

Jake wriggled his face muscles, feeling the crusted blood on his forehead. His head still ached. His swollen lip felt like it covered half of his face. But he had to forget about all of that now. As he approached the palace, he could make out the large, paved landing pad covered with Vernitions and a few pirates scattered here and there. He scanned the entire pad, but there was no place to set down. He couldn't simply plow through fifty or so Vernitions.

As he flew over the pad, he saw a small circular opening in the crowd. In the middle of the opening his eyes caught sight of the capsule. *Good, there's still time,* Jake thought. The crowd was maintaining its distance from the capsule without any guards holding them back. They had to be concerned about the plasma booster burn. That meant Sloan was close to launching it. He also noticed one large man in a black trench coat standing on the stairs to the capsule. Even at that distance, it was unmistakably Sloan.

Jake sat his fighter down in the deserted city streets near the palace, jumped out, and ran. His head throbbed with every stride, reminding him of everything he had been through to get to this point. The harder he ran, the more it pounded. And his whole body still ached from the g-force experience. But he had to get to Diane.

He was forced to slow down when he hit the crowd at the edge of the launchpad. For a moment, he thought he saw the old blind man in the crowd. He stopped and looked closer but couldn't find him. At that moment, the words of the old man returned to him: *"I can only warn you . . . if you choose to help the galaxy, you may lose the one closest to you."* Jake now realized what he'd meant, but what did the old man know anyway? He talked in riddles.

Jake was not going to lose Diane.

Jake continued to push and shove through, but it was slow moving. Too slow. He felt frustration and his old nemesis, anger, building up inside. The movement had reopened his head wound and his sweat mixed with the blood as both ran down his face onto his neck. He didn't want to draw the attention of any pirates or Sloan's men, but he had to clear a path to the capsule. He pulled out his sepder and fired twice into the air. Screams came from the crowd as people searched for the source of the noise. The mass of people started to disperse from around him. Eventually, he could run again with his sepder held out in front to clear the Vernitions before him.

He could make out the capsule up ahead. He was almost there when a sharp pain pierced his left shoulder blade. He pulled up, grabbing at his back. The worsening pain turned into a burn. His grappling fingers felt an object sticking out of his back. He pulled out a small dart. He turned to see two pirates in a clearing surrounded by people. A dark-skinned human and a blue-skinned creature from Neptune.

The pirate from Neptune smiled. "You have ten minutes until the neurotoxins paralyze you. But don't worry, you'll be able to think and hear. And it'll wear off in time for Mr. Sloan to inflict some real pain. He's been expecting you."

Jake didn't have time for this. He turned and continued forward, but he was already feeling sluggish, and the pirates quickly caught up with him.

A blue arm flashed across Jake's face and then tightness and pressure squeezed his throat. The blue-skinned pirate had put him in a choke hold. He gasped for air.

"Not so fast," the pirate said. "We can't have you spoiling the festivities. You still have nine minutes."

Jake had had enough. He used to fight with anger, but learned it was more of a weakness than a strength. He was finished controlling his anger. He had to get to Diane and these pirates were in his way, so he allowed himself to unleash all of his pent-up frustrations on them. He drove his elbow deep into the pirate's gut. Once, twice, and a third time. On the third blow, the pirate moaned, released his hold, and doubled over, trying to breathe. Jake's peripheral vision caught the human pirate coming at his side, a sword raised to strike. Jake assumed Sloan had instructed the pirates to take him alive, but he didn't have that restriction. He still couldn't shoot them, though. There were too many Vernition bystanders. Jake turned and blocked the strike with his sepder, spinning low in a complete turn. Coming up out of the spin, he plunged his sepder into the pirate's chest.

Jake turned to face the blue-skinned pirate. His vision started to blur. He wobbled but kept his balance.

The pirate glared at Jake. "It's time for me to take you down."

Jake returned the glare and spoke slowly and deliberately. "You will try."

The pirate raised his sword and charged, attacking with a slash, a stab, a sweep, and a crush. Jake parried each blow but was too sluggish to get off a counter. His inability to move was angering him even more.

The two combatants continued to clash weapons until the pirate shoved Jake, clearing space between them for a disabling blow. Jake was now seeing triple. Three blue-skinned pirates were looking at him, swords raised. Jake shook his head. That did nothing.

The pirate smiled. "Trying to figure out which one of me to strike?"

The pirate charged. Jake stood his ground, leaving his sepder dangling at his side. The pirate tilted his head in a look of confusion, then hesitated just as he reached Jake, who quickly brought his sepder up hard into the pirate's throat. The pirate stood for a moment in front of Jake, gurgling.

"The one in the middle," Jake said before the pirate toppled over.

Jake started to fall too but used his sepder to support himself. He hobbled like that to the edge of the clearing around the capsule. He could hear and think clearly. But he was losing his motor skills, and his vision came and went.

The capsule door was closed, but he could see Diane through the window. She was looking down, not out. His heart ached even more at the sight of her. What had they done to her? She looked beaten to the point of near death. Her face was covered in blood, her right temple swollen, and her chin split wide open.

Jake shouted, "Diane! Over here. I'm here, Diane!"

She never moved. From her lack of reaction to everything, he knew she couldn't hear in there. Sloan now stood alone with Jake in the clearing. He slowly walked over to where Jake stood. Jake's legs gave out, and he fell to his knees in front of Sloan. He wanted to shoot Sloan. He wanted Sloan dead. Then he could get to Diane. He tried to raise his sepder, but his arms wouldn't move; they hung at his sides. He tried again, and the sepder slipped form his numb hand and clanked onto the pavement.

Jake's speech was still fine. "Let her go, Sloan. She didn't do anything to you. Let her go. Send *me* in the capsule. I am the one you want."

"Jake Saunders," Sloan said. "You were the one I wanted. I offered you a chance to join me. If you had, none of this would have happened." Sloan shook his head.

"We took back Earth," Jake said. "The war's over. You've lost. There's no need for any of this."

"Oh, young man, this war has only just begun. What you call a war, I call a battle. You might have won this battle, but I assure you, I will win the war." He leaned down toward Jake with narrowed eyes, his expression serious. "And I will have your planet and your galaxy." He put his face next to Jake's. "You think it hurts losing her," he pointed to the capsule. "Wait until I destroy the rest of your world. And there won't be a thing you can do to stop me."

Jake narrowed his eyes. Anger raged inside him. He wasn't worried about Earth. Earth would be ready the next time and could take care of itself. All he cared about now was Diane and Sloan. One, he would give anything to keep alive. The other, he wanted dead.

Jake's cheeks burned as he spoke. "That's where you're wrong Sloan. You've already destroyed my world. You've taken everything from me. You killed my father. Because of you, my Uncle Ben was slaughtered. You destroyed Earth, my home. You killed Commander Cantor in front of me. And now you're taking Diane from me."

Jake had regretted the years he lost seeking revenge against Romalor. But now he didn't care if he lost the rest of his life in search of revenge. He didn't care because the rest of his life wouldn't have Diane in it. He summoned every ounce of his strength. With adrenaline coursing through his veins, he got his legs underneath him, and stood stiffly to face Sloan eye to eye. He spoke through gritted teeth as he leaned into Sloan. "I've got nothing left. NOTHING! You've taken it all. So, you'd better kill me right here and now while I can't move. Because if you don't, there is no place in this universe that you can hide. I will spend every last second of my life hunting you down. And I WILL find you! And I WILL kill you!"

For the first time ever, Jake caught just a glimpse of concern on Sloan's face, which immediately disappeared as Sloan continued to look directly at Jake. "Launch the capsule," he shouted.

Flames soared out of the boosters on the bottom of the capsule. The capsule moved slowly at first as it lifted off the pavement. But seconds later it accelerated faster and faster as it rose into the sky, turning into a tiny dot.

"NOOOO!" Jake shouted. "DIANE!"

Jake tried to step in the direction of the capsule, but his legs gave out again, and he fell face first, unable to move his arms to break his fall. His chin smacked the hard pavement, opening a large gash. He felt little pain, though, due to the paralysis. He tried to push himself up, but his arms still wouldn't work. Sorrow overwhelmed him. Diane was gone, and even worse, she was gone thinking that Jake no longer cared about her. What hope could she possibly have?

Jake heard nothing around him. He just lay there, unable to move, sobbing. His vision was now completely gone. And between the toxin, the head injury, and the emotional stress, he was losing consciousness. Then the sorrow faded as anger took its place. Not just anger. This time it was hatred. Rage overtook every part of him.

He was able to shout one last word before plunging into unconsciousness.

"SLOAN!"

EPILOGUE

E zekiel shifted in his chair. For the first time ever, he felt uncomfortable sitting in his seat at the large table in the meeting hall. He took a sip of water and wiped a bead of sweat from his forehead with a handkerchief. He braced himself for another barrage of questions from the Chamber.

"Let's call it like it is," Martock said. "Your mission failed, right?"

Ezekiel paused before responding. He had not completely failed. At the end of the day, Sloan wasn't in control of the Milky Way.

"No," Ezekiel said with authority. "I did not fail. Diabolus lost. He did not take over the galaxy. He was forced to retreat."

"But your report said that he all but destroyed the planet Earth," Esau interrupted in his broken voice.

"Earth is very resourceful," Ezekiel replied. "It will recover." He paused. "As I was saying, Diabolus has left the Milky Way galaxy and has lost the support of the Permidiums, all without interference by Lotox. I consider that a victory."

Martock spoke again. "Without interference by Lotox, you say? Your report is vague on what you did. How is it not interference under the ancestral code?"

"I merely helped two foes become friends against a common enemy and provided a couple directional hints," Ezekiel replied. "It was as simple as that."

"Enough of what Ezekiel did and didn't do," Cleoptara said loudly. "Let's figure out what we are to do next. Do we know where Diabolus is now? Do we know his plans?"

Purss chimed in. "One thing we do know is that he isn't finished. We haven't heard the last of him."

"You are correct," Ezekiel said. "He isn't finished. And no, I don't know where he is at the moment, but I will find him. That is the easy part. I'm pretty certain he hasn't given up on the Milky Way galaxy. The hard part will be apprehending him and getting him back here. He knows about the serum."

"Yes," Martock said. "I read that in your report. How does he know?"

Ezekiel shook his head. "I have no idea. But he knows, and he'll be ready for us."

"We have no other way of subduing him, right?" Cleoptara asked, raising an eyebrow at Purss and Ezekiel. "Or do we?"

Purss shook his head. "No, there is nothing more I have kept from the Chamber. The serum was our only option."

"Then we send more people," Cleoptara said. "Or even recruit an army of our own."

Purss leaned forward. "No, we've already been through the risks with involving too many people and the interference it would cause. And it would still do no good. Diabolus would see that coming from even farther away and be even more prepared."

Ezekiel shifted in his seat again. "Stealth is still our best option."

"And look where that got us the first time," Martock retorted sarcastically.

"This time I will approach it differently," Ezekiel said. "Diabolus will see me, or any of us, coming with the serum. But he won't see a human coming. He won't expect it."

Cleoptara raised an eyebrow again.

But Purss spoke first. "The Saunders boy?"

"Yes," Ezekiel confirmed.

"He's alive?" Cleoptara questioned.

"Yes, I saw to that. I got to him before Diabolus's men could, while he was unconscious. He's alive, safe, and in good hands, and still doesn't know a thing about Lotox or who Sloan really is."

"And just how do you plan on bringing Saunders into this?" Esau asked. "Especially without explaining everything to him. By finding the girl for him?"

Ezekiel turned directly toward Esau. "Finding the girl for him would ensure his assistance, but I don't know where Diabolus sent her. And I cannot foresee where she's heading. Another action of Diabolus from which I am blocked. But I don't need to bring Saunders into this. He already is in. Diabolus has taken everything from that boy." Ezekiel paused and looked around the table. "I won't have to explain anything. He'll go after Diabolus on his own. He'll go after him with a vengeance. All I have to do is better equip him."

"I like it," Cleoptara said.

"Me too," Purss said.

The rest of the Chamber members acknowledged their agreement as well, all except Esau and Martock.

"I've never liked this plan from the start," Esau said. "But no use voting. I can see Martock and I are in the minority once again."

Purss turned toward Martock. "Martock?"

"Fine. But I'm going on the record as opposing this as well." Then he turned his attention to Ezekiel. "You are placing a lot of hope in this Saunders boy, a mere human that Diabolus has beaten down time and time again. What makes you think Saunders has a chance against Diabolus?"

Ezekiel leaned forward and placed his hands on the table. "Because, just as you say, Diabolus has beaten him down time and time again. And Saunders gets back up every single time. He has a will and a drive like nobody I have ever encountered." He paused and looked into the eyes of each Chamber member, ending with Martock. "Don't underestimate Jake Saunders. Diabolus already has. And that will be his downfall."

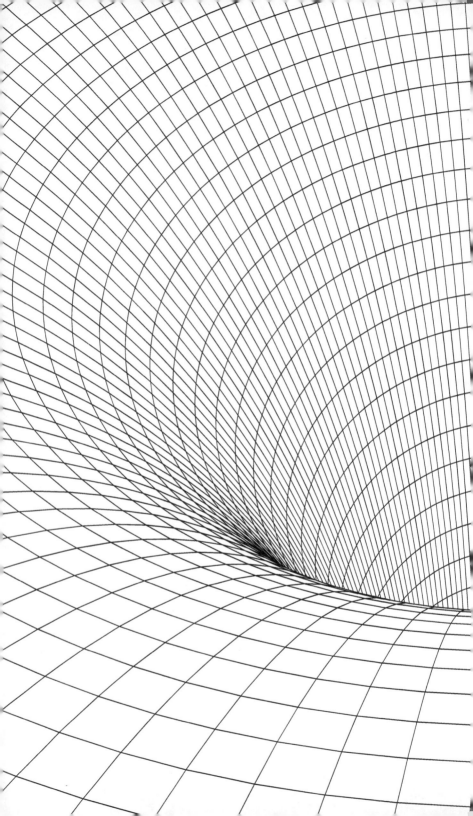

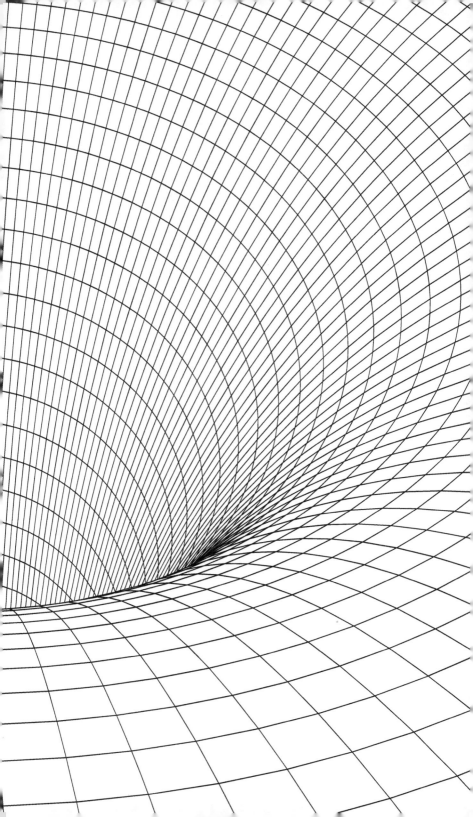

ACKNOWLEDGMENTS

I would like to personally thank the following people for their contributions in helping me to create and refine this book.

First, I would like to thank my family. My wife, DeAnne; son, Luke; and daughter, Lucy. They encouraged me to write this sequel and constantly support my writing.

In addition, I would like to thank the team at CamCat Publishing for all of their hard work and helpful advice in bringing this book to life. A special thanks Bridget McFadden, who read and reread my manuscript, edited it, and provided outstanding recommendations. She also put up with my many typos. Thanks to Maryann for coming up with the perfect cover design as usual, Bill Lehto for his business assistance, and the excellent marketing team of Laura Wooffitt, Gabe Schier, and Abigail Miles.

Finally, I would like to thank all of the other CamCat authors for all of the support and cross-promotion they provide. CamCat has assembled the finest group of authors and I couldn't be prouder to be among them.

ABOUT THE AUTHOR

Bryan Prosek is a young adult writer and business attorney. He focuses his writing on science fiction and dystopian universes. Along with his debut novel, *The Brighter the Stars*, and his latest novel, *A Measure of Serenity*, he has published books and articles in legal trade journals and magazines.

When he isn't writing or practicing law, you can probably find him watching science fiction movies or television shows. He loves the big screen and the small screen. There's a good chance that he'll be watching one of the numerous Star Trek movies or series, but he could be watching anything from *Guardians of the Galaxy* to *The Conjuring*.

You can find more about Bryan at his website,
www.bryankprosek.com

Taking you to new worlds.

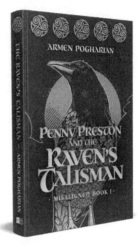

VISIT US ONLINE FOR MORE BOOKS TO LIVE IN:

CAMCATBOOKS.COM

CamCatBooks   @CamCatBooks   @CamCat_Books

CPSIA information can be obtained
at www.ICGtesting.com
Printed in the USA
LVHW101749110922
727532LV00002B/2/J